# Suburbilicious
## vignettes from Jasper Lane

# Eric Arvin

*Dreamspinner Press*

Published by
Dreamspinner Press
4760 Preston Road
Suite 244-149
Frisco, TX 75034
http://www.dreamspinnerpress.com/

Suburbilicious

Cover Art by HvH    http://hvhexpo.blogspot.com/
Cover Design by Mara McKennen

ISBN: 978-1-61581-043-7

Printed in the United States of America
First Printing
September, 2009

eBook edition available
eBook ISBN: 978-1-61581-044-4

For Equality

# Suburbilicious: Vignettes from Jasper Lane

Two unassuming lesbians move onto a white-as-Donna-Reed suburban street," Asha Fields mumbled as she stood in the drive and fiddled with her necklace, an anniversary gift from her wife-*bian* Keiko. She surveyed the street, ever suspicious of perfection.

"What?" Keiko inquired, picking up a small box of dish rags from the pavement. The big, butch movers (V-Haul, they were called) had at last driven away, and now it was left to Keiko and Asha to find a place for all of their things—most of which belonged to Keiko. "What did you say about two lesbians?"

"That's what they're saying," Asha replied, referring to their neighbors. "They're all watching us as we move in, and they're saying, 'Two lesbians move onto a street.' We're the start of a bad joke."

"Oh, hush! Just grab that box over there, and let's have some wine. We can celebrate our new home. Just you and me alone. Now that you finally have some time off, we don't need to worry about getting a call in the middle of the night."

Asha picked up the box as she was told. It was slightly heavier than Keiko's, filled with plastic cups and the like. Asha much preferred plastic to glass. She had quite a collection too. Almost every theme park in the country was represented.

"Besides," Keiko joked, "it's not us being lesbians that'll trip them up. Wait until they learn we're Wiccan! Now, *that's* a real stereotype—Wiccan lesbians." She laughed, and despite herself, Asha did too. She could never stay serious when she heard Keiko laugh. Who could? It was such a light and airy thing, Keiko's laugh. Like the ghost of a cloud.

Asha persisted as they entered their new home, "Seriously, have you seen the people around here? They all look like models. They're way too attractive. The women look like Barbies, and the men look like gay porn stars. It's just strange. They're watching us. I can feel their eyes…. Oh, jeez! What if Jasper Lane is Stepford?"

"Ash, honey, you're crazy. But then, that's why I love you." Keiko placed her box on the kitchen island and gave Asha the expected peck on the cheek after such a comment. "And remember, we're not the only new residents here. There's that man across the street. The older guy? He's doesn't look like a porn star. Maybe he'll distract everyone from our nefarious doings."

"He doesn't count." Asha began unpacking her box of plastic and Tupperware, though she didn't know where to put them yet. She placed them around the box from whence they came on the kitchen island. "He's renting. Renters don't count. Me and you are going to be here for a while. We bought the house. He'll be gone in no time. He's not the type to stick around; I can tell."

Keiko didn't say so, but she hoped that Asha was right. She didn't like the man across the street. There was something about him; hidden trouble. And Keiko was never wrong about these things. He was a bad actor. And she knew something about bad actors. She could sniff out a good dog from a bad one, and, given what Asha did for a living, she knew she too would soon be able to ascertain the truth about the guy.

"Get some cups, baby," Keiko said, as she pulled the wine from her huge bag, which lay in the corner of the kitchen. "Let's celebrate." She grinned with that "look what I've got for you" expression, shaking the wine bottle playfully.

Asha chose two sippy cups they had bought on a trip to Disney World a few years earlier. Keiko poured a generous amount of wine into each, and they made their way outside again. The previous resident had left behind a swing in the front yard, and it was good sitting weather.

"You'll be fine," Keiko said. "We'll adapt."

"We're good at that," Asha agreed with a smile.

2

And that was very true. They were both very good at adapting to new situations. Why, adaptation had been the key to survival for both of them. Big situations, larger-than-life problems, had always come up, but they lived through them and remained together. Like all great couples, they drew strength from those experiences.

When they separately told their parents they were gay, that was the first grand hurdle. (Damn, they had to stretch their legs to get over that one!) Asha's parents, Southern Baptists to the last, were none too pleased at first, but they eventually warmed to Keiko, even if the exact nature of Asha and Keiko's relationship was never discussed. Asha was allowed to bring Keiko to family gatherings, but only as a "friend."

Keiko's parents were different, though. They had still not come around; they could still not reconcile their older beliefs with who she was. There had been little to no interaction between them for two years now. Asha could tell it hurt her, but Keiko never said anything, and Asha was not the type to pester a wound.

Asha still dreaded the thought that her parents might one day find out, on top of the whole "lesbian thing," she was a Wiccan too. *Lord save us all*, she thought.

Keiko believed she would never have the chance to lay that particular shock on her own family. It was a sad, strange relief to her. Divisions, she reassured herself, are saviors and killers at the same time.

But still, laying aside all their varied issues with family and world tradition, they were a happy couple. Yes, they were content to at last have their first house together. Not an apartment, not a rental, but an actual house, a house for them and their *future* family.

"I feel them," Asha said, breaking into the suburban quiet around them.

Keiko was at first alarmed. She thought maybe Asha had been attacked by bugs or ants crawling on the swing. It did look a little worn, after all. "Feel what?" she asked. Then she realized what Asha had really meant. "Honey, they're all probably just normal people like you and me. You're making them out to be some crazy caricatures of suburbia, some nutty writer's fantasy. We're not in a book or TV program, babe. Their lives are just as ordinary as ours. They have the same simple worries that every other American suburbanite has; nothing more. There's not a mechanical Katharine Ross in the bunch."

Asha swallowed some of the sweet wine. Together they pushed the swing ever so slightly, a squeaky hinge responding to their efforts, and a new summer breeze glided past.

"Their eyes." Asha peered mercilessly up and down the street. "I just know they're watching us right now." She said this with a hint of playful dramatics, trying to make Keiko laugh again. "They're all probably hidden behind the curtains at their windows. I wonder if they know I know they're watching us."

"I WONDER if they know we're watching them," Melinda Gold remarked. "I mean, it's not like we're hidden behind curtains here on the patio."

She sat properly, not a wrinkle or crease anywhere, clothing *or* skin (she had recently discovered Botox), and drank her morning coffee opposite Cassie Bloom, Becky Ridgeworth, and Vera on the large front patio of Cassie's magnificent and much envied cul-de-sac. The morning coffee at Cassie's was a ritual now. It had been for a while. Each morning the four of them gathered at Cassie's to discuss the worthiest news and gossip from the night before. And there was always gossip. Always. What was the point of living in the suburbs otherwise?

Melinda had given up the expensive coffee she had been intent on drinking for a while—the infamous kind that came from a monkey's bottom and was somehow suitable for human consumption. She had seen it on *Oprah*. Aside from disgust at the thought of drinking coffee strained through monkey intestines (she had given up eggs as well; in fact, anything that came out of a living creature's backside was now out of the question), she found she much preferred to brew her own anyway. Or better yet, to run down the street and purchase some of the fresh-made cappuccinos from the cute little coffee and pastry shop that had just opened. Still, to this day, she really couldn't figure out what had possessed her in the first place to drink monkey diarrhea, Oprah or not. It wasn't as if it was a book, gosh darn it!

"They're certainly a lovely looking couple," Becky said, peering down at the new arrivals as they swung delicately on the swing in their front yard.

"I introduced myself this morning," Cassie informed them all, her voice as regal as ever. "There's something going on there. I'm certain of it."

"How do you mean?" Vera asked, ready for the juicy details.

"Well," Cassie began as she set her mug down and leaned forward, as if her voice might carry down the hill and throughout Jasper Lane, "I saw one box in particular—some of their things—and it had some very strange symbols scrawled across it. Pentagrams and stars and half-moons."

"What's it mean?" Becky inquired. "Are they Satanists?" It sounded an absurd question, something a third-grader might ask, and they all broke into a fit of giggles.

"They're most likely Wiccan," Cassie recovered herself to reply.

"Oh, Wiccan lesbians." Vera yawned. "How tired. How... *Willow*."

"So, they worship Satan?" Now, Becky was deathly serious. This sort of gossip had never hit Jasper Lane before.

"No, dear," Melinda said gently. "There's no devil in Wicca. The devil is a Christian invention." She and Becky had of late been getting along. It was an attempt for both of them to stay in the good graces of Cassie.

Everyone at the table stared at Melinda with some surprise.

"What?" Melinda shrugged. "I do research every now and then. One can't stay in the dark all their lives, can one?" She took another sip of her coffee, proud that she had shown herself unpredictable to her friends. The computer had exposed her to whole new worlds. Melinda loved to hang ten on the Interweb.

"Well," chimed in Miss Vera, "I'm just happy I'm not the only sista living around these parts now."

"What are their names?" Becky asked of Cassie.

"The Nubian princess," she winked at Vera, "is named Asha. Her partner is called Keiko. They've been together for some time. I know Keiko is in filmmaking, but I don't know what Asha does. She's on leave for a while from whatever it is. Intriguing, isn't it?"

"What about that strange man who's renting Cock Ring Girl's old house?" Vera asked. Cock Ring Girl, whose real name escaped them all, had left Jasper Lane recently. (Her hubby had become the spokesman for a prominent sex toy maker after using, and thoroughly enjoying, the cock ring his wife had won for him at one of Cassie's gay porn parties. He had written the company, saying how much he enjoyed the product, and a star was born.) "Any news on that creepy mother fella?"

"None," Cassie said, with a hint of indignant mystery. "I went to welcome him to the neighborhood this morning as well and couldn't get him to so much as open the door for me."

"Very odd… and rude!" Melinda exclaimed.

"I thought so too. We'll just have to see if our resident hermit ever shows himself."

Vera stirred in her seat. "Child, this has got Hitchcock written all over it!"

"Just you wait, my darling," Cassie assured her close friend. "I'll figure that man out."

"I know you will." Vera smiled, shaking her head with knowing.

"So," Becky interjected. "How's life with Jason? Are things going well?"

Jason, Cassie's son, had only been back on Jasper Lane for a couple of weeks. Still, whenever his name was mentioned or he walked into Cassie's presence, she lit up as if she were seeing him for the first time in years all over again.

"It's heaven having him around again!" Cassie exclaimed.

"I haven't seen him out much. Does he have friends in town?" Melinda asked.

"Some… but he spends a good amount at home with me."

"Be careful, honey," Vera warned. "You don't want him turning out like our resident Norman Bates down the street."

"He'll be fine," Cassie said, even as her smile hinted worry. "Jason has always been what others might call 'strange'. He's unique— an artist. And artists are loners." She looked to her friends for corroboration. They all smiled politely.

"Patrick called," Melinda chirped up, ending the awkwardness. "He'll be coming home soon, I should think. Maybe he and Jason could get to know one another better. They never really had much of a chance growing up."

"Yes. That would be lovely!" Cassie appreciated the shift in subject. "And how is Patrick?"

"He's well," Melinda proudly explained. "He's doing very well in his courses. I'm so proud of him."

"And his girlfriend?" Cassie inquired.

"Oh, I'm afraid they're broken up." Melinda put on an affect of disappointment.

Cassie, Becky, and Vera said, "Oh," with faux commiseration.

It was a teenage crush, after all. Not really worth devoting a full-out fall-to-pieces cry over, and they all knew it. *Heck*, Melinda thought, *I didn't even fall to pieces when the divorce from Frank finally happened.*

"What's this Becky tells me about you dating again?" Vera asked, all playful insinuation and marvelous wide eyes.

"Yes," Melinda admitted, somewhat embarrassed. "I'm dating a wrestling coach from Patrick's old high school. Patrick never knew him, because, well, he never wrestled of course, but…."

"A wrestling coach," Cassie said hungrily. "Sounds hot! It's been a while since you've been pinned, Melinda."

"Well, to be honest, after Frank I was kind of worn out. And it's true that all the nice, clean, attractive men really are gay. That's not just a cliché. I was desperately hoping it was something women just told one another."

"There was that man you met at the Joneses' Fourth of July party last year. He was very attractive... and straight," Becky reminded Melinda.

"And a porn star!" Melinda said, as if that in itself explained everything.

"Aww! There's the old Melinda," Cassie teased, tilting her head in mock adoration.

"Malcolm—that's the coach—he's just what I'm looking for. He's just the right sort of man to jump back into the dating world with." Secretly, there were a couple of things about Malcolm that bothered Melinda. One of these was his name. His first name, Malcolm, was a good, respectable name, very classic. "Melinda and Malcolm" sounded like a respectable couple. But it was his last name that set her on edge: *Nipple!* He was known as Coach Nipple!

She was certainly not going to tell *that* to any of her friends.

"My dear," Vera said. "I've never seen you more relaxed. He must be doing something right." She winked.

Melinda blushed. "Vera!" She turned her gaze to the coffee in her mug, praying that her friends might never discover she was dating... a Nipple.

*Oh, that word!*

A clatter from the large front door of the house brought the foursome's attention to Jason as he joined them on the patio. His hair was long and tangled, and he was a week's gone from shaving. He looked every bit the American expatriate he had been while traveling through Europe. Barefoot and wearing a hole-ridden pair of paint-speckled jeans and a T-shirt, he carried with him an easel, a choice of

8

paints, a glass of water, and, in his mouth, a couple of paint brushes. He unburdened himself without much trouble, setting the easel so that it was turned to him and he could paint Jasper Lane.

"Well, hello, darling!" Vera exclaimed. "Aren't you gonna give us a kiss?"

"Hello, ladies," Jason spoke lightly with a half-grin. He put his paints down and came to his beaming mother, kissing her on the cheek.

"What's this?" Cassie asked, touching the painted heart on his jaw.

"My heart," Jason answered. "Just a whim this morning. I wear it where I can see it now." He gave Vera a quick peck on the cheek and returned to his easel.

His heart comment had struck Cassie, but she did her best to hide it. Of course, she knew Jason would wear his heart in the open now. It had been hurt plenty when hidden on the inside, hurt by his very own father. Cassie still carried guilt for remaining with Jackson for so long, for not getting herself and Jason away from him sooner.

Melinda sighed. "I should be going," she said. "I have things to do before I see Malcolm tonight." She rose, ever the lady. "Thank you, ladies, for a lovely morning."

*God, her smile*, Becky thought. Good Housekeeping, *here she comes!*

"I should be going too." Vera pushed her chair back gracefully. "The club doesn't run itself. I've got a host of hot gay boys to prepare for tonight."

The ladies all said their goodbyes for the morning to both of the Blooms on the patio. Cassie saw her three friends off with the class her position required, waving at them as they made their journey down from the cul-de-sac to Jasper Lane. After this, she sat once again at the patio table, watching her son as he eyed canvas and subject.

"Are you happy here, Jason?" she asked. "Are you truly glad to be back with me?"

He didn't look at her, but instead put color to canvas with a couple quick flicks of his wrist. "It's good to see you, Mother," he replied. It was honest enough.

"That's not what I asked, darling."

"I know. But that's all the answer I can offer you right now."

"Jason, I wish I could…. Oh, I don't know, do things differently for you."

"Mother," he said, at last looking at her. "I'm past whatever anger I had toward you. You did what you had to do for me. I know that now."

The way he said it made her wonder if he knew the truth. Did he know just how far she had gone for him? As far as murder, or at least, an accomplice to it?

"I'm very happy to be with you again, Mother." He smiled, charming and uncertain at the same time.

She was enchanted by his face; she always had been. How he could make her smile with a simple look. Which, she supposed, is why the opposite expression made her feel the failure as a mother. "Do you think you'll ever be happy here again? In this house?"

Jason continued his frenetic painting. "This is not a jab at you, Mother, but I don't think I ever was happy here. Not with Dad. Not with all the pressure to be what he wanted me to be."

"I understand, darling," she lightly replied. Still, in his sad answer Cassie did not hear a denial to her inquiry. Could he be happy again in this house? He hadn't said no.

She rose, gathering the coffee mugs by their handles with the long, elegant fingers of one hand. "I'm going to fix myself a cocktail. Would you like one?"

"That would be lovely, Mother." His attention never left the canvas.

Cassie walked toward the door, pausing to catch a glimpse at his work; the beginnings of an impressionist's-eye view of Jasper Lane. Fragments, dots, and blurs fusing to form recognizable forms. But if one looked too close, it was nothing but a befuddled mess. She ran her hand gently along his shoulder. "Looks good," she encouraged. "I'll be right back, sweetheart."

SINCE Rick had been working as the supervisor of Hot Body Gym, he had come to classify bodybuilders in two distinct categories: the ones who did it right, following the rules of safety and evolutionary intelligence and doing it for more than just superficial reasons (what those reasons were he could never discern); and the roidtards. Rick groaned every time one of the roidtards came into the gym. They primped and preened, strutted and flexed, were loud and obnoxious, and were at their most contemptible while doing squats. Everyone must look at them. They needed that attention. "Look at this, fellas," they would say as they flexed in the mirrors, even as their undergrown genitals poked up like sprouts from their too-tight Lycra shorts. Rick imitated them at home sometimes, to James's amusement.

The man who stood in front of Rick now, red-faced and embarrassed, wearing a barely there tank top with a dip that exposed a huge, veined chest and strangely protruding nipples (*God, you could nurse on those!*) was indeed a complete and utter roidtard. He held to his crotch with both massive hands as if, by some chance, his dick would suddenly spurt length past its pre-pubescence and he would need to restrain it from ravaging the gym membership. It seemed his tight shorts had finally given way as he struggled to save himself from an awkward and dangerous position.

Just before the defrocking of the diminutive dick, Rick was walking around the gym (he had numerous responsibilities, and making sure the fitness center was clean and uncluttered was one of them), and he noticed a small gaggle of people standing around a weight bench, watching the chemically enhanced Jerkules bench an unreal amount of weight… without the recommended spotter. The looks on the faces of the observers were of nervous fear, not adoration. Before Rick could make it over to the bench to put an end to the non-testicle spectacle, however, the roidtard's arms simply gave out. The bar crashed down on his chest, forcing a loud fart from him and a horrified gasp from the group of spectators. Immediately, Rick and the others standing nearby were upon the meathead, helping dislodge him from the outcome of his foolishness. And as the roidtard rose, freed from his metal weight, his shorts, unable to contain his thigh muscles any longer, ripped and fell to the floor.

Once he had frantically drawn up his shredded shorts again, he stood surrounded by snickering gym-goers and the one-eyed stare of a disapproving Rick Cooper. The roidtard didn't look Rick in the eye. Instead, he bounded as fast as he could to the locker room. Rick rarely needed to say anything to any of the gym's patrons if they did something unsafe. His look said it all. The eye patch, of course, was a little intimidating, but beyond that Rick just didn't look like a happy-go-lucky man. He never had. Even his smile seemed forced. Ever since he was hired on as supervisor, he was constantly told, "Smile, Rick! Customers like to feel welcome. You're a good-looking guy. Show those pearly whites!" But his smile was even more unsettling than his natural broodiness. In the end, though, he did his job well, and that was all that mattered.

The truth was, despite his appearance and demeanor, Rick had never been happier nor more content. He had a great job, he had a beefed-up body due to his hours at the gym, and he had a great home he shared with the love of his life, James Tucker.

"Turn that frown upside down," James always teased in rhythm.

"What, and scare the children?" Rick replied.

James was everything to Rick. That's why it was especially difficult on days when James came to work out at the gym; Rick could never get any work done. All he wanted to do was be where James was, see what he was doing, smell his scent, touch his sweaty shoulders. More than once while James was doing bicep curls in front of the mirrored walls of the gym, Rick had found himself hanging lazily from the pull-up bars and watching his partner like a bedazzled kid or a curious monkey with a sick love. Rick was drawn in James's direction. He had no motor control when James was in the building. And so this day was no different.

# Suburbilicious: Vignettes from Jasper Lane

Before Rick even got to the area of the gym where the free weights for bicep curls and shoulder shrugs were located, he heard a kind of ruckus, a *whoop-whooping* from a small crowd. "Oh, Lord!" he thought. "Not another roidtard."

As he made his way past the laughing men and women, however, he saw that it was not the brainless exploits of another uneducated meathead after all. Instead, in front of the mirror and the delighted group of fitness enthusiasts, Rick's pride and joy, James, and James's rugby teammate, Seth, were dancing, keeping in perfect step like two members of a boy band, to Celine Dion's "That's the Way It Is." Rick stood and folded his arms, stoic but giggling on the inside to the boyish charms of the two; these two large, muscular men, bouncing and arm-waving to a pop song. James had met Seth through the gym itself. They were both members of the all-gay rugby team, the Sacred Band of Thebes, and had immediately connected like frat boys, or, in James's case, army buddies.

It was Seth who first noticed Rick standing in the crowd of onlookers. He stopped, returning the gaze with his happily surprised, gap-toothed grin. He was a masculine-looking man, square-jawed and hair shorn like James's had been when Rick had first met him. Seth liked to work out in his rugby gear. He said it made him feel the part, as if being a tax attorney wasn't his real job. His legs were as thick as redwoods, and while the rest of him was large and beefy as well, he always seemed to Rick to be bottom heavy… and that included a rather large ass. He had two teeth missing from playing rugby on and off all of his life, so when he smiled, as he did now, it always caught Rick off guard. It was a bit menacing.

Seth nudged the still-dancing James, who seemed disappointed that their floor show had ended. The crowd began to disperse, but not before giving a scattered applause.

"Dude," Seth said, like a buddy-buddy schoolboy. "Your BF looks pissed." He nodded, still grinning in Rick's direction. His hands were set on his thick waist.

James shrugged. "He always looks that way." He crept to Rick playfully, reaching around and pinching him on the behind. Rick swatted at his hand.

"This is a gym." Rick played the regulator. "Not the set of *Can't Stop the Music*."

Seth lifted his hand to his forehead. "Yes, sir!" he said, that strange grin still there.

"Don't be like that, babes." James took Rick by the hand, leading him behind one of the large circular pillars in the gym. Once there, Rick's severity immediately lessened.

"You know," James said, forehead to forehead with Rick, "Seth is gonna think you don't like him."

"I don't know him. How can I not like him?"

"You didn't like Ballser right off the bat either, remember?"

"Ballser was a cum stain. Seth is an okay guy, as far as I can tell." Secretly, though, Rick did have a growing suspicion about Seth's intentions. It was nothing he felt compelled to voice yet, however.

The back of James's hand brushed down Rick's chest and stomach on the way to a more tropical locale. Rick grabbed it, his eyes lighting in caution and delight. "We're in public!" An honest smile formed on his face.

"That's it!" James laughed. "Smile again, baby."

"James, you sex-crazed fiend! Stop." Rick was tickled by how James, once the very poster boy of frightened closet cases, was now able to top even their flamboyant friend Terrence in outward and open displays of affection. "Save it for later. All this working out has got your testosterone flowing, hasn't it?"

"I've got a flow, all right." James winked.

Seth peeked around the pillar. "You two homos done? If not, can I join in?"

Rick's stoic, no-nonsense expression returned.

"I'm a-comin'," James said, pulling his hand from Rick's clasp. "Seth and I have gotta get this workout in. We've got practice in about an hour."

"Good," Rick grunted. "The sooner you're out of here, the more work I can get done."

"Hear that, Jimmy?" Seth remarked, putting his arm around James's shoulder. "You're a distraction. Can't say I disagree with him, ya big piece!"

Rick did not like that at all. Yep. James was right, Rick concluded. He didn't like Seth.

"Are you coming to the game?" Seth asked.

"Of course," Rick answered.

"He's gonna wear something sexy as hell, aren't you, babe?" James lifted his brow. "He's my own personal cheerleader. You could wear one of those little skirts and do flips so I can see your panties."

"I can't cheer."

"Terrence can teach you. Wasn't he a cheerleader in college?"

"He and Christian went on that father/son thing in the woods."

Seth was pulling on James's arm to get back to the weights. "Oh, that's right," James remembered. "Well, at least wear the skirt and panties." Seth pulled him away.

Yeah, Seth was coming remarkably close to being cum stain–like.

"On second thought," James yelled from the weights, "forget the panties!"


TESSA, the name of Terrence's one-night tryst with the puzzle that was heterosexuality, had put together the trip to the father/son camp as a surprise for both Terrence and their son, Christian. She had done this because she knew that they needed to spend more time together. Of her own admission, she hadn't even let Terrence know about Christian (Terrence called him Chris, for reasons of obvious aversion) for the first sixteen years of their son's life because she wanted him to be raised with her own ideals. She realized the folly of this now and sought to rectify the error by any means she could.

It was a long drive from Jasper Lane in the compact minivan; an all-nighter. They would have been there sooner, but Terrence insisted on stopping by every antique store they passed, and there were a lot of them. Chris liked browsing, so this was not something he fussed over in the beginning. But by the time they were through browsing (or the shop owners had thrown them out), the minivan kept getting more and more compact.

"Dad, no more!" Chris eventually had to put his foot down. He said it with a bright smile, though. He said everything with a bright smile. He could have said "Rupert Murdoch is President" and still be smiling as the world collapsed around them.

Chris realized this was par for the course with his father, this semi-parenting of Terrence. For their trip, Chris had packed a few items of basic clothing that he could reuse; he had also brought camping gear, and Terrence had helped him pack the tent in the back. There would be plenty of room for them in the minivan, he had first supposed. But that was all before Terrence began loading his "basics" into the van. Terrence had brought luggage. He had packed every creature comfort he could think of: an electric toothbrush, his iPod, his laptop (and a small library of the best of Falcon porn), and the latest issues of every magazine he subscribed to, all twenty-six of them. Chris just laughed as he stood alongside David and Cliff, the three watching Terrence struggle with his load of unnecessary necessities. "That's our Terry!" their expressions seemed to say.

Once they finally arrived at the camp, which consisted mostly of pines and lakes spotted by barren patches designated for the tents (the only stable structures were the check-in and the latrines), it was Chris who realized exactly what type of vacation his mother had planned for the two of them. He wondered when Terrence would notice, but, thankfully, he didn't seem to be paying too much attention to what was going on.

*God, thank you for laptops and gay porn DVDs!*

Terrence had completely missed the three crosses at the camp's entrance, and, to Chris's relief, his father had even skimmed over the rather obvious Christian feel and look of the check-in as they approached it. Chris held his breath the entire time, but there was no grand explosion of horror. Terrence was completely unaware, even without his DVDs. Chris thought it would have been humorous, if it weren't so sad. Instead of paying attention to the crucifix-decorated welcome forms he was signing or the "Jesus loves you" pen he was holding or the collar-wearing older man who was welcoming them, Terrence was busy checking out the only other father to arrive as of yet, a cute *GQ*-ish number with gorgeous, executive hair and a plaid shirt. Chris was thankful for this; otherwise, their vacation together would have ended sooner than… well, a gay man's vacation at a bible camp.

The old priest or preacher or shaman—whatever he was—the old man who had welcomed them shook Terrence's hand, but Terrence hardly noticed. He had caught the other father's eye, trying to reel him in. Quickly, Chris acted. He pulled at his father like an anxious child ready to go to the fishin' hole, and soon enough they were out the door with the directions to their designated campsite.

"Did you get a look at *that*!" Terrence whispered. "Oh, daddy!" Then, remembering he was with his son, he straightened up, somewhat embarrassed.

"This ain't the Dunes in Saugatuck," Chris jibed. "Here are the directions. It's not too far. I'll drive."

They first carried the large green army tent they had borrowed from James (well, Rick gave it to them, technically, without telling James) from the minivan. Setting it down, they surveyed their surroundings. They were given a spot at the rear of the campground near the woods and the lake. Terrence liked this. From here he could watch the other fathers arrive and slowly divide and conquer.

"I wonder where Paul Bunyan from check-in will be?"

Chris shook his head in mock disappointment. "This isn't a monastery, Dad. Mom sent us here to spend more time together."

"And we will," Terrence assured him. "But I'm sure there are going to be times when you want to be alone with the other boys your age."

"Right." Chris smirked.

"I'll start unpacking!" Terrence proclaimed excitedly as he sauntered back to the minivan. It was the sauntering that made Chris giggle. Terrence was like a chameleon; he changed every five minutes, trying the butch routine here, the more fem there. Turned on by superheroes one day and cowboys the next. Even his hair was a constant show of changing personal taste. When Chris had first met Terrence the year before, his head was shorn as clean as a cue ball. Now he wore a stylishly messy blond mop. Chris sighed. *What a great dad!*

Chris busied himself with unpacking the tent so that the canvas lay square on the ground. He set the pegs and rods to the side, knowing that one of the competitions described at check-in was the raising of the tents. Kind of like a barn-raising, he supposed, but pointless. When done he squatted on the ground as Terrence fumbled his way in and out of the minivan. It was immediately an enjoyable show, so he tore open the beef jerky he had bought at one of the previous nights' numerous pit stops and chewed hungrily.

"Hello, young man," came a kindly voice from the dirt road near the campsite. The preacher/pastor/shaman who had checked them in earlier was walking toward their site, kicking up dust onto his black ensemble with his shiny black shoes. "Christian, right?" he said, coming to a stop in front of Chris. Terrence remained by the minivan, still fighting with his luggage. Chris was able to keep an eye on his father over the preacher's shoulder.

"That's right," Chris replied with his trademark smile. He was hoping desperately that Terrence would be too consumed with his testy luggage to recognize the old man was actually an old man of the cloth, and was relieved when the old man didn't repeat his name: Father Donaghan.

"Very appropriate for this place, your name is." He chuckled. "I just came by to tell you something I forgot. Check-ins are always so confusing for me. The older I get...." He wasn't a bad old man, Chris thought. Rather grandfatherly, in fact. Wilford Brimley-ish, but not as hefty. "I came to invite you to the prayer circle this afternoon," (Terrence straightening, ears seeming to perk up to the sound of danger), "a circle of Christian and brotherly love," (Terrence turning in their direction, a deer caught in the headlights), "a joyous praising of the Lord."

At once, Terrence dropped his luggage and bounded into the woods, desperate for escape. Father Donaghan heard the luggage drop but was too slow to see Terrence flee into God's wilderness.

"Looks like you've over-packed, my boy," he said, noting the spilled luggage.

"Looks like," Chris agreed anxiously.

Kindly refusing the old pastor's generous and continuous offers to help him get things settled, Chris finally saw Father Donaghan off and at once leaped into the forest after Terrence. It didn't take him long to find his father. The sounds of a cell phone's keys being punched frantically led him around a thick wall of ferns and brush.

"What are you doing?" Chris asked.

"Calling your mother," Terrence hissed. "She did this on purpose. Did you know about this? Oh, it's an evil plot! I've never been more Barbara Stanwyck than now."

Chris took the phone from him without much struggle. Terrence simply wasn't expecting it.

"What are you doing? Give that back!"

"You'll get it back when we head home. Not a moment before." He closed the phone before Tessa could answer and stuffed the cell into his pocket. "Now come on. Let's get things unpacked. Christian or not,

19

you're going to have fun here. And you're going to have that fun with me. Got it?" He turned to go, expecting Terrence to follow.

After a few steps he heard a rustle in the brush and turned to see Terrence still hidden behind leaves and trees. His fingers pulled away the leaves just slightly enough so that he could see out. "Is he gone?" he whispered loudly. "Is the church man gone?"

"Stop that!" Chris whisper-shouted back. "Stop hiding behind bushes. You look creepy!"

"Don't talk to your father in that tone of voice!"

"If you don't come out from behind there, I swear to God, I'll—"

"You'll what?"

"I'll scratch every DVD you brought with you!"

There was an audible gasp, more rustling, and then Terrence emerged from nature as if nothing had happened. "Let's go raise a tent," he said, walking briskly past his son.

CLIFF'S large, legendary, muscular ass was right in the middle of being plowed by a well-hung Austrian named Leopold when Steve got the call. As the new CEO of GetchyaSome! Productions (he and Cliff had both been lured back by sizeable raises), Steve made it a point to visit the sets of all of his gay porn films in production. He wanted to show his stars and crew that he cared about the end product. There had been a need to prove himself. After all, he was a straight man running a gay porn powerhouse. There were always whispers behind his back. To keep his position on top, as it were, he had to show that he had every intention of producing the best in butt sex and blow jobs out there. After a few choppy weeks and a sweeping PR push, he had gained the begrudging respect of the industry. It didn't hurt that he had experience in the gay-for-pay subgenre. That had made his acclimation to the biz much smoother. Still, though, respect had been obtained. Steve visited all of his sets, especially those sets with his biggest stars. And Cliff was the biggest, in every sense of the word, as well as a good friend.

The sound of Steve's cell phone jingling in his pocket (he had forgotten to set it on vibrate) interrupted the entire awe-inspiring scene being filmed, eclipsing Cliff's line "Come over the Cliff, baby!" as Leopold the Austrian plunged and tried to rend the porn superstar in two. Steve's home phone number appeared on the ID, letting him know his wife was calling.

"Sorry," Steve shouted to the crew as he clicked open his cell. There was a sigh of disappointment and a call for "Cut!" The Austrian dismounted Cliff, and they sat chatting on the makeshift dock in the backyard of the large production house until the director was ready to roll again. Steve walked a few feet to the other side of the pool, a film set that for once was not in use. "Sweetheart," he spoke gently, "I thought we'd agreed that you would never call during working hours unless there was an emergency." Then he paused in panic. "Is Amy all right?" His heart had begun pounding before the thought had even finished. Had something happened to his Amy? His baby girl? His pride and joy?

"Amy's fine," Sandy choked out through loud, squeaky sobs. "But I'm a bad mother!" Here she let loose a wail that caused those nearest Steve to look in his direction.

Steve calmed himself, closing his eyes in relief, and walked farther away from his employees. "No, you're not," he soothed. "Why would you say that? You're the best mother in the world. Any orphan would be lucky to have you."

She seemed not to notice his attempt at levity and continued trying to speak in a choking, halting, whimpering plea for understanding and reassurance. "I love our daughter, Steve. I love Amy."

"I know you do, baby. Who said any different? What's this all about?" He could see her now, sitting at the dining room table, using her hair as a snot rag. She never used to act like that, but since Amy's birth, things had changed.

"I had this dream, see?"

"Is that all?" He ran his hands through his dark hair and then took a glance at his watch.

"I had this dream that I was five hundred pounds and we had ten children and the house was a sty, a complete mess, infested with roaches. I couldn't keep anything under control. All the kids were mean to me and looked like Lindsay Lohan. They said I was a bad mom." Wheezing, choking, phlegm.

"That's ridiculous," Steve assured her. "We'll never have more than five."

Again, levity failed, and Sandy let him know it by her exasperated wailing.

"Okay! Okay! I'm sorry. I'm serious now. That won't ever happen, darling. I mean, look at you. You're more beautiful now than ever. And come on, Lindsay Lohan? Amy is much better looking."

"Really?" Sniff sniff. "I'm more beautiful now than I was? I'm still pretty?"

"Absolutely."

"Well, that makes me feel a little better. But that wasn't the worst thing about the dream. The worst part was that you had a mistress."

"Now, that *is* ridiculous. You've always been the only one for me. Even when I was doing gay-for-pay and had a dick up my ass I was thinking of you. Honey, you have to watch what you eat before you go to bed. Food can have an effect on your dreams."

"I guess so." She was calmer now. "I guess I just feel useless, Steve. I mean, being a mother is great and rewarding. It's, you know, all those things the talk shows say it is. But I'm just so anxious. What am I missing out on? The world's going on without me while I change diapers and watch PBS with Amy. Maybe I just need a hobby."

Steve saw Cliff approaching from around the pool. He walked with large strides, the meat of his frame shaking with each heavy footfall underneath the white terrycloth robe. He was like a steroid piñata. The sun glittered off his dark blond hair, and his smile told Steve he knew exactly what was going on.

"I'm on break," Cliff whispered. "Do you want me to talk with her?"

"Honey," Steve gently cooed into the phone, "your best bud's here. Do you want to talk to Cliff?"

There was a pause and a sniffle. "No," she said timidly. "Not just yet."

Steve shared with Cliff a confused grin. "Why not?"

"Because in my dream you were fucking him too."

THE empty halls of the high school in summer echoed the clip-clop of Melinda's impressive heels. She was dressed in her best, knowing that the way she looked went a long way toward making her the region's number-two Avon representative. A long, flowing skirt and a light blue summer sweater rounded out her outfit. Though no one was around, the noise her heels made on the cold floors was causing her a great deal of embarrassment. She was a nice, petite woman. Women like her didn't echo down hallways! So she was relieved when at last she came to the rubber floor of the gymnasium where Malcolm was holding practice with his top wrestlers, ever in preparation for the next school year. He had the top wrestling team in the state for two years running.

And there he was, all six feet gorgeous brawn of him in a blue T-shirt and sweats. Melinda had met him at Patrick's graduation. He had glanced her way then, giving a flirtatious wink. She smiled back, red-faced, but she hadn't followed up with anything more. She wasn't ready. She needed to "defragment" herself (a computer term she had recently learned). Deconstruct and reconstruct. It was like starting over completely new with men, as if she were a virgin. She nearly was. Frank, her ex-husband, had been paint-dry boring. But now she thought, with all that behind her and a respectable period of solitude, she was as ready as she would ever be to get back "out there." When she ran into

Malcolm again and he asked her out for the seventh time (she had kept count), she agreed to a date.

To have someone now as new and exciting and handsome as Malcolm in her life was... well, it was amazing. His presence scared away any memory of Frank. She was happy with the woman she was becoming, if a little scared. The woman that she had been was becoming a distant memory, a woman of someone else's construction.

Melinda watched the coach with his wrestlers. They flipped and struggled and pinned one another in their sweats, not in the singlets they usually wore for competition. And they got themselves into the most astonishing positions. Why, they were almost foul! Perverted even. Melinda found herself blushing and had to look away several times. She doubted very much that she would be able to sit through a wrestling match. She smiled to herself. That must be what the Boys do. She imagined David and Cliff, Terrence, Rick, and James, all flipping and flopping around but going much further with the play. *And doing it naked.* She smiled more, thinking that not a year earlier such a thought would have set in her more turmoil than she could have handled. The thought still shocked her, but it didn't disgust her.

Malcolm's fierce coach persona lifted as Melinda waved from the gym door. He seemed to become a different person entirely. His brow unfurrowed, his stance relaxed, and a smile replaced the scowl on his rugged, unshaven face.

"I'll be right back, guys," he shouted as he jogged across the gym to Melinda.

She was delighted by him. Sometimes he seemed so innocent and free, ready for anything. He kept his eyes to her as he approached. He had a nice body, and it showed through his sweats. It wasn't sculpted like David or James, and certainly not anywhere near the size of Cliff, but it was nice. He was simply a man who took care of himself, yet never refused a piece of pizza if he so desired one.

"How's my girl?" he said, his smile a mischief-maker.

Melinda blushed again. "I'm well." She swung a little, like a girl with a crush. "I just thought I would take a break from selling Avon

24

and come see you. These boys should be outside in summer, Malcolm. Not in school."

"Ah," he said, turning to look at his wrestlers. "These are my best guys. I gotta keep them focused and fit. Besides, they're having fun."

"Are you?"

"I am. But," he whispered, "it would be more fun if you were on my wrestling team. What do you say? If I opened it up to girls, would you join? You could pin me down."

Melinda giggled and felt all the more foolish for doing so. Malcolm continued to watch her adoringly. He had a deep cleft in his chin. She was beginning to love that cleft among many other little things about him, and they hadn't even been dating too long.

"Wanna pin me? Huh? Wanna pin me?" He hunched his shoulders, drawing near and poking her playfully in the sides.

"Stop! Stop!" She laughed until she let out a huge squeal that echoed through the gym. The wrestlers looked and whispered with smirks and lurid glances. Melinda turned beet red.

Malcolm turned to the boys. "Practice!" he warned. Turning back to her, he said, "I better get over there. Are you ready for tonight?" He flashed a playful grin.

"Yes," she said, delighted and nervous. Her redness was fading now as the boys' attention had waned. "Our first night together."

"If it's too soon...," he offered, though his expression was pleading with her not to back out.

She paused for a moment, thinking she might. But then said, "No... no. It's the perfect time, I think. I want to. I really do."

"Me too." He drew her close and kissed her. Not one of those gentle romantic kisses, nor one of those boring obligatory kisses Frank had given her, but a kiss like she had never had. Rough, hard, and animal.

"Nipple!" one of the boys yelled. Melinda nearly screamed, jumping at the word ringing through the large gymnasium. It bounced off the walls and continued down the halls, a thousand "nipples" filling the air.

The coach gave her a last flirting look then went back to work. She watched him walk away. She never imagined she would ever date a man like him. He was so masculine. So perfect. So different from Frank. And that was all that really mattered, wasn't it? Malcolm seemed to really care for her. He hadn't let up asking her out until she had said yes, and she was glad she had. But what if things progressed? What if they fell in love? Her heart jumped at the thought of marriage. Could she ever really take his name? Could she ever let herself be referred to as Melinda Nipple?

CASSIE was happy to indulge her son Jason's artistic endeavors. In fact, it brought her quite a bit of personal joy. She lay in a plastic tub Jason had pulled up on the deck; she was draped in a white robe with a white towel wrapped around her head and one arm hanging limp from the side. (Jason wanted to re-create the artist David's controversial *Death of Marat*.)

After the morning's coffee gossip with the ladies, when Cassie had come back outside with the cocktails for her and her son, Jason had momentarily disappeared. He was so very different since he had returned from Europe, hardly the same boy at all. He was no longer the gleeful, boisterous boy he had been. Now he was quiet and introspective. His laidback attitude was refreshing to Cassie in that he seemed at last somewhat content. But this also worried her because she had no idea what he was thinking. He would never let a word about that be known. Was there still resentment there for her? Perhaps she should have told him the truth about his father's disappearance and what led to it, after all. He still didn't know about any of that.

Soon enough Jason reemerged onto the deck carrying a robe and a towel and pulling behind him the plastic tub he had once used as a toy box.

"Wherever did you find that?" Cassie wondered, staring with nostalgia at the object. It brought to mind happier times when it was just her and Jason, times when Jackson was away on business.

"It was up in the attic. I found it the other day." He handed her the robe and the towel. "Here. Go put these on. I'm going to make you a martyr."

She gasped in delight and ran inside, excited to be the subject of her son's art.

And there she was, a diva in a tub play-acting a villain as a martyr. She relished the chance to overact with dramatic aplomb whenever the opportunity presented itself. She even let out a few sighs to get in the mood as she draped herself over the edge of the tub. Of course, her cocktail was never too far away, sitting just in reaching distance beside her trusty cell phone.

When the phone rang, Jason paused. He knew his mother would answer so he didn't bother trying to stop her.

"Sorry, darling." She stretched for the cell. "I won't be a minute." She knew he knew that was most likely a lie. She liked to talk.

"Hello, Vera!" she exclaimed as she played with the towel on her head. "Oh, I'm in a toy box on the deck. I'm posing for Jason. Yes. He's brilliant." A wink to Jason. "What's wrong, dear?" she asked Vera, recognizing a slant to her friend's voice.

Jason watched as his mother stiffened and began peering down the cul-de-sac at the street below. "You don't say," she said, the venom coming out in her voice. "Thank you, Vera. I'll look into it directly."

Cassie continued to eye Jasper Lane, searching for something. She seemed to have forgotten completely about the painting.

"Mother," Jason spoke, reminding her of why she was in the tub. "What's the matter?"

Cassie turned her attention back to her son, the villainess in her voice not apparent in her expression. "That was Vera at the club," she said. "She said on her way out this morning she saw that strange man, the one who's renting down the street, she saw him with binoculars in a tree… watching *our* house."

"Is she sure it was him? Maybe it was some kid or someone building a tree house." Then, "What's Vera doing paying such close attention to other people's trees?"

"Apparently whoever it was wasn't very well hidden. I suppose, though, you could be right; it could have been someone else. She did say she didn't get a very good look."

"There you go then. May we continue?"

"Of course, darling," she said sweetly. Cassie knew that Vera was rarely wrong about anything, though. In all the time Cassie had known her, Vera had only really been misguided once: before she became Vera, she and Cassie had dated exactly one time. When Vera called in the middle of the day about seeing a strange man in a tree watching the house, Cassie knew to take it seriously even if she didn't particularly show it. Yes, Cassie would get to the root of this. She'd find out all about the mystery man and his Tarzanic espionage. *Oh, the excitement of a new project!*

"One moment, sweetheart," Cassie said as she rose from the tub, standing and facing Jasper Lane.

"What are you doing?"

"If somebody wants a show, I'll give them one." The robe dropped to her feet. "Forget *Marat*, darling. Paint *The Birth of Venus*."

THEY stood proudly for the Lord at the center of the campground. It was just after noon, and they were soon to have their first meal together as a godly group right after the prayer circle. Terrence was quite knowingly the limp dick in this particular daisy chain. He held hands with Chris to one side of him, and a large man with bad pores who smelled of garlic to the other. The man's fleshy paw was sweaty and uncomfortably tight. Terrence tried to wriggle free, but it was of no use.

Garlic Man was holding on relentlessly, clearly enraptured by the old pastor's prayer—the old pastor's long, long, long prayer. Terrence had never been averse to prayer. No, he had indeed prayed quite a few times in his life. He had prayed for a good night at a bar, for the right price on a pair of boots, for the chance to meet his favorite porn star. Yes, he had probably prayed more than all those in the circle combined. Christ! His life was practically a religion in itself.

Terrence found it difficult to keep his eyes closed for prayer. Couldn't Father Donaghan just mutter an "amen" and get it over with? Does the length of it really matter to God? (He giggled internally at the question.)

Directly across from him stood the hot *GQ*-looking father he had noticed at sign-in. Terrence took advantage of the moment. Now that all the other eyes in the circle couldn't see him ogle, he studied the man. Quite attractive. Not at all the type Terrence usually fell for, though. After all, he wasn't a muscle boy. Terrence imagined the man's name was something classy like Frederick or Timothy. He took care of himself, it seemed. His shoulders were broad, and he definitely looked to have some muscle beneath his manly plaidness. Hmm. Physical fitness. Strange for a straight man. *Very strange indeed.*

"Timothy's" son looked quite a bit like his father, Terrence noted. They could be brothers. Chris didn't look as much like Terrence as the resemblance that existed between these two. In Terrence's mind, there was now a contest between him and Chris and "Timothy" and his son for best-looking father and son at the camp. Yes, there was definitely competition for that title now that Terrence examined things more thoroughly.

*Damn that Timothy!*

He realized with a start that Timothy was staring back at him now. How long had his eyes been open? Terrence felt himself turn red, and he quickly closed his eyes. As he tensed, Garlic Man tightened his grip even more.

*God, was this prayer ever going to end?* God knows we're grateful, Terrence thought. This is bordering on harassment.

He opened one eye just a little. Timothy smiled and then stuck out his tongue and scrunched his nose. Immediately, Terrence snorted. He couldn't help it. The laugh came up so suddenly he was powerless to stop it. Another wave of supreme embarrassment came over him.

He could feel Chris looking at him, tightening his own grip on Terrence's hand as if chiding. On the other hand—literally—Garlic Man loosened his grip, perhaps aware he wasn't next to the most pious of men. Father Donaghan seemed to stutter over his words but then continued.

When Terrence was certain the danger had passed, he once more opened his eyes slightly. Timothy made yet another face, this time crossing his eyes and sticking his tongue out sideways. An effective variation.

Terrence couldn't hold back the laughter this time either, but it was much louder. Garlic Man at once let go of his hand. *The circle was broken! The circle was broken!* Father Donaghan stopped and stared, baffled. Chris pulled at his father's hand with a forced smile, covering his own embarrassment.

"Dad! Hush!"

Then there was Timothy! *That Timothy*—or whatever his name was—smiling innocently even as Terrence tried uselessly to point at him.

"It's just… he… I'm sorry," Terrence stammered as he regained his composure.

"Something funny, Brother?" Garlic Man huffed.

"No. Nothing. I'm sorry." He locked playful eyes with Timothy. "I guess something just got into me. The power of the Lord."

RICK opened the door to the house with a satisfied sigh. He was done for the day.

## Suburbilicious: Vignettes from Jasper Lane

He had gotten up early in the morning before it was even light out and crawled over James, who was sprawled on the bed, wrapped in covers and snoring. He took a shower, dressed, and then kissed James on the forehead before he left, knowing that the evening was *their* time. The fitness center and work claimed most of the day, but the evening was set aside for recreation. It was the time of day Rick loved most. Now, finally home, he could relax the night away with James. They would probably watch a movie, cuddle, drink some wine, the usual. The wonderful, ever-comforting usual. It was nice to have a routine now. James's fondness for routines had rubbed off on Rick, and he liked being rubbed off on by James.

He heard the splash of water in their bedroom bath. James was home already. He hadn't taken his Jeep to the fitness center that morning. Instead, Seth had picked him up. Rick thought when he got home James would still be at practice and Seth would drop him off later.

"James," Rick called, walking to the bathroom.

"Taking a bath," James answered.

"A bath? Not very green, James. Showers are better." The bathroom door was wide open. Rick couldn't help but smile at the sight of James in the tub. Such a large man, surrounded by bubbles, his hair wet and face dripping. His knees shot up out of the water, dirty and scuffed.

"I know. Call Al Gore. I'm bad." He was all innocence. It was enough to make Rick start undressing on the spot.

"Looks like you need a good scrubbing."

"Then get in here and give me one." James set his arms on the bathtub's edges and arched his brow as if he were a romantic hero.

Such talk was embarrassing. The stuff of bad romantic novels, but at the moment the blood had gone to their dicks, not their brains. Maybe poets and playwrights had clever sex with witty flirtations. Rick and James just wanted the cheap, dirty kind.

Rick crawled carefully into the tub and leaned back against James's stomach. He felt James's penis getting harder against his back,

31

and James hugged Rick tight to his body, nibbling on his ear. The water was plenty warm. The heat they were creating would surely cause it to boil.

"I could have fucked you right there in the fitness center today," James mumbled.

"I got the keys. Maybe we can go play some night when nobody's there."

"Oh, I want to get you on the squat machine!"

Rick chuckled and rubbed James's dirty knees.

"What are you doing home so early?" Rick asked. "I thought you'd still be at practice."

"We quit early. We'll practice extra hard tomorrow. Tonight the guys want to go get a drink so I came home to get cleaned up."

Rick's plans for the night dissolved right there. There was now a bump in the routine. "I was hoping we could spend some time together."

"What are we doing now? Besides, I won't be long. We're going to JR's, just up the road. Why don't you come?" He gave Rick a kiss behind the ear.

"No," Rick mumbled, defeated. "No. Those are your friends. Maybe I'll just get hold of David or Becky."

"Are you angry with me? Baby, don't be mad. This is my team. I'll be back in no time. Then I'm gonna ravage you." He began chewing on Rick's ear with ravenous attention.

Rick couldn't help but laugh. "Ouch!" he squawked. "Too hard."

"Will you wait up for me?"

"I guess so. I can postpone our night for a few hours. You'll probably be kicked out of that blue-collar bar anyway. A bunch of gay guys in a straight bar? Unnatural."

"We're not all gay. There's Will."

"Oh, yeah. I forgot about your token straight guy. I guess every team has to have one," he joked. "Do you need a ride? How much are you planning on drinking?"

"Don't worry about that," James replied. "Seth is picking me up again."

SANDY was playing with Amy on the floor, still sniffling from her breakdown earlier on the phone with Steve, when the doorbell rang. She handed Amy the teddy bear they were playing dancy-dance with and rose to answer. She realized she looked in no way appropriate to answer the door. Her clothes were wrinkled and stained with baby food, her hair was all loose ends, and her eyes were puffy from crying all day. And if she thought about how inappropriate she looked to be answering the door any longer she would only end up crying more.

Elizabeth Trump stood stoic and proud when Sandy opened the door. She was the president of the Gay Porn Wives Club, an organization that Sandy was a part of but rarely participated in. The reason for this rare to non-participation on Sandy's part being said Elizabeth Trump. The very demeanor of the woman was irritating to Sandy. She was a pretentious bitch who looked down at anyone who didn't have that certain car or wear those specific shoes. She always reminded Sandy somehow of how Eva Perón was portrayed on stage and film. Elizabeth's hair was pulled back tight, and she wore tweed suits even in the summer.

Standing beside her was her husband/hag fag, a prominent porn star ridiculously named Eddie Licious. What his real name was Sandy didn't know. But Cliff had done a few films with him and never had anything too wonderful to say about him. From what Sandy gathered it was a case of "All About E" between Eddie and Cliff. Eddie would do anything to be number one in the porn business, and at the moment, Cliff was the only man in his way.

"Hello, Sandra," Elizabeth said. She spoke like she was thinking of taking up a new accent, something from across the pond. Sandy had to restrain herself from pointing out to Elizabeth the fact that she was from North Dakota and everybody knew it. Her true accent was probably more Marge Gunderson than Princess Di.

"It's Sandy, Elizabeth. You know I prefer Sandy. Every time we talk I tell you to call me Sandy."

"You look tired, dear."

"You look constipated. What do you want? My daughter and I are playing." There were certain people Sandy could successfully hide her contempt for when she spoke to them. Elizabeth was not one of them. Eddie smiled politely from behind like a good pocket gay.

"Children," Elizabeth muttered. "So pleasant. I'm glad I couldn't have any."

"I imagine they are too."

Elizabeth grew impatient. "Enough with the pleasantries. I'm simply here to tell you that the Gay Porn Wives annual presidential dinner will be held next week. You, of course, being a member of the GPWC, are invited, though I don't see the point in you coming." She paused, hoping it had the effect of bringing Sandy down a peg.

"Is it time for a new president already?"

"Well, no. I mean, there's no one running against me. There hasn't ever been actually." Eddie corrected her with a mumble. "Ah, yes. There was that one, but after she was exposed as a lesbian she couldn't truly be expected to win the race as a Gay Porn Wives President, could she?"

Amy hollered happily from inside.

"Fine. Great. Sounds fun," Sandy said, exhausted. "I'll be there."

As she started to retreat inside and close the door, Elizabeth, who hadn't moved to leave, reached forward, forcing the door to stay open. Her eyes showed shock and displeasure. "You're coming?"

"Sure. Why not? I have nothing else to do. It would be nice to be around some other grownups for a change."

"But… what about the child? You can't just leave the child here by herself? And I hardly think it would be appropriate to bring her along."

"Well, of course not! I'll get a sitter." She noticed the exchange of looks between Elizabeth and Eddie. "If you didn't want me to come, why did you invite me, Elizabeth?"

"It's the duty of the president to make certain everyone knows about certain events. Even those who…."

Sandy folded her arms. "Those who what?"

"My dear, the GPWC has some dignity. We're a classy organization. You can't come looking like that!"

"I don't intend to, Elizabeth. I can shower." Then the most delicious little notion popped into her head. Their looks of disgust had prompted it. They had no one but themselves to blame. "I'll see you then, Elizabeth." She shut the door on their faces and walked back to Amy, her arms still folded and a grin creeping across her face.

Yes, if she ran for president of the GPWC, it would kill two birds with one sharp-edged diamond stone. And she could win. She knew she could. She was much more likeable than Elizabeth, after all. By running and winning she would finally have something to do outside of being a mother to Amy, and she could defeat Elizabeth Trump at the same time.

There wasn't much time, though. She had only a week to prepare. She had to make the other ladies of the club see that her non-attendance at the meetings had nothing to do with any disgust or disrespect for gay porn, and everything to do with Elizabeth Trump. Yes. Sandy felt a second wind in her life. She would start at once. She would make her intentions known to all.

"Your momma's going to be president, baby girl," she said as she picked Amy up from the carpet and made for the laptop to type out a few e-mails.

TERRENCE sat comfortably outside the tent flap chatting on his cell phone with David. He had begged and whined until Chris relented and gave it back to him. Chris stared at his father, feeling a mingling of things. He was proud that he and his father had won the first contest, that of the tent raising. But he was also a little embarrassed that the other fathers and sons were still nowhere near finished. When Terrence had hollered "Done!" and the pastor came striding over and pronounced them the winner, all the other teams had stared in disbelief. Garlic Man had even insinuated that they had cheated somehow, a notion that Terrence challenged, saying he could tear it down and build it three more times "before you could even pitch your tent once, you smelly old fatty!"

Father Donaghan gave Terrence a chiding look. "We're all brothers here," he said. "This is all in the spirit of godly fellowship."

*GQ* Guy, or "Timothy," gave Terrence an impressed nod, though, afterward, and that calmed Terrence down. In fact, he went nearly bashful.

"How did you learn to put that tent up so quickly, Dad?" Chris asked. The other groups' progress was now slowed by discouragement. They had misjudged the fruity-acting guy and his cheerful son.

"David taught me in college. We did a lot of camping. I pitched a lot of tents." He giggled with adolescent fervor.

So now there was nothing left for Chris to do but watch the tents slowly go up. The sky grew darker, and the other fathers and sons had a harder time getting their own tents raised because of it. Still, they looked to be having a lot of fun. Chris was a bit jealous of the father/son back-and-forths he was seeing.

"I'm going to see if anyone needs help," he said, rising from the Scooby-Doo cooler. He was hoping Terrence might offer to come along.

Terrence simply nodded as Chris walked away. "Oh, this daddy's a real hottie!" Chris heard his father explain to David on the phone. "And I can't be sure, but I think he might be interested in me too…. Oh, Chris is fine. You should see how proud he was when we won the first competition…."

Chris made his way around the grounds, getting curious looks from some of the teams, distrustful looks from others, and even a "hello" or two. But no one wanted his help, so he continued walking until he came to *GQ* Guy and his son, *Seventeen* Boy.

"Hey there!" *GQ* Guy said immediately.

His smile was welcoming, and Chris felt relieved enough to walk right up to them.

"Hi. Need some help?"

*GQ* Guy looked at his son. "Sure! We're not going to win anyway. Who cares if we get disqualified? I'd rather that then come in second place."

"We're not a very competitive family," his son added.

"Believe it or not, us neither." Chris thought a moment. "Well, I suppose Dad's a little competitive in some things…." (Like men.) "But I don't think there's anyone here that's going to give rise to his edge." He helped *Seventeen* Boy in his task of getting the pegs firmly in the ground. It was a large tent.

"What?" *GQ* Guy asked. "Does he like to rassle?"

Chris laughed self-consciously at the joke. "Close."

"I'm Harry, by the way," the father said. "This is Jordan."

"I'm Chris," he introduced himself. "My dad's name is Terrence."

"So, Chris, what's a nice boy like you doing in a Christian place like this?"

Chris laughed. He liked this family. They weren't at all the religious zealots he was expecting or like the type he had met growing up. "We were tricked by my mother."

"Your mother?" Harry stopped working and regarded Chris.

"Yeah, but she and my dad aren't together. He actually didn't even know I…." He caught himself before he divulged family secrets. "They're not together."

"I see. Maybe I'll go introduce myself."

Chris swallowed. "He'd probably like that." Yes, he probably would. And he'd probably faint just so Harry would catch him in his arms.


VERA stood behind the glass window of the VVIP Room (that is, the Very *Very* Important Persons' Room), high above her surging patrons. Normally neither she nor anyone she knew would frequent this room of her club. It was originally designed strictly for the elitist snobs of the gay world, the ones who felt they needed a space from which to look down on all the others. Vera hated those types, even if they kept her club on every gay man's "place to be seen" list. But tonight, for the first time, she found the room to be truly useful. She sipped her apple-tini mindlessly and watched the bodies below shake and crawl over one another. The strobe lights and pulsing music facilitated their sense of tribal dance and unity.

"So now we need to decide what to do," Cassie said from behind her at the table where she sat with David and Becky.

Vera had closed off the VVIP Room to everyone else so there would be no one else there to hear their conversation, a conversation that was going to be rife with secrets.

"And you're sure this guy was watching Cassie?" David asked Vera.

Vera walked back to the table, her face etched in worry. She took slow, gorgeous, deliberating steps. "What else could he be doing? He wasn't bird-watching. We ain't got no special birds around these parts."

"Vera's right. He had to be watching me," Cassie said. "We could hope that he's just some lunatic or pervert. Hopefully a *harmless* lunatic or pervert...."

"The world's full of them," chimed Becky.

"But we must also think on the most unpleasant of possibilities."

"That he knows about Jackson." David stared at the table surface in front of him. He breathed heavily. "And this had started out as such a good day. Terrence only called me once."

Vera sat down, rubbing her forehead with her long fingers. Her fabulous nails, each pasted with flawless faux rubies and emeralds, glittered under the sparse light. "Do you think the crazy son of a bitch, whoever he is, knows your husband is buried around your house and flowerbeds?"

"I don't know," Cassie replied quietly. "But he knows something."

"Maybe he's a private eye, a detective," Becky offered.

"Maybe." Cassie leaned forward, moving her wine out of the way, and took Vera's hand, holding it tight. "Don't you worry too much, Miss Vera. Not yet. Let's find out who he is first. Then we'll make plans to deal with him in the best way we can."

"What have I got to lose?" Vera said. "I've killed one man. Why not another?"

"You know that's not what I meant."

"I know, hon." She squeezed Vera's hand in return. "I wish I could have seen whoever it was more clearly. It's been gnawing at me all day."

"If he is a detective you wouldn't know him. None of us would," David said. "So, what's our plan, Cassie?"

"*Our* plan?" Cassie pulled back and drank her wine. "You and Becky have nothing to do with this any longer, David. This is for me and Vera to deal with now. We just thought you should know what was going on since you helped us clean up matters in the first place."

"Bullshit!" David exclaimed. "We helped you cover that bastard up, and we're gonna make damn sure he stays covered up. Got it?"

"We're helping out, Cassie," Becky agreed. "Now, what's our plan?"

Vera and Cassie smiled at each other, appreciative of the loyalty of their friends. "Guess there's no getting rid of them, Cass," Vera remarked, the concern still evident in her voice and demeanor.

"We need to find him," Cassie said. "We need to dig him up, every troublesome piece of him we hid around the house. And we need to get rid of all of them. That last part I already have figured out; I just need to reassemble the bastard."

"Do you know where he's at?" David asked.

"Mostly. I won't forget it easily. It'll be like excavating a dinosaur. We'll dig until we find the complete skeleton. We'll have to do it very late, though." She was tired of dealing with Jackson. Even dead he was causing her problems. How to keep what was going on from Jason was going to be the true task. He was an inquisitive young man, and what was about to take place around the house would surely make him suspicious of things.

"What then?" Becky inquired.

"Then we cremate him," Cassie spoke resolutely.

"THAT was… a lovely dinner," Melinda lied as she placed her fork on the finished plate of ravioli. She dabbed at the corners of her mouth with her napkin.

When Malcolm said he would cook for her she thought he had meant it, not simply crack open a can of store-bought food and serve packaged salad as a side dish. Still, it was the thought that truly mattered, she supposed.

"I honestly tried to really make something," Malcolm apologized. A CD of power rock ballads played softly in the background. "I bought this Mediterranean cookbook. Was gonna make you something out of that, but I set the kitchen on fire."

Melinda couldn't help but laugh. "That's okay. Really! It's very sweet that you went to all this trouble. My ex-husband wouldn't have bothered. You've made the place up... quite nicely."

She studied his home as if to back up her claim with something in particular. The candles about the house were a nice touch. Other than that, though, the place looked like he really didn't spend too much time there. There was an enormous plasma TV on the wall and a cushy leather sofa, of course. There were copies of *Sports Illustrated* fanned thoughtfully on an end table. And there were a couple of life-sized wall posters in the shape of various sports players she was unfamiliar with. *What a strange decoration for a grown man!*

"The bedroom's better," he whispered with a grin, having followed her eyes.

"Pardon?" Melinda acted surprised.

"The bedroom looks better. I don't decorate the front room too much. It's just seen by my buddies usually when we watch the games. They don't care about how the room looks as long as the plasma's there and a pizza's on the table. But the bedroom...." He winked.

"Spend a lot of time in there, do you?" Melinda teased.

"I'll be honest; I have dated quite a bit. But it's all a search, isn't it? For that right gal?" He rose from his seat and took her hand. "Would you like to see it?"

Nervously, Melinda let herself be led through the house to the master bedroom. They passed a trophy case of bronze and gold wrestlers.

"My victories." Malcolm beamed. "Back in college mostly."

"There are quite a few of them. You must be very good."

When they reached the bedroom door, Melinda was speechless. This room was indeed very different from the front part of the house— but no less tacky. In fact, the tackiness might have actually risen a couple of notches. The room was dark, lit with candles. Leopard and zebra prints covered the bed and chairs. A giant naked bronze wrestler was posed in the corner. And there were not-too-subtle hints of leather here and there. The rock ballads were being piped through the entire house by an expensive sound system. Hearing the music in the bedroom, Melinda thought it reminiscent of a scene from some serial killer movie starring Jodie Foster.

Malcolm walked to the bed and sat down, seductively massaging the area next to him. "See? I told you it was better."

His smile was so adorable and proud that Melinda did everything she could to seem dazzled. "It certainly is!" she exclaimed, perhaps too flamboyantly.

She approached the bed, and Malcolm took her hands, bringing her down with him to lay on the leopard print. She couldn't help but keep her eyes open as they kissed; the leopard print was staring back at her. Malcolm rolled over on top of her in their embrace.

*This is nice*, Melinda thought. *So what if he's not the most sophisticated man? He's a fantastic kisser. And his body!*

As she thought this, and her nerves began to settle, a set of angry lyrics jarred her. "I Wanna Fuck You Like an Animal" blared throughout the house.

"Shit!" Malcolm said as he quickly untangled himself from Melinda's arms. "How did that song get on the playlist? I'll fix that. Be right back." He raced from the room.

Melinda was left on her back, staring up at herself. A mirror! On the ceiling! Over the bed! She hadn't the time to utter anything in horror. Malcolm came bounding back into the room and threw himself on the bed, covering her mouth with juicy kisses. He had thankfully turned the music off now, and all Melinda could hear was the sound of her own nervous kissing and the beat of her heart.

But she couldn't keep herself from looking at the mirror. Was this how she always looked making love? Horrified and clumsy? She was lovelier than this, surely. More elegant. But then, maybe years of being with Frank had done this to her. Years of not having any intimacy at all had made her look frigid.

The thought of Frank and what he was responsible for fueled a spark of anger in her, and that anger made itself apparent by a bite to Malcolm's lip. He growled in pleasure and kissed her back roughly. She enjoyed that and ground herself into his strong, vibrant body. She rubbed at his crotch, the first penis she had felt in too long. She felt a twinge of shame for allowing her hands to wander. Her eyes in the mirror, the eyes of a Melinda she was trying to let go, chided her. So, to ignore the eyes in the mirror, to chastise them in return, Melinda put her weight into rolling over and on top of Malcolm. They had rolled around so much, though, that there wasn't a lot of space left on the bed, and they went tumbling to the floor.

Malcolm caught his breath. "Forceful," he growled. "I like that in a woman!"

"Sorry. Guess I misjudged how much room we had."

"Nothing to be sorry about, baby." He flung his arms above his head, clearly turned on. "Dominate me! Do what you want. I wanna be punished."

Melinda rose on her hands in alarm and confusion. "What?"

"I've been bad. All men are bad. We need to be spanked." He turned over beneath her, sticking his rump in the air.

"I would agree that men sometimes are—"

"Do it! Hit my ass! Smack it!"

Melinda had no idea what was going on. Was Malcolm into S and M? She had just recently learned what those initials stood for after stumbling into an e-mail in her "bulk" folder.

"Come on, baby! Smack it." His voice was muffled by the carpet.

Melinda hesitantly obliged, giving his rear end a slight tap.

"Harder! You can do better than that."

She slapped it again, harder. She had to admit, it was a bit freeing to let go of some pent-up energy.

"Just whale on it. Think of all the men that have done you wrong. Take it out on me. I'm begging you. I need it!" He wiggled his tush at her. "Think of Frank."

That did it. She let loose with a spanking that could have been argued as abuse. But slap after slap Malcolm groaned in delight.

Melinda stopped suddenly, disbelieving what she was doing. Malcolm sat up, his eyes glowing with desire. "Why'd you stop? That was hot."

"I don't understand. What are we doing?"

"We're having fun. We're two consenting adults having a good time on my bedroom floor."

"But I'm hurting you."

"No, you're making this a great night. It makes up for my ravioli screw-up."

Melinda smiled and kissed him gently. "You're a sweet, strange man," she said. "But that ravioli *was* awful. You need to be punished! Let me see that rear end." She pushed him back down on the carpet.

"Yes, ma'am!"


MORNING in Hot Body Gym: The die-hards and soccer moms filled the place. Rick Cooper had other thoughts on his mind.

"Seth came by this morning and picked James up again." Rick thoughtlessly hoisted some scattered light weights onto their racks as he confided in his old college friend David and Steve, the porn producer. "He never drives anymore; Seth always offers to take him to rugby practice."

"I don't think there's anything to worry about, Ricky," David said. He stretched his shoulders and arms, preparing to do some chest exercises.

"James is obviously still crazy about you," Steve interjected, pulling on David's arm. The two and their very significant others were becoming the resident cool couples of Jasper Lane. David and Cliff and Steve and Sandy. It sounded like a sex comedy from the 1960s.

"I know, and I feel awful," Rick monotoned. "It's not like I don't trust James."

"It's not?" David lay down on the bench press. Steve stood behind to spot.

Rick thought for a moment. He trusted his boyfriend; sure he did. James couldn't lie, couldn't cheat or be dishonest. It just wasn't in his nature. Rick picked up a light EZ curl bar just to have something in his hand. "I just don't trust this Seth guy. Do either of you know him?"

"I've met him," Steve said. "Thighs of death. Would love to get those on film."

David rose from his set. "He's a nice enough guy. Very friendly."

"Maybe that's it. He's just too friendly for my taste. Maybe James is right, and there's no reason to be jealous at all."

"Maybe." David shrugged. "Ricky, you're acting a bit like Terrence here. He's the one who usually freaks out like this. I've never seen you act this way before."

"Must be true love," Steve teased.

Rick sighed hopelessly, letting the bar in his hand swing a little too broadly, nearly hitting Steve in the knee.

"Whoa, killer!" Steve took hold of the bar. "Man, you *are* distracted."

"Maybe I should head out for a bit—take a break before I hurt someone," Rick reasoned.

"Sounds like a good idea, Ricky." David stood and patted his friend on the back. "James loves you. There's no need to worry. You've marked your territory on that one."

"That's kind of gross, David."

Rick found someone to cover him for a few hours, one of the chipper underlings who would do anything for more money—and had. He started driving, thinking he would stop and get a coffee or a cappuccino or something more suitable to ruin his diet. He could blame it on the stress and worry and not feel too bad about it. As he drove listening to a Josh Ritter CD, however, his worries took over. They would not be silenced, and Rick soon found himself driving in the direction of the rugby field, just a large, bare patch of land behind the local high school.

Rick parked and walked around the corner of the school. He peered cautiously and saw thankfully that he could easily get close enough to practice to watch James without being too obvious and make certain he went unmolested by Seth. There were a couple of large minivans parked in the grass, and a sizeable crowd had assembled to watch the Sacred Band of Thebes charge up for the big game the next day. Included in this crowd were some of the members of the other teams—the other, *straight* teams—the Sacred Band would face. They wore mocking or condescending grins on their faces. Rick was reminded of that scene in *A League of Their Own* where the idiot in the bleachers yells "Girls can't play ball!" That's how these guys looked. Like big, dumb, cocky, straight idiots.

Rick found them useful, though. He hid unnoticed behind a group of those straight idiots and tried to find James amongst the huddle of shorts and thighs. He recognized James's ass before he saw his face. Rick knew that ass anywhere. That ass that looked so good in running shorts, that ass that looked as if it were poured into khakis, that ass that should be in porn, that ass that—*had just been smacked by Seth!*

Rick was furious. How dare Seth! He had to look away to restrain himself from pushing the ogres in front of him aside and doing some American-style football tackling on the rugby field. He turned his back to practice and seethed in silence.

*I should just go home. Just go home and get control of myself. It's just a game. Guys always smack each other on the asses in games. JUST. GO. HOME.*

But before he took one step toward the high school parking lot, he heard a high-pitched shrill voice rip through the air, making everyone turn in his direction, even the rugby players. In front of him, a little girl holding her mother's hand had stopped, pointed at Rick's eye patch, and screamed, "Look, Mommy! A pirate!"

*Damn Johnny Depp!*

The mother quickly hushed the obnoxious child, apologized, and hurried away. Rick decided he and James would never have children.

"Rick?" James called from the field. Rick turned to see James running toward him, and everyone else's eyes focused on his eye patch. "What are you doing here? I thought you had to work?"

"I—I do. I am," Rick stammered. "Just taking a break. Thought I'd come to see how you're doing."

James smiled. "We're doing great. These straight guys don't know how good we really are."

Seth came up from behind. "Heya, Rick!"

Rick nodded. "Well, I better get back to the gym. I was just… uh…."

"Checking up on me," James interjected.

"What? No! I had a break." He swallowed at being caught in a lie. "I had a break and now my break is through, so I'm leaving." He turned around stiffly and walked away.

"See you tonight, baby!" James called, amidst what Rick was sure were straight idiots snickering.

"Bye, Rick," Seth hollered.

*Fuck off, Seth! And hands off my man's ass.*


VERA again spotted the man in the tree immediately. He wasn't too well hidden. He was a grown man in a small tree and looked just this side of ridiculous. Vera had just finished her morning chit-chat with Cassie, Becky, and Melinda and was heading to her car parked along Jasper Lane when she sighted Mr. Obvious. He didn't see her as she approached the tree. His binoculars were focused intently on Cassie, who rested decadently on the front deck of her house in an elegant lounge chair, so Vera didn't need to sneak to get to him. Women of her fabulous distinction didn't sneak anyway. They made themselves known. She flashed her flamboyance with her colorful spring gown and ravishing wide-rimmed purple hat. Her high heels sank into the grass as she left the sidewalk and stood at the bottom of Mr. Obvious' tree.

"That limb is not going to support you much longer, sugar," she said in her loud, pay-attention-now voice. Vera didn't holler. Ladies don't.

The sound of her commanding voice shook him, and he dropped the binoculars to the ground. He nearly fell after them.

"Can I ask what you think you're doing?" Vera inquired. She looked calm and collected but was ready for a fight if the strange man decided to jump from the tree like some jungle animal—a rabid sloth.

"I'm…." Vera saw him trying to think, trying very, very hard to think, the poor imbecile. "I'm…." She also saw the way he looked at her. She knew that look. That was a look of a man with a crush. "I'm…."

"You're a terrible spy, honey. And not much of a liar, either. Now get down from there before you hurt yourself."

The man did as he was told. Once on the ground he collected himself, wiping the dumbstruck expression from his face. He was not a terribly intelligent-looking man. He was impish with small features: tiny eyes, a tiny nose, and a tiny mouth. His face seemed incapable of showing any emotion but displeasure or momentary surprise. Only, his eyes showed that hint of enchantment that Vera was all too familiar with. Men adored her. At least until they found out she had been born with a penis. Then most of them ran away, afraid of what that said about them and what their attraction to her said about the true nature of love.

"I'm watching birds," he finally sputtered.

"Really? And what's that bird up there?" Vera pointed to a small sparrow on a limb.

"Well... it's complicated. You see—"

"Cut the crap, sweetie. You were watching Miss Cassie. I want to know why."

He said nothing. He simply stared at her, falling deeper for her the longer he stood there. Finally he spoke. "A fine woman like you shouldn't be privy to the wrongs that horrible witch has done."

Vera controlled herself. Normally, upon hearing any man insult Cassie, Vera would have laid him out flat. But she had an idea. She could use his infatuation with her to their advantage. She saw she needed to pull out all her acting prowess. Miss Dorothy Dandridge lives again!

Vera softened her gaze on the round little man in his crumpled suit. She leaned in closer as if about to whisper a secret. "You're right," she said. "She's a vile woman." It hurt her to say it, but the play must go on. "She's done things—"

"What things?" the man responded caringly, excitedly, to her newly exposed, delicate womanhood.

"Oh, the things I've seen! She has this neighborhood under her thumb. She has us all doing what she pleases. There's no escape once she has you. You must get out!" Vera flung herself on the man, too dramatically, she thought. But he responded with a gasp.

"You poor creature," he said, holding her in his short arms. "Why do you stay with her? Why do you have coffee with her every morning?"

"What else are we to do? If she suspects any of us are disloyal, she'll...." Vera turned on the waterworks and wept defenselessly onto his shoulder. Bending so far over was straining her back. She would need to make an appointment with her chiropractor when she got home.

"There, there." He rubbed her shoulders a little lustily. "Don't you worry. I've got plans for Cassie Bloom. What's your name?"

"Vera," she said as she pulled from their embrace. It wasn't hard to do. She was much stronger than him, a fact that seemed to excite the little man. "What's yours?"

"Let's not worry about that," he said with a nervous grin.

*Dammit!* Vera thought, though she continued to smile and wipe away fake tears.

"You know," she offered. "I should really leave you alone. If you're going to catch Cassie doing the evil that she does, you need all the time in the world. She's a clever one."

"Don't I know it! But not as clever as me." He winked.

They stood for a moment, the little man undressing Vera with his eyes, Vera trying to erect a psychic force field around her body. "Well," she finally said. "Back in the tree you go!" She gestured as if she were giving him a hoist.

"Oh, right!" he said, struggling to climb the old arbor again.

"You should go higher than you were," Vera offered. "People can see you otherwise."

"Thanks!" the man called shakily as he climbed.

Every so often he would stop and look down at her, as if to say, "High enough?" "Higher!" she would encourage. This continued until all Vera could see was a pudgy ankle in black socks through the foliage of the trees.

"That's high enough!" she called.

"But I can't see anything!" he yelled back.

She couldn't hear his response, however. Vera was already in her Escalade, cruising slowly down the tree-lined drive until she came to the house he was renting. Making certain the imp hadn't followed her and that no one else was watching, she quickly got out of her car and cautiously opened his mailbox.

"Sales, notices, junk," she said as she fanned through the contents. It was all addressed to Current Occupant, everything except the very last one, clearly a porn magazine wrapped in brown and addressed to a Mister—

"Sweet Jean Marie!" she said aloud.

Across the street, another of Jasper Lane's newest arrivals, Asha Fields, came out of her home to check her mail and was watching Vera curiously.

"Hey, girl!" Vera beamed, hiding her surprise at being caught going through someone else's mail. "I'd stay and chat, but I gotta get to the club. We should get to know one another. Later!" She threw the letters back inside the mailbox, hopped in the Escalade, and drove off.

As she drove, shaking her head in total shock, she said to herself, "Cassie is going to flip!"


"THIS is my sister, Candice."

Malcolm had done the introduction as his sister joined him and Melinda at The Bread Room Café on Barbour Street where they were meeting for lunch. Candice was a very thin woman, full of outrageous gestures and loud, joyful proclamations. The whole café looked her way when she spoke, much to Melinda's embarrassment. She was abrasive and opinionated right from the start.

"We're all illegal aliens!" "Why not legalize marijuana? Cigarettes are legal. Gateway drug, my skinny ass!" "The government subsidizes illness; there's no money in healthy people!" "Sam's Club is a cult!"

Malcolm encouraged her by laughing at everything she said. Melinda tolerated her, shielding her face as best she could from the other patrons of the café. Melinda smiled pleasantly at Candice's jokes, all the while picking politely at her Caesar salad (light Italian dressing on the side). Was it even appropriate to be meeting members of Malcolm's family so soon? Their relationship had just started. It wasn't as if they were going to get married anytime in the near future, though,

Melinda thought with naughty delight, their romantic encounters together certainly seemed like those of a committed couple. At least, a committed couple in those glorious cheap reads one finds in the supermarket, which Melinda had become addicted to.

"So." Melinda took the initiative to find out more about Malcolm's sister. "What is it you do, Candice?"

"Please call me Candy. Everyone does." She then went on to explain that she was a police officer and proceeded to extol the virtues and hardships thereof. Melinda couldn't help but focus on the name: Officer Candy Nipple.

Candy Nipple. Melinda felt she was constantly surrounded by variant degrees of ridiculousness of late. Like the real world was still out there, but she was an unwitting actor in some adolescent teenage boy's favorite show. A show filled with funny names and flatulence—that last gag played very well by her very own mother and her... gas problem.

Melinda watched Malcolm taking in his big sister as if everything she said was new, as if he hadn't heard it a million times before. The truth was they probably talked every night. Their family bond was tight. But was that refreshing or troubling? Malcolm would occasionally flash a grin at Melinda as if to say "Isn't she great?" and Melinda would smile back, waiting for the end of Candy's life story. A story told in stereo, it seemed, for the entire café to hear.

"... and that's when I told the governor to lick my pussy!"

At last, with that disturbing anecdote, Candy was finished. Melinda rose to escape to the restroom and freshen up.

"I'll join you," Candy said with excitement.

"I'll be waiting." Malcolm beamed at them both. "Don't you ladies talk about me too much in there."

The restroom was very small. Only three stalls. It was a small café, after all. But Melinda only wanted to check her face. (What a silly phrase! As if her face might have fallen in her salad during lunch.)

Candy seemed to have the same idea and stood remarkably close to Melinda. They bumped elbows more than once.

"My brother really likes you," Candy said. "He really does. Haven't seen him this worked up over a woman since high school, when he dated Nora Dunkstall."

"Oh, really?" Melinda was pleased. She grinned thankfully at Candy in the mirror above the sink.

"Yeah. Unfortunately, I had to drop-kick the bitch when she broke his heart."

Melinda's heart leapt, and she froze, staring back at the now glaring Officer Nipple. "I—I don't plan to…." What could she say? How was she to know how things would work out between Malcolm and her?

"I'm just pulling your leg!" Candy screamed, laughing and nudging Melinda playfully. "I mean, I really did kick that slut Nora's ass, but Malcolm takes care of his own heartaches now."

"Oh," Melinda sighed, relieved.

"Had you going, though, didn't I?"

"You certainly did."

"Ah, come here, you!" To Melinda's extreme displeasure, Candy put her in a headlock and gave her what she believed was referred to as a *noogie*, a first for her. She had never been more humiliated! At least there was no one else in the restroom to bear witness to what was happening.

Candy released her and headed for the door. "You can't fool me, Melinda. You act all prim and ladylike, but Malcolm told me what a fine wrestler you are."

Melinda stared at herself in the mirror. Her blouse crumpled from the struggle in the headlock, her hair messed, her eyes wide with shocked embarrassment. She was wrong. This moment was far more humiliating than the noogie.

TERRENCE was bored and depressed. In fact, his depression had led to his boredom, and his boredom had led him to the stash of alcohol hidden in the glove compartment of the minivan… and the alcohol in the side-door pocket… and under the seat… and in his luggage. He had hidden the good stuff everywhere, determined not to go without his cocktail when he needed it. And he knew he was going to need a few cocktails on this trip. After all, this wasn't one of those fun camping trips with the Boys, the kind where everyone coupled off and didn't see one another again until dawn's light. This was a father/son thing with a bunch of straight men who knew nothing about having a good time. Not really. They roasted marshmallows and told ghost stories at the campfire. Very pedestrian stuff. Terrence felt left out.

"You feel that way because you don't get involved," Chris chastised him. "Just go hang out with the other dads. They're cool, from what I know."

But Terrence's painful adolescence had ingrained in him a fear of groups of straight men and boys. He always went off on his own to avoid them, always played by himself on the playground in school. He still hadn't resolved his issues with childish name-calling and the threats of violence. He was glad Chris would never have to go through all of that.

Also, Chris and he hadn't won at anything since the tent raising, and Terrence felt he was letting his son down. He thought he was a terrible father, and he thought Chris felt that way as well. Tessa was right to keep them secret from each other for so long.

"It doesn't matter, Dad," Chris had said sweetly. "I just like being here with you. That's the whole point of this, not how many contests we can win." Such a kind, endearing boy.

"*How did he come from me?*" Terrence wailed as he gulped down a baby bottle of scotch. Then he made a disdainful expression. He hated scotch. Why did he have scotch?

Chris was hiking now with the other fathers and sons. Chris never pleaded, but he did ask for Terrence to come along. When Terrence had said no, he wasn't sure if he saw disappointment or relief in his son's eyes. Had he broken Chris's heart or given him the chance he needed to escape, hitchhiking his way from the camp and back to his mother? It was midday now, and Terrence was alone, sitting outside the tent in his camping chair with attached foot rest. He'd already been drinking for an hour, but he had just started to turn into a crying, runny-nosed mess.

"I'll be good and hammered when they come back. Then I won't care. Then I'll be able to do anything." Terrence believed he was kind of similar to Popeye when he drank his drinky-poos, except without the deformed forearm muscles. "They'll see!"

He struggled to rise from the chair; it hung low, so it was a difficult feat when mixed with his mild inebriation. "I'll win every contest to come! Me and Chris will. There'll be no stopping us." His foot got caught on the chair, and he fell to the ground. "I want to go home."

To make matters worse—worse than being a disgrace to his only son, worse than being on a camping retreat with mean, mean hets, worse than falling on his face in the dirt—the hot dad from sign-in hadn't flirted with him yet. Not since the prayer circle, if that *was* his idea of flirting. Even when he came over and introduced himself during the tent-raising contest, he had done nothing but smile his way through his introduction. There were no telling winks or "accidental" brushes against the arm. And to top it off, his name was Harry, not Timothy. Funny. He looked much more like a Timothy than a Harry to Terrence. They didn't talk much afterward, either. It was actually rather awkward. Possibly because Terrence was drooling over the guy.

"I'm so stupid!" Terrence pounded his head backward into the dirt. "Ouch."

He realized he should have said something; he should have made a move on the guy.

"Oh, how beauty confounds me!" He stared at the sky. The sun was bright, and Terrence shielded his eyes. "There's only one thing I can do," he said decisively.

At once, he rose and got his backpack from the tent, filling it with his beverages. Bottles and bottles, most of them travel-size or stolen from hotels. They clinked as he hoisted the bag over his shoulder. The backpack's weight nearly brought him to the ground again, but he found his balance. He was going to find the group. He was going to catch up with the hikers, with Chris, with the pastor—with Harry.

Terrence was going to make his move and become a new man. Everyone would be so proud. He took a swig from a new tiny bottle of vodka and set off on his journey.

ELIZABETH TRUMP stood at the podium in the Civic Center looking out across the two dozen faces of the Gay Porn Wives Club. She stood as haughty and severe as any queen, and had on more than one occasion referred to the group as her "subjects," but only to Eddie or when no one else was around. She was a taskmaster, a hard woman, because she had to be. That's what the job required. Being president was no easy thing. It wasn't a job that any simple housewife could handle, certainly not someone the likes of Sandra Jones. So her husband Steve had gone far in a short time in the biz; so what? Elizabeth was a porn producer herself. She made sure the films got made. Without her, all gay-kind would crumble and fall.

Elizabeth Trump knew she was fabulous!

Eddie Licious sat obediently beside the podium. Even though he was not officially part of the club, every woman there knew he was the second in command, no matter if Joyce Brummet held the office of VP. Eddie's dark skin and eyes made many of the women lose track of what Elizabeth was saying. It had happened more than once that someone had to be reminded what the weekly meetings were for. No, they were chided, they were not there to fantasize about Eddie and his strong back and large dick that they had all seen in numerous films. The point of the club was to expose the beauty of gay porn to the world and to fight off the religious zealots that picketed their industry. Of course, it didn't help that Eddie always wore the tightest faded jeans he had and the most chest-hugging, bicep-grasping T-shirts he could find. Women didn't go to the restroom to touch up their makeup when he was around; they went there to drool in private. Eddie was Elizabeth's Trump card. As long as she had him, she would always stay in office. No other Gay Porn Wife had a husband who could compete with Eddie's popularity and looks.

Roll had been taken, and the meeting was coming to order. A few minor issues were discussed—stores that would no longer carry gay films, new actors to watch out for being posted on the *Buckstar Bulletin*, possible new inductees to send invites to. It was all done very quickly and efficiently.

"And now we come to the issue of the presidency," Elizabeth spoke in her commanding tone. "Since it seems there will once again be no one to challenge me, what say we do the election now, just as a formality, and get it over with?"

"But not all of our members are here, Elizabeth," Joyce objected. "Sandy Jones needs to be here for the vote. It's in the rules that all members should be present."

Elizabeth looked at her VP with extreme agitation. There were murmurs of agreement passed among the club. Elizabeth had heard of the e-mail Sandy had sent to the other members. Elizabeth herself had not received one, but she could only guess as to what Sandy had said. "Sandy Jones hasn't shown up to a meeting in months," Elizabeth explained calmly. "Why should she vote?"

"Because she's a member," Joyce reminded her.

Elizabeth gave in. "Very well. I don't see what difference it will make her being here or not, but we shall have the election as originally planned." She eyed Joyce suspiciously. Joyce never liked Elizabeth. What if she and Sandra were planning an overthrow? But Elizabeth knew that even if the two of them refused their vote for her, she would still win. What was their game?

As if answering Elizabeth's inner inquiries, the double-wood door at the back of the hall opened with a loud, echoing thunder. There Sandy Jones stood, dressed in her finest, most lovely attire: a business suit that was neither too harsh nor too girlish; one that showed off her shape quite nicely and gave her an air of importance. She carried a briefcase and whipped off her sunglasses as she approached the podium, sweeping her hair back in a gesture of assuredness. Strapped to her back, in a pouch, was Baby Amy, giggling and laughing as the women made adoring sounds to her. Sandy's entrance certainly got everyone's attention, just as she had planned. Sandy had been waiting outside the meeting hall door, listening for just the right moment to dazzle.

Elizabeth kept her composure at the podium. "This is a closed meeting! Role has already been taken."

"I'll reopen it," Joyce said, taking out the roster and her pen. "Sandy Jones, are you here?"

"I'm here."

"She's here," Joyce said to Elizabeth. There were mumbles of both approval and disapproval from the group. They were already divided on whose side they would fall. Clearly, Sandy was a more pleasant person, but Elizabeth had experience and Eddie Licious.

"I'm throwing my hat in the ring," Sandy said, standing directly in front of the podium, staring Elizabeth down. "I'm running for president of the Gay Porn Wives Club."

"I second the nomination," Joyce said at once.

A third chimed from somewhere in the group in support.

Elizabeth looked about ready to blow. "Fine!" she hissed. "But I don't see the point. She's barely here at all. What do you know about leadership, Mrs. Jones?"

There were shouts of agreement with Elizabeth. In fact, the crowd seemed more in favor of Elizabeth at the moment. Sandy was going to have to prove herself in the next few days, and she felt she was up for that.

The women began talking among themselves, excited by the prospect of having an actual say on the new president, the first democratic vote in a very long time. Elizabeth leaned over the podium so that only Sandy could hear her and spoke sharply. "There's no way you're going to win, Sandra. I could run this organization with my eyes closed. What have you got to show? Diapers."

"Maybe that's the problem," Sandy replied. "You've been here too long, old guard. Maybe a little variety would be just what this club needs."

"It runs fine. You shouldn't fix what isn't broken. You're just looking for an excuse to get out of the house, you poor thing. You don't care about this club; not like me. This is *my* club, sweetheart!"

"Please! You and your husband need to go. There's new blood, Elizabeth, and I'm it."

Elizabeth's face went white at the word "husband" and she shot a quick glance at Eddie. "There might be blood, indeed," Elizabeth replied. "You prepare yourself, Sandra! This is going to get dirty, and I'm not responsible for what will be going down."

"Oh, I'm ready," Sandy assured her. "You've never had to fight for anything in this club, so I'm not too concerned. And the name is Sandy, you egomaniacal bitch!"


WHEN Seth came into the fitness center, Rick was relieved that James was not with him. Yes, Seth getting his workout in without James anywhere near was a good thing. Since rugby practice and the ass slap heard around the world earlier that morning, Rick had been eaten up with jealousy and insecurity. To make things worse, he was nibbled on by guilt for not fully trusting James. Now, however, he exhaled with relief and glanced down at the employee chart he was writing up for the next week.

Adjusting names and shifts on the schedule, Rick soon felt as if he were being watched, though, and looked up. Sitting on the pec-dec, looking quite fierce and determined as he did his sets, was Seth. Rick couldn't tell if the scowl on his face was from physical exertion or anger. Either way, Rick returned the gaze, and his own face definitely held an expression of challenge.

Would they have a fight right here? A rumble? A tussle? Should there be a referee? Rick was prepared to fight for what was his, dammit. He'd leap over the desk and take on the rugby player without delay, even if Seth was two times his height and thrice his width.

"I'm ready, big guy," he growled beneath his breath as he continued the weight room stare-off.

Rick had never felt more masculine, more animalistic than he did right then. It felt good to have something, someone who he felt so passionately about. He understood all the old romances now; how all those fools died for love. He was one of them now.

Rick flung the folder and charts to his side on the desk, his breath heavy and measured. He popped his neck. Seth stared back. *Oh yeah! There was going to be a throwdown at Hot Body Gym.* And it didn't matter to Rick that he would be fired or that he'd be in excessive pain from the beating he was about to incur. The high afterward would make up for it. There are some things worth sacrificing one's health and sanity for. James was the worthiest cause Rick could imagine.

Just as Rick was set to pounce, to leap over the counter like a love-struck, swashbuckling bandit, Seth seemed to wake from a daze and noticed Rick staring hard at him. He immediately smiled. "Hey there, Rick! Sorry. My mind was elsewhere. Have you been standing there for long?"

Rick suddenly felt unmanned. *Abort! Abort!*

"N—no. Not long."

Seth rose from the pec-dec and walked over to Rick. "Practice was a bear. Man, your boyfriend packs a punch."

"I'm sure he does. I wouldn't know. I've never given him cause to hit me."

"Right," Seth laughed. "You two are the perfect couple."

*Was that a dig? Would there be a tussle after all?*

Seth leaned in closer. "Just how perfect *are* the two of you anyway? No troubles?"

*Oh, the tussle is definitely back on!* "What do you mean, Seth?" Rick tried to put as much contempt onto the pronunciation of the rugby player's name as he could, but his natural monotone wouldn't let his disdain shine through as clearly as he would have wished.

"I just mean… never mind. Listen, we should get together, the three of us. You've got a good man in James, Rick. A real good, solid guy."

"Yes, I do."

Seth stood awkwardly and quiet for a moment under Rick's one-eyed stare. "Well, I best get the ol' workout done. I'll chat at ya later, okay?" He walked away with a slightly less-assured gait, and Rick breathed again.

It wasn't an obvious victory, but Rick was certain he had won some small battle. His stance became proud and erect behind the desk; he hadn't realized he had placed his hands on his hips like some undefeated superhero.

"That's right, bitch. Just keep walking." He kept his eye on Seth as the big man disappeared behind some racks. "Jesus! He's got a huge ass."

THANKS to Vera's investigative efforts, Cassie now felt she was getting a handle on the mystery of the strange man down the street. She didn't have the upper hand, but that would come. She was a little concerned as to how, though.

Cassie had heard her brother-in-law's name before; Jackson had said it upon occasion, but she had never met the man in person nor seen him in photographs. Jackson kept his life and relations hidden even from her. They didn't have a wedding, just a quick dash to the justice of the peace witnessed by one of his own government compatriots. But now Vera had discovered who the little tree sprite was: none other than Jefferson Bloom. Indeed, it was worse than having some tired detective on the case. As Jackson's brother, as family, he wouldn't give up until he had discovered what had happened. To protect Vera, to protect Jason, and to protect herself, Cassie would need to do some serious thinking. Could she kill a man, just as Vera had done? A man who had done nothing to her, as far as she knew? Would she be able to do it if the time came? It would be about self-preservation, fighting for one's way of life. War was no different. Only then it was justified under some large banner of patriotism, but it was still about the protection of a certain ideal of living.

Cassie walked through the house, cocktail in hand in the best crystal. She liked using her best crystal when she drank, no matter what time of day it was. And today, especially, a little extra comfort was required.

If she went to prison, would they send her where they had sent Martha Stewart? Or would they just electrocute her and get it over with? Did they electrocute in civilized countries anymore?

Vera had explained to Cassie her plan to find out more information, to discover the precise nuances of their new foe's actions.

"Vera, no. I won't allow it!" Cassie had said over the cell phone. Vera was at the club, more concerned with their new problem than anything involving business or boys.

"This isn't up to you, hon," Vera replied. "This is about both of us. More directly, it's about me. That man has nothing but hate for you, and he's never even met you. But with me… well, he was practically drooling. You should have seen the spectacle! He wants to see you hang for something you didn't do—something I did. I can get close to him; I can see what he's got."

"Oh, Vera, be careful!"

"Don't you worry about me, sugar. Vera will be just fine. It's that little man who needs to worry. Now, we better get off the phone. We're not being very covert, and we need to start watching ourselves."

Cassie hoped Vera could pull it off, but there would be no talking her out of it either way. Besides, if Vera was right, Cassie wouldn't be able to get close to Jefferson. He was watching her all the time. From what Vera told her of her run-in with him, though, he didn't seem a very intelligent man. She supposed high-tech wiretapping and the like was beyond his skills. Jackson was the government man in the family. From what she was told, Jefferson sold ice cream out of the back of a van in California. But that could just as easily have been a lie as well.

One thing was certain: Cassie needed to rid the house of Jackson's remains once and for all. That was something that needed to be done soon, before Jefferson gathered enough courage to come closer and snoop around.

She wandered out back to the pool area where Jason was doing laps completely nude. His clothes were scattered around the poolside carelessly. He had never been self-conscious about his body. That's one thing Cassie was proud to say she had instilled in him—pride in how he looked, no matter what his father said.

Cassie had been fighting the urge to tell him what had been going on since Vera called about first spotting Jefferson in the tree. Truth was the best way with Jason. His life had been filled with lies and secrets. They had nearly destroyed the relationship between him and his mother. And still, the hint of truth was what drove him away. The truth of his father's feelings for him, he didn't want to hear. Cassie knew Jason still suspected she had killed Jackson, but the subject had not been brought up once since his return to Jasper Lane. Jackson was rarely mentioned at all. Still, his ghost, his putrid memory, hung stubbornly around the house like a foul odor.

Yes, he would have to be gotten rid of very quickly. It was silly not to have done it sooner. But the question remained, would Jason believe the truth? And if he did, what would he do?

Jason saw her standing there with her cocktail and made his way to her. He rested his arm on the edge of the pool, saying nothing, his long, shaggy hair pushed back from his face by the water.

"I haven't seen you in the pool for a while," Cassie said, crouching down.

"Yeah. It felt like a good day for a swim. Besides," he reasoned, "if there's someone watching us, I can't have you getting all the attention." She swore he almost winked with mischief. It made her heart leap in delight.

"Jason…." She was going to tell him; she had to. His innocence, his future depended on it.

"Yes, Mother." He looked into her eyes. She saw that he knew. There was no way he couldn't know. With that one glance Cassie saw for certain that Jason knew his father was dead. Maybe not the specifics of his death, but he knew that his mother did indeed have some part to play in it.

"Nothing, darling." She drew her hand over his wet hair.

"Mother. How I love our short conversations about nothing. And I think we both truly understand what 'nothing' really is, don't we?"

She studied his face for some clarity.

"I think I'm becoming happy to be home." With that, he did a backstroke into the water and continued his laps as if uninterrupted.

"Darling, I wish I knew you again," Cassie said, slightly above a whisper.

MELINDA had left Malcolm and Candy in the café after her ladies room degradation, taking a taxi back home. Malcolm pleaded with her to stay, to let him explain, but Melinda was furious, as furious as her hushed demeanor would allow her to portray in public.

"How could you!" she hissed, still straining to keep a smile in case others were watching. They were outside of the café, fewer tables but still a patronage. "I can't believe you told your sister about what we did in the privacy of the bedroom."

"She doesn't care." It wasn't the most soothing explanation.

"Well, I do! That was something completely new to me, and I don't want it getting around that I spend nights… spanking you." The taxi drove up, and she quickly got in, chased, she was certain, by stares.

"Okay. I'm sorry," he said. "Can't we talk about this?"

"I don't know. Maybe later. Not now." She slammed the door, yelled politely at the driver, and headed home, turning around and watching Malcolm diminish in size as the taxi sped away.

She knew Malcolm thought nothing of what he had exposed to Candice. Perhaps he and his sister talked about private matters all the time. But that was not Melinda's way. That was not any normal person's way, as far as she knew. Brothers and sisters didn't talk about their sex lives with each other. She certainly never had with her sister.

Yet at home, after a while Melinda began to second-guess herself. Maybe she had overreacted. Clearly, Malcolm was very fond of her; that was evident by him introducing her to his loud, obnoxious sister. The minutes were weakening her resolve, eroding her anger. Still, she refused to answer the phone when Malcolm called. She let it ring and ring. Let him suffer. Let him think she was still angry with him even though she was becoming more amused by the situation as the hours went by. This surprised even her.

She did try to call Becky Ridgeworth once, but her unlikely friend wasn't picking up her cell; and Melinda's son Patrick called as well, just to say hello and ask her how things were.

"Heard from Dad?" he asked, not truly concerned about his father.

"Not in over a year," she answered, even less concerned.

And that was what brought the truth of the matter to her. Frank, who had known her most of her adult life, didn't care about her. Malcolm, who had just met her recently, was nuts about her, nuts enough to introduce her to his sister and then to keep obsessively calling her when he thought she was angry with him. The notion that someone cared about her that much, that someone found her so desirable made her giggle and blush. The grin wouldn't leave her face.

*Yes*, she thought. *I did overreact.* And even if she didn't believe that deep down inside, even if she thought her actions were completely warranted, couldn't she just deny them for the sake of what she had finally found after all these years? Malcolm was just what she needed.

Melinda was about to reach for the phone and call Malcolm when there was a knock at the door. The silly grin still lit up her face as she absentmindedly answered it. Malcolm stood under the porch light, solemn, apologetic, with his hands behind his back. He looked at her like a punished puppy, and she laughed.

"Get in here!" she said, pulling him by the arm into the house.

"I thought you'd never talk to me again," Malcolm said. "I really didn't mean anything by telling my sister about us. I'm just excited to be with you. I had to tell someone. Candy won't tell anyone. I promise."

"Excuse me for saying so, darling, but your sister doesn't seem to me to be the most discreet woman in the world." This truly worried her, but she couldn't help grinning all the more.

"She can be. She can be if asked to be... by me. She won't say a thing, not to anyone." He paused, hoping for a kiss. "Am I forgiven?"

Melinda let him wait for her answer just a few more seconds. But her stubborn smile couldn't hide how she felt. "You are forgiven. Just don't let it happen again, Mister." She shook her finger at him like one would a naughty boy, and then too late wondered if that might have aroused him given his bedroom predilections.

"Good," he replied, leaning in to kiss her tenderly. "I got you something. A gift to say I'm sorry."

From behind his back he brought a little, shiny, black gift bag. Melinda took it gleefully. This is something else she had missed all those years with Frank, little gifts to say "I love you" or, at least, "I think about you." She reached into the bag and brought out a violet velvet mask.

"Pretty," she said, trying to discern exactly what it was. "What is this, sweetie? A sleeping mask?"

"Better," Malcolm replied. "And there's a whip out in the car that goes with it. It's a set. I just couldn't fit the whip in the baggy."

She stared at him in confusion.

"It's for you to punish me with. After all, I've been a naughty boy today."

AT THE Joneses' house, Sandy had put Amy to bed and was enjoying a drink in the kitchen with Cliff. She loved their late-night get-togethers. She loved that she had the most muscular, gay best friend in town. When they went shopping together, it was a sign of pride, Cliff in his tight sweaters or stretched-to-the-limits tees, carrying her bags and laughing at her jokes. She still had a longing to be the popular girl despite the fact that it had been years since things like that were supposed to matter, and with Cliff she always was the "it" girl. She supposed that's why she adapted so quickly when her husband Steve had told her he was secretly doing gay porn to pay their bills. Though outraged at first, her neighbors' curiosity and her immediate rise in neighborhood standing had lessened her ire. And things had worked out, after all. Steve was now the CEO of GetchyaSome! Productions and was making a good deal of money. He no longer acted in the porns, of course; he just made them. Thank goodness Steve had never fucked or been fucked by Cliff during his brief tenure as a gay-for-pay superstar. That would have been awkward, probably destroying her friendship with Cliff. And she hated that thought. Sandy adored Cliff; she loved him to pieces!

They drank their bottles of beer amidst light talk and gossip, catching each other up on the workings in their daily lives. Their significant others, David and Steve, had gone out for a drink with Rick, who, they had learned, was having some jealousy issues.

"Do you think they're talking about us?" Sandy asked. "What do you think they're saying?"

"What are we? In high school? Of course they're talking about us. They always talk about us when they get together. They're like boys in a locker room."

"Good. They better. We're pretty."

Cliff laughed. "Yes, we are. Better than they deserve."

"Let's drink to that." Sandy raised her bottle, clinking it with Cliff's over the granite tabletop.

"I heard about the commotion you caused today at the Civic Center during the Gay Porn Wives meeting," Cliff commented. "Looking to be the next president of the club, huh?"

Sandy shrugged. "Problem is I don't think I can win. But it sure was fun to see Elizabeth squirm under the eyes of the others."

"Why couldn't you win? You've got just as much business in that office as she does. She's only there because she has money and produces our industry's films—and not even the best ones. You're married to the CEO of one of the classiest porn companies around." He took a drink, keeping his eyes on Sandy.

"You think so?"

"Absolutely."

"I don't know. I mean, I have the VP, Joyce, on my side, but the other women seem to be siding with Elizabeth." Her finger traced the words on the bottle wrapper.

"Because she's safe; because they know what to expect. They all probably like you better; Elizabeth's a raging bitch. But you need something else. You need to bring something new to the orgy, baby." He reached over and grabbed a handful of nuts from the bowl in the center of the table.

"Like what? Elizabeth has Eddie. He's her golden cock ring. I have nothing that would compare with that guy. I mean, the ladies of the club like Steve, but they lust after Eddie."

Cliff grimaced each time Sandy mentioned Eddie's name. "I hate that guy!"

"See, if I had you," she joked, "if I had married you instead of Steve, then I'd win for sure. We'd just have you there on election day in all your naked sweetness."

Cliff lit up. "You *do* have me," he said, reveling in a new idea.

"I was joking… I think." She stared at him attentively. "What do you mean?"

"I mean, why don't I help you? That's what friends are for, right?"

"And how would you do that, Dionne Warwick?"

"You just watch me and have some faith. I can make some calls. You have Steve. This is perfect!"

"I don't get it. What are you going on about?"

Cliff rose from his seat, clearly excited about something, and began pacing the kitchen. "I've written a porn. Not just any porn, though. This is the greatest gay porn that will ever be filmed. I just need a backer. We can put your campaign on its back with Steve's okay, and those ladies will be sure to vote for you, especially once we hint at its scope. You hate Elizabeth; I hate Eddie. If I help you defeat her, I get my idea for the ultimate epic porn film finally realized. And you," he said, swinging around, pointing at her, "you become the new president of the Gay Porn Wives Club!"

His excitement was contagious. Sandy found herself standing as well. "Do you really think we can pull it off?"

"There's a change a-coming, Sandy Jones. And we're right at the forefront of it."

Sandy grinned with enthusiasm. "My friend, the porn star!" she squealed as she ran and jumped into his arms, wrapping her legs around his waist.

TERRENCE cursed himself for never watching *Survivorman* as he stumbled through the woods in search for Chris and the others. He should have listened to David and Cliff when they said "The show might save your life one day." Oh, how foolish he had been! He was certain he would be lost forever in the forest of the campgrounds, never to be seen again. One day, some ten-year-old survivalist would wander across his decaying, stinking corpse tangled in the vines; that is, if he hadn't already been eaten by cougars or insane deer. Yes, Terrence was cursing the sky as it darkened, saying his farewells to Chris and to his beautiful life back on Jasper Lane. He trudged on, leaving behind him a trail of small, empty bottles as he finished drinking one after the other. (*Like breadcrumbs*, he thought. *It worked for those two chubby kids in that fairy tale.*) Perhaps it would have helped if he had stopped drinking altogether, but that was all he had to battle against the despair of his impending, most likely painful death.

Just as his hope for a way out of the woods was about to vanish after having run through a big, sticky cobweb, Terrence saw a path before him. Joyously he ran along it in drunken, hobbling strides. His backpack was miraculously lighter now. He would soon be reunited with Chris. The poor boy must be worried sick. They would embrace with all the lovely trimmings of a Spielberg film—soaring music, swooping camera. But upon emerging from the trees, Terrence was bewildered. He had come out onto an abandoned campsite far from their own. It hadn't been used for quite some time. Terrence had no idea where he was. On that very first day at the camp, traveling through the grounds in the minivan with Chris, he had seen hundreds of sites left unused. This could be any one of those, and the darkness didn't help matters. The crickets chirping now sounded to him like a "tsk-tsk" as in, "Look what you've done gotten yourself into now!"

He kerplunked himself down on the cool grass in front of the ancient remains of a campfire. The night was huge and uncaring. The trees were tall and angry, pointing at him with their strong, healthy limbs. "Fuck you!" Terrence shouted, taking the last gulp of his tequila. He belched and lay down, using his backpack as a pillow.

Just as he got himself settled, ready to pass out, he realized he had the undeniable urge to urinate. Cautiously, he rose to his shaky feet. The world was swimming around him. How was he supposed to find a toilet if the world kept moving and stayed so dark? Unable to find a suitable place to relieve himself, Terrence finally just undid his pants and peed where he stood, which, from the sound of it, was a gravel road; one of the park roads. Maybe he wasn't so lost after all. Maybe in the morning he would be able to find his way back to camp.

With this in mind, he thought it a bad idea to leave the newly found road of hope and hunkered down beside it for the night, rolling over into a ditch before he had even remembered to pull up his trousers.

The sky was still dark when Terrence awoke from his alcohol-induced nightmare about woodland creatures in top hats and finding the secret meeting place of Concerned Women for America in the vagina of a donkey. His head was beginning to grumble with that dull ache he knew would eventually lead to one hell of a hangover. In the distance he heard voices and saw lights.

"Dad!" he heard Chris call.

It took Terrence a moment to become cognizant enough to respond.

"Here! I'm o'er here," Terrence groaned in the ditch.

There was the sound of a scuffle and the shaking of flashlights as Chris and whoever it was with him came rushing to Terrence's side.

"Dad! What are you doing in a ditch? Are you okay?" Chris was peering down at him, concerned. He held Terrence's head in his hands.

"I'm fine. I wenta looky for you. I felt bad, so I wenta looky...."

"Dad, are you drunk?"

Terrence held up his fingers in a gesture meaning "a teensy, tiny bit." Chris immediately released his head back onto the ground with a thud.

"Chris," Terrence whined. "I'm gonna have a headache."

"Serves you right. What made you think you could find us by yourself? We've been looking for you all afternoon."

"Chris here's been worried sick," another voice said. Terrence gasped. It was Harry! Perhaps, Terrence thought, if he acted as if he passed out, Harry wouldn't think him a bad father. Just sick.

"No use, Dad. We know you're drunk."

So, he had done it again. He had disappointed Chris.

"Let's get you up," Harry said as he and Chris got Terrence to his feet. The fallen trousers nearly tripped him up anew, so Harry gently tugged them up and fastened them like a good man. Terrence didn't notice the sweet grin on the hunk's face.

"I think I need mouth-to-mouth resuffocation," Terrence swooned to Harry.

Harry grinned. "Well, you're talking to us so I don't think it's necessary. Otherwise, I'd be happy to… resuffocate you."

"Nuts!" Terrence griped in defeat.

"Just hold still here for a few," Harry continued. "My son went to get the Jeep back at camp. You'll be right as rain in the morning."

Terrence could feel his son's resentment even as he struggled to stay up. "Sorry, Chris," he said.

There was no reply, just the sound of chastising crickets.


THE bar was crowded and noisy. Rick rarely ever ventured into JR's. It wasn't the type of place that called to him on those rare occasions when he wanted a night out. Rick much preferred small, quiet pubs where waitresses came carrying baskets of cheese fries to one's table and a one-man acoustic was strumming in the corner. At JR's there was music blaring from an old jukebox playing honky-tonk that could barely be heard over the karaoke and steady stream of fights that erupted among the mostly straight, mostly out of shape, and seemingly bitter patrons. He was a bit uncomfortable, especially without James by his side. But Steve and David had promised him a good time. They frequented JR's and seldom had cause to throw a punch.

They sat in a back booth, away from everyone. The room was low lit and hazy from smoke. Rick sat, shoulders hunched over his drink as if he were afraid it might be stolen or he might be noticed by some unseemly rabble-rouser. "James went straight to bed when he got home tonight," he told David and Steve. "I was hoping we could spend some time together, but that's happened less and less since he's joined the rugby team. No sex for me tonight. He says he won't have sex before a game. He wants to save all his energy for tomorrow. Sports are dumb."

Steve commiserated. "Sandy hasn't wanted to have much sex since Amy was born. They say that's natural. We've become a cliché."

David broke the mould. "Cliff wants to fuck all the time." The others looked at him with playful contempt. David shrugged. "What can I say? I married a nymphomaniac gay porn star. I'm actually glad he gets some of his sexual energy out during the day on set or I'd never get any rest."

"We hate you, Dave," Steve said, taking a drink from his mug and staring off into the crowd where yet another quarrel had erupted.

"Are you feeling better about the whole Seth situation?" David asked Rick.

"Not really. I saw him in the gym today; thought he was staring me down. Turns out he was just spacing."

"Probably thinking about James naked," Steve teased.

"That's not funny."

David asked, "Why don't you just confront the guy? Just ask him, 'Hey, are you hitting on my hubby?'"

"I prefer the term 'partner' now. It holds less of a religious connotation. Plus, there's less likelihood someone will picket your home."

"Whatever. It's all the same. But personally, I think 'partner' sounds like you're in a law firm together. I like to call Cliff my hubby."

"'Hubby' suits Cliff." Steve nodded in agreement.

"To answer your question, I'm very close to doing just that; confront Seth about things, I mean," Rick said. "I'm just afraid that when I do, Seth will tell James, and then all hell will break loose because James will think I don't trust him."

"Maybe you should just drop it," Steve weighed in. "I mean, your fears, they're your own insecurities. We all know James is not going to sleep around on you. Pardon me for saying it, Rick, but you do have a lot of baggage. There are a lot of reasons for you not to trust due to your previous relationships."

"I know. And I'm letting them cloud what James and I have." He sighed heavily, and leaned back in his seat. "I wish I knew what to do. I wish I could quit obsessing over the matter."

"Sorry we can't be of more help, buddy," Steve said. "Let's just get drunk, eh? Maybe the solution is under all this alcohol."

"Uh-oh, fellas," David interrupted. "Looks like we're being checked out."

Three scantily clad female urbanites were headed their way. They walked—nay, sloshed—with a mixture of sensuality and rum.

Rick slid down into his seat. "I don't need this."

"Look at this fine table of gorgeous men!" the first young woman said in a faux breathy voice. "Do you mind if we join you?"

Rick: "Gay."

Steve: "Married."

David: "Both."

THE next morning, Terrence awoke in his tent with the headache he knew had every right to be there. He didn't care how he had gotten to the tent; he momentarily didn't even care about his embarrassing actions from the night before. All he wanted at the moment was a mimosa or a Bloody Mary. He squeezed his temples and groaned, regretting now that he had not left at least one of the baby bottles of gin to help cope with the morning-afters.

"He wants to see you, Dad. Wake up."

Terrence heard Chris's voice over the pounding in his brain.

"What? Who?" He opened one eye and peered up at his son, who towered over him.

"Father Donaghan. He wants to talk to you about last night." The words sounded like a death sentence coming from Chris. None of his usual mirth could be discerned in his voice. He wasn't even smiling.

"Tell him to call back later." Terrence rolled over on his side; his brain bumped and clunked in his head.

"Now, Dad," Chris demanded, pulling a corner of the sleeping bag from his shoulder. "Get up now. Do this for me. You owe me after last night."

"Ugh…. Damn you for playing the guilt card so early in the morning."

"It's eleven o'clock. I let you sleep in." He leaned over and spoke clearly in his father's ear: "Now get up."

Terrence grumbled incoherent curse words as he rose, stumbled, obviously still drunk, and then whispered incoherent apologies to Chris as he tumbled out of the tent after his son—incoherently.

The march to the check-in where the pastor was waiting was somewhat foreboding for Terrence, and that was aside from the length of the walk itself. Chris led the way like a guard in a prison film. The other fathers and sons watched from their tents. Terrence avoided looking at them. He would have enjoyed the dramatic effect of the moment if he wasn't still so nauseated and drunk. Terrence imagined he looked like hell. But that was still a sight better than most the other fathers at the camp. Well, except Harry.

Where was Harry anyway?

"Can't we drive to check-in?" Terrence grumbled.

Chris didn't answer.

"Okay. I deserve the silent treatment. I realize I was a complete asshole, okay? But I said I was sorry, didn't I?" He couldn't remember now what he had said.

Inside the check-in at the long table Terrence had first seen him at sat Father Donaghan. He still looked sweet and understanding. But there was villainy beneath, Terrence was certain. That's how they get you! It's all blessings and holy water in the beginning. Then it's private prayers in the nude under pornographic renderings of the Virgin Mary. Terrence had seen it on the news.

"Good morning, Terrence and Christian," the old man said kindly, gesturing them to the seats in front of him.

As they took their seats, Terrence noted Harry was there with them as well, seated in the corner. Harry smiled. Terrence quickly looked away.

"Terrence," the pastor began, "do you know why you are here?"

Terrence shrugged. "Because I got lost?"

"Dad, please!" Chris sighed with exasperation.

"Well, so to speak. You're here because of your... problem."

*Here it comes!* Terrence thought, folding his arms in preparation for a showdown. *These biblical types were all alike! Trying to put the gay man down! Well, this gay man doesn't go down.* He giggled at his mind's choice of words.

"Your alcoholism," Father Donaghan said.

"I am a proud gay.... My what?"

The pastor repeated, "Your overindulgence of the spirits. There's nothing wrong with imbibing a little, but—"

"I'm not an alcoholic," Terrence nearly shouted, somewhat more relieved than when he first came into the building, though still combative.

Father Donaghan looked at him with a compassionate, if condescending, expression. "There were tiny bottles littered throughout the forest. Empty bottles. Not a drop left. As if they were licked clean."

"I was thirsty!" Terrence offered. "And I was worried about Chris. I had been thinking about him all day. I was worried he...."

Chris was looking at him thoughtfully. "Worried about what?"

"Nothing. I was just concerned is all." Terrence caught the slightest hint of understanding on Harry's face as his eyes grazed the corner of the room.

"Well," the pastor continued, "whatever you call it, it's clear there are some issues you're trying to mask with it."

"What are you, a shrink too?"

"Dad! He's trying to help."

"Well, I mean, the guy doesn't even know me. Besides, if I was an alcoholic, believe me, I'd have reason to be!"

Father Donaghan sat patiently. "Just promise me you're through with the alcohol, at least here at the camp."

"Oh, I can definitely promise you that. I drank it all."

Harry snickered in the corner, bringing a look from the pastor. Terrence felt more comfortable now. At least Harry seemed to be on his side. Harry, a prince among men. Did they kiss last night? There was some memory of a dream, something like a princess in a fairy tale being awakened from a long slumber by a charming, broad-shouldered, big-dicked prince—just like in the Disney movies.

"I'll have to have you kicked out of the retreat if alcohol is found again. Do you understand?" For the first time the pastor looked serious.

Terrence swallowed. "Yes, sir," he said timidly.

"Good. And no more wandering about in the woods by yourself."

"I promise. One wrong turn and I could have been lost forever."

"Well," Chris cut in, "at least until you remembered the cell phone in your back pocket."

"Fuck!" Terrence shouted.

That moment of realization was one hell of a knee-slapper for Harry in the corner.

A CAKE is a surefire way into a man's heart or home. Vera's mother had told her that years before, and Vera had always remembered this piece of advice. She had taken to baking at a very early age just for that reason. The morning after she and Cassie had fumbled through their one sexual experience together, Vera had risen early after coming to certain conclusions about her life and baked a magnificent strawberry angel food cake for her soon-to-be new boyfriend. She took it to him before classes began, and they spent the day feeding it to each other. The next morning, after their first night together, it was cheesecake. She didn't make cooking for men a habit, though. She didn't want her or her new beau gaining too much weight.

So it was with her mother in mind that Vera put together a scrumptious coffee cake for Jefferson. She thought about adding some rat poison at the last minute, but, unlike Jackson, Jefferson might actually have other people who noticed he had gone missing. Jackson had been a fan of coffee cakes; Vera guessed Jefferson was as well. Maybe their mother, whatever type of infectious beast she was, baked them coffee cakes in her lair. Vera thought that perhaps a little sugar and sweetness might get her invited into Jefferson's rented home, where she could snoop around for a bit. Maybe then she could see exactly how dangerous he was.

Vera saw Keiko bringing out the garbage. They smiled and waved at each other. "Lord," Vera said to herself. "I hope the rumor doesn't circulate that I'm actually interested in this fool!"

She rang the doorbell. Waited, rang again, and then knocked. There was no answer, but Vera thought she heard something coming from the back of the house. Not one to have her plans thwarted, Vera carried the coffee cake around back.

"Yoo-hoo!" she called. "Mister Obviou—Curious!"

The backyard was fenced off by aging wood that was in need of some repair. She went to push open the back gate, but it opened of its own accord; Jefferson stood nervously, holding onto its handle on the other side.

"Well, hi there… Miss Vera," he said, a mixture of delight and worry in his voice and apparent on his face. "What brings you…?" He was distracted; he looked at the cake like a hungry bear.

"I brought you something." Vera offered up the cake. "I just wanted to thank you for your kindness. Can I come in? I baked it myself."

Jefferson smiled, clearly in love (though with Vera or the cake was uncertain). "Yes, please."

Vera looked around the overgrown backyard. Nothing had been done about it since he had moved in; not a blade of grass shorn. Vera saw he had been having instant coffee at a wobbly old table left behind by the previous residents, Cock Ring Girl and her young husband. A disheveled pile of papers lay in one of the chairs.

Practically drooling, Jefferson took the cake from Vera and set it down on the table.

"Shall I go get a knife?" Vera offered, eager to get a look inside the house and maybe see something telling.

Jefferson blocked her way to the patio door. "No! No, that's all right. I'll get it. You just have a seat."

"Oh," she said, disappointed. As she could make her way to the chair with the pile of papers, Jefferson (though he had yet to tell Vera that was indeed his name) raced in and grabbed up the clutter before she could pretend to remove them carefully and with only mild interest.

*Damn, he's quick!*

Jefferson went inside with the papers, closing the patio door behind him, and soon returned sans clutter but carrying a butcher knife.

"It's just a cake, darling," she said. "We're not slaughtering a pig."

Jefferson looked at the knife. "It's all I could find."

He set to cutting the cake at once. Vera offered to do it, but he seemed not to notice. He wanted that cake. He took a large, hastily sliced piece and gnawed on it greedily, seeming to forget Vera's presence altogether. "So good," he mumbled with his mouth full.

"You're welcome," Vera said, trying to mask her disgust.

He opened his eyes, remembering her. "I—I'm so sorry," he said, embarrassed. "I'll get some plates."

"Don't bother, hon." Vera touched his arm gently. "I made that cake for you. I haven't much of an appetite this morning."

Jefferson sat down opposite her, his eyes on her, but his thoughts on the cake as he continued to shove large portions in his mouth.

"My heavens, baby! When's the last time you ate?"

"I don't get real food often. Most of the time I eat fast food. Nothing like this." Bits of coffee cake shot from his mouth, but he seemed unaware. He swallowed hard, pushing down a mouthful that could have choked a cow.

"Well, maybe you should let me into your kitchen sometime, Mr.… uh… I'm sorry. I don't think I know your name," she lied. "Isn't that odd?"

"Jeff. My name is Jeff."

"Well, Jeff, why don't you show me that kitchen, and I can—"

"No need!" he said, stopping her as she rose. "It's a mess. You know us bachelors. Messy. I'd be ashamed for you to see it."

"Oh, it'd be no shock to me, darling. I'm not one to judge."

"Still, I'd rather you not. And," he continued, cutting her next idea at the root, "the restroom isn't working either. The plumbing is all haywire." There was a stare-off of sorts before Vera smiled and settled back in her chair.

"Well, it seems the former tenants didn't leave this place in such good shape, did they?"

Jefferson shrugged in befuddled agreement. He was filling up on the coffee cake, his attention more and more focused on Vera as the plate emptied.

"So what have you learned about Miss Bloom? Anything new?" Vera was determined her baking for this odious man would pay off with *some* bit of information.

"Cassie? Uh... yes. Well, I can't discuss that. An ongoing investigation. You understand."

"You can tell lil' ol' me," she pleaded, leaning over the table with her willowy arms, taking his heavy hands in her slender ones. He seemed absolutely stunned by this.

"Go out with me!" he blurted.

*Oh, for Christ's sake!* "Excuse me?"

"Go out with me tonight. I mean... please. You're divine! You're magnificent! You're everything I never thought I could have. Let me take you to dinner."

Hmm. However horrifying this turn of events was, it had possibilities. "We could eat here. I'll cook," Vera offered. "It would be much more intimate."

"I'd rather take you out. It's not so nice in there." He gestured at the house with a nod of the head as if the house walls might overhear.

"Fine," Vera replied, through gritted teeth. She didn't realize how tightly she was squeezing his hand.

"Ouch," Jefferson whined.

"Oops! Sorry, baby. I guess I'm just... excited." She decided then and there that the next cake she would make him would be Death by Chocolate... literally.


DEATH and sweat were in the air. The pitch was crowded with steely eyed determination; the thirst for the win. Gay (plus a token straight) against straight (plus a couple questionable but closeted guys). The Sacred Band of Thebes versus the Bravehearts. Rick watched the pitch intently, though with more interest in the proximity to which Seth came to James than with any care for the actual game. Still, he had to admit, it was a fierce spectacle. Very masculine. Whether the Bravehearts would admit it or not, this game reeked of homoeroticism, enough to make poor Terrence pass out, if he had been there. Big, bulky men in tight shorts, muscles alive and twitching. It was definitely a turn-on. How did the gay players concentrate?

James had told him it wasn't like that. They weren't turned on during the game. They had their purpose in mind. Besides, it was hard to even think about getting turned on while being pushed and pummeled by stinky, sometimes overweight guys. In the scrum (a term Rick had just learned) it was the exact opposite of sexy. Rick took James's word for it. From the outsider's point of view, however, it was something to see.

The game was going well for the Sacred Band. At the outset, the Bravehearts and their fans were merciless in their guffaws and outward knowledge of stereotypes. Even as big as the Sacred Band was, the Bravehearts still believed no team full of queers could beat them. As the game went on, though, as the first try was made by the Sacred Band, the sarcastic sneers on the opponents' faces began to disappear and were replaced by concern that they might actually lose the first game of the season to a bunch of fairies. At the ten-minute half point in the game, after the Bravehearts hadn't made goal one, they were already a defeated lot.

Rick had been told a bit about the game of rugby by James. James told him that they played by rugby league rules, whatever that meant. Rick knew that a game lasted two hours and forty minutes; he knew there were fifteen players and seven alternates; he knew that the field was called the pitch; that the props pushed the scrum (Rick noted that this sounded particularly hot and naughty, and he must keep an eye on Seth); that the token straight guy was the hooker (he remembered this because it was funny); and that James was one of the two quarterbacks.

"It's a hell of a lot more fun than American football," James had said.

And while Rick now knew some of the superficial rules and terms of rugby, he still felt a bit like Sally Kellerman in the football scene in

*M*A*S*H* ("He got a red flag! He got a red flag!"). He didn't want to be *that* guy, so he made certain to keep his cheers and jeers internal throughout.

James was turning Rick's shit on, though, as he played all fierce and testosterone-filled. There was no escaping that fact. Maybe sports weren't so bad after all. James glared and grunted, barked and hollered; Seth and the others joined in too, sounding more like some tribe of hot Tarzan motherfuckers than their regal namesake. And this was all during halftime to put some fear into their opponents. When the game started again there was absolutely no hope for the Bravehearts. They were as nervous as Mel Gibson at a synagogue of gay Jewish bodybuilders. They managed to score once, and this only enraged the Sacred Band more.

The game ended soon thereafter. Rick was ecstatic that there was not a game the next day. He wanted some of that extra ferocity James had stocked up now. If he could just tear him away from Seth, they could have a very fun night together.

Through victory hugs and yells, Rick watched James congratulate each teammate and then shake hands with each Braveheart. James spotted Rick and, wearing the grin of the victorious and proud, trotted over his way. He wrapped a sweaty arm around Rick, slapping his ass with a loud smack and a lusty squeeze. "What do you think about your hero?" he growled.

Rick was again surprised by the outward display of affection that just a year earlier would have been so out of character for James. "I'm thinking I can't wait until tonight. Make sure you save some of that energy for me."

"Don't you worry. I will. You've got a whole lotta trouble coming at you tonight." James's eyes were those of a soldier who hadn't had sex in years. "In fact, we've got time before the victory party at JR's if you wanna get off home for a little somethin'. I need to shower first anyway."

James's fingers were pressing so hard into Rick's ass that it was beginning to hurt—in that good way.

"Let's go then," Rick said without hesitation.

"And you're coming to the victory party, by the way. Whether you want to or not," James explained as he and Rick hurried off to the car. "That is, if you can walk after I'm done with you."

Rick wondered if he could even concentrate on the road as he sped out of the parking lot. He wanted to go down on James in the car; he'd never done that before. He knew they would be completely bare-assed before they even got home.

MELINDA had joined Becky Ridgeworth's power-walking club earlier in the spring, once she and Becky had become better acquainted and saw that they really could stand to be around each other. The other women in the group were scattershot as far as their participation went. Some walked two days, other three. None of them but Melinda and Becky walked every day of the week. For them it had turned into a kind of therapy, something that each looked forward to. Melinda could tell Becky about Patrick's latest news or Nanna's newest threats of eternal damnation, and Becky could tell Melinda about her struggles to find the perfect man or the very juicy details of the porn industry, for which she worked behind the scenes. It always gave both of them something to think about—and whisper to others—as their days went on. Though they were unlikely to admit it, Melinda Gold and Becky Ridgeworth were becoming good friends. How on earth had that happened?

This day it was just the two of them puffing down Jasper Lane, their arms swinging in time like those of a locomotive. Becky was telling Melinda about an altercation on one of the sets between two actors who had become lovers but were now split up. They were both hired for the same project, saying that, yes, they could keep their past relationship off the set. That hadn't lasted very long, however.

"…and so Markus was rising up out of the pool to get ready for the next shot," Becky huffed out, "when Robert came over there and heeled his penis into the concrete! I mean, *heeled* it. It even hurt *me* to see it, and I don't even have a penis."

"Oh, my good Lord!"

"Needless to say, filming was halted. I don't know how they're going to finish the shoot."

"I can't imagine. That poor man."

"They took him to the hospital. There's a sprain." The two of them agreed that they were very grateful they did not have penises of their own to keep track of. They seemed to be more trouble than they were worth, always getting in the way, swinging this way and that. How distracting it must be to be a man!

"So what about the coach?" Becky asked with a playful nudge to Melinda's side as they walked. "Any news worth sharing?"

Melinda furrowed her brow in thought. "Well...."

Becky gasped. "There *is* something! What is it? Does he like to cross-dress? Tell him to move to Jasper Lane; we haven't got a cross-dresser here yet."

"No, he doesn't cross-dress. At least, I don't think he does. But...."

"Melinda! For heaven's sake, just tell me. You're killing me here."

"Okay. But you have to promise not to tell a soul."

"You have my word," Becky said gleefully.

"Of course I do." Melinda looked at her, uncertain. She had to tell someone, though. Having to hold all the shock was very taxing. "He likes to be spanked."

Becky let out a squeal of sheer delight. "No!"

"Yes." Melinda found the excitement in Becky's voice strangely enticing; it made her want to tell Becky more. So she did. She explained the whole lurid affair. How things had started off so innocent and romantic. But then, their first night together, Malcolm had become this passive man in bed who liked to be told he was a bad boy and that he should be spanked.

"And I couldn't spank him hard enough. He always wanted it harder! My hand hurt afterward."

"You spank him? Melinda, that's so unlike you!"

"I have never seen a man so turned on in my life. It was very strange, but, honestly, the sex afterward was simply incredible."

"Really?"

"Mind-blowing!"

"Mind-blowing?"

"My mind was blown." It felt so good to finally get it off her chest. And why should she feel guilty about it? Malcolm had told his sister, so they were even now. "And Becky," she said in a much lower voice, "I find that I rather like doing it as well."

"Get out! You're a dominatrix?"

"What? No! What is that? Well, whatever it is, no. That doesn't sound like anything I would be. A dominatrix?" She made a mental note to look the word up on the Interweb when she got home.

Becky kept her eyes wide on Melinda. "You are so a dominatrix. Mistress Melinda. It's very sexy. You could sell your own brand of whips or something."

"Would you hush!" Melinda laughed at the teasing. "But it's definitely the best sex I've ever had. I never knew it could be so exciting."

"Honey, you need to come to Cassie's next porn party. We'll teach you some new stuff; get you some new whips. There is a whole world you probably never knew existed under the thumb of that mother of yours and married to that driftwood of a husband."

"Well, I intend to find it all out now." Melinda was determined. "There's nobody in my way. Being with Malcolm is so... so...."

"Liberating?"

"Yes! Liberating." She stopped, her face taking on that look of concern again. "Except there is one thing I'm having issues with."

Becky waited, watching Melinda closely as they both stood on the sidewalk under a tree. Whatever Melinda was about to say, it was going to be good. Becky could tell that from the expression on her face.

"It's his name, Becky," she finally said, biting her lip.

"His name?" Becky repeated. "I don't understand. Malcolm is a very classy name. I thought you would like that."

"I love his first name, but his last name... it's Nip... Nip... Nipple. His name is Malcolm Nipple."

"Oh, my God!" Becky cackled. "Coach Nipple!"

Melinda tried calming her friend's hilarity, but it was no use. Becky was a ball of boisterous bouncing in the broad daylight. Her shouts echoed down Jasper Lane.

"Melinda," she said, calming down enough to put her hand on Melinda's shoulder. "You know when I said I wouldn't tell anyone? I'm sorry, but I can't keep that promise; not on this."

"You're going to tell Cassie, aren't you?"

"Come on, hon. I'll buy you an ice cream to make up for it."

WHILE Vera was keeping Jefferson Bloom busy and fed in his backyard, Cassie was trying to remember exactly where she had planted her husband. There wasn't any method or pattern to where his bits and pieces lay. They had simply been hidden deep in the dirt that year as Cassie and Vera had taken it upon themselves to re-landscape the property.

"It will be a nice surprise for Jackson when he comes back," Cassie had explained to the nosy neighbors.

"But where has he gone?" Nanna had inquired, her evil eye unrelenting in its stare.

"Who can say?" Cassie responded pleasantly. "You know how secretive the government can be. I wouldn't be surprised if he didn't come back for a very long time."

But now that it had been a few years, Cassie couldn't really remember exactly where all of Jackson's parts were. She knew, of course, the general locations; a woman never forgets where her husband has been. But whether he was under this rosebush or that one was a mystery. And she certainly didn't want to go about digging up her entire lawn. It would give Jefferson pause if he saw large mounds of fresh-turned earth as he looked down at her from his perch. No, Cassie had to be stealthy about things. The excavating of the ex would need to be done at night, and all the house lights would need to be off. She couldn't risk the slightest hint of recognized movement as she, David, and Becky exhumed Jackson Bloom.

Her first thought was to dig for that large, bulbous head of his. She knew exactly where that was: out back, beneath the lilacs and tiger lilies. But since that was the easiest bit of him to find she persuaded herself to try to gather the other bones first.

As far as Jason was concerned, she was just acting as strange and flamboyant as she always had. That's what she hoped he thought anyway. But one could never tell with Jason. She would just have to make certain all the digging was done when he was spending a night with a friend or had gone to sleep. But what a ridiculous idea! She knew she was not going to be able to hide what she was doing from her son. He would find out. He already suspected her of his father's death.

Down on Jasper Lane life went on as usual. Gayhound, now cared for by Terrence after Ruth Goins had died and left him the house and the dog, chased a cat across the shaded street; Melinda and Becky were speed-walking and laughing (it was good to see them finally take a liking to each other); and children from neighboring streets ran through the yards of the Jasper Lane residents. How gentle and perfect everything seemed on the surface.

# Suburbilicious: Vignettes from Jasper Lane

THE news spread like crabgrass through the e-mail vine of the Gay Porn Wives Club. Not only was Sandy Jones challenging the domineering Elizabeth Trump, but she now had an ally in her fight. And what an ally it was! One could almost hear the support leaning toward Sandy when Cliff announced that he was backing her in her campaign.

Elizabeth did not react well to the news. Eddie followed her about the house trying to calm her down as she smashed plates and rattled the air with coarse language such as her home had never been witness to. Meanwhile, the VP Joyce sat at her home after reading the news and had a victory martini. The other women envisioned all sorts of dramatic showdowns. Some envisioned an Alexander Hamilton situation involving Sandy shooting Elizabeth. Or better yet, others thought, Cliff and Eddie whipping their dicks out at opposite ends of the street like in some old Western, giving a whole new meaning in their minds to "shootout."

Satisfied that she now had a real chance of winning the election, Sandy devoted herself to other matters, if only for a few hours. She played with Amy, chatted on the phone with Becky, strategized with Cliff on his breaks during filming, and baked a pie to take over to the new couple in the neighborhood, Asha and Keiko. She had yet to introduce herself and thought it best to do so while she was in such a spectacular mood. The other new neighbor, the mysterious man who resembled in her mind a child molester, she ignored altogether. As a mother she had gained something of a sixth sense about people, and hers was telling her he was not a good man. But the two new women— they were top-notch people.

"I hope you like cheesecake," Sandy said gleefully when Asha opened the door. "I'm Sandy Jones. Me and my husband Steve live just across the way. I'm sorry it's taken me so long to introduce myself, but busy, busy, busy!"

Asha took the pie with a smile. "Well, thank you! I love cheesecake, and so does Keiko. Won't you come in?"

"I can't stay. My daughter is napping, and I need to get back." She gave a sideways glance at the mysterious man's house.

Asha raised an eyebrow and leaned in to say, "I understand completely. The man gives both of us the chills too."

Sandy sighed, relieved that someone else wasn't quite comfortable around him. "So, where is Keiko? I would love to meet her."

"Actually, she's working. She's directing a commercial for a local mattress store or something today."

"She's a director?"

"A very good one. But getting her name out there is hard, so she takes what she can get."

Sandy was hesitant to even bring it up, but then, why not? Things happen the way they are supposed to; at least, that's what she had started believing lately. Maybe meeting Keiko and Asha was something like fate. "You know, my husband is in the entertainment business. He runs a studio, actually. He might have something a little more... creative for her than a mattress commercial. I could talk to him, have him look into things if you want."

"Really?"

"I don't suppose her being around a bunch of naked men would be a problem for you?"

Asha looked at her suspiciously. "Clearly not."

"Clearly. You see, my husband... he's the CEO of a large gay porn production company. I mean, it's not Hollywood—"

"But it's not Mattress Mania, either." Asha was thinking. "Hold on," she said as she left Sandy at the door. Shortly she returned with a business card. "Keiko's card. Have your husband give her a call. This might be an interesting opportunity."

AT DINNER at the campground the food was set along a lengthy table in the center of a broad circle of tents. All the fathers and sons were encouraged to eat at the table, to join in the fellowship, but it wasn't required. Terrence, feeling that he had nothing whatsoever in common with the others there, usually ate alone at his tent. Chris could sense his discomfort and would always get his father something to eat, a plate full of stuff he thought Terrence might like, and then he would go and eat with some of the other sons. The younger men usually didn't eat at the long table either.

"You can come join us if you want," Chris offered, handing Terrence a paper plate of greasy fried chicken, slaw, and potato chips.

"That's okay," Terrence replied. "Go enjoy yourself."

"I feel terrible you hate it here."

"It's not your fault. And as much as it pains me to say it, it's not your mom's fault either. I'm just not one for cozy gatherings like this, I suppose." He tried to stretch out a smile. "Go on. Have fun."

Chris slowly walked off with his own plate, every now and then looking behind with worry at his father. They were so different from each other; the only thing they could agree on was a love for antiques.

Terrence had made it through his plate of homemade food, nearly retching from the amount of grease he had eaten, when he saw Harry, who up to that point had been eating at the long table with the normal dads. He was heading Terrence's way with a small plastic bowl. Terrence quickly wiped his mouth of any residual grease that might be there from the chicken and struggled to sit up straight in the camping chair.

"Hey there," Harry said as he seated himself on the Scooby-Doo cooler. "Brought you a little something."

Terrence looked cautiously into the little bowl. "Thank you. That was very nice. But I don't like ambrosia salad."

"You don't?" Harry exclaimed in false shock. "Come on. You'll love it. I made this myself."

"You did not."

"I did. Been packing it in my cooler to share with someone who might appreciate it." His smile melted away all of Terrence's self-pity and resentment. A small breeze ruffled Harry's bangs, which hung just slightly over his forehead.

"Well... all right. I'll give it another try." The truth was, Terrence had never actually tasted ambrosia salad. It just always seemed like one of those things he would never like. It sounded like nursing home food. He leaned in to pick up the spoon from the bowl's edge, but Harry grabbed it first.

"I got it," Harry said, scooping up a large helping and bringing it to Terrence's mouth.

Terrence could feel himself blushing as he was fed by the flannel-wearing piece of hotness. He couldn't help but keep eye contact even as he tried to swallow the huge portion that had been spooned to him.

"Got some on your lip." And Harry wiped it away with his salty thumb.

*Oh, how perfect and predictable!*

Terrence was glad he was sitting. His knees were jelly.

"Why don't you eat with us at the table?" Harry asked. "We'd all like to know you better."

Terrence smiled and looked at his feet. Why was he suddenly a bashful flower now? This wasn't his persona. He always went after the guys he wanted with gusto, no excuses. Even when the guys shrugged him off initially, he would always wear them down with his determination. Yet with Harry he felt goofy and awkward and disoriented. Maybe he had caught something when he had gotten lost in the woods. Been bitten by a bug or sneezed on by a bird.

"I have to be invited." Terrence just made up any excuse he could to explain his solitude from the group. "I have to feel welcome."

"We don't make you feel welcome? Well, that's a damn travesty on our part. I need to fix that. You are certainly welcome, and from now on I will personally invite you to every little thing that goes on around here, okay?"

Terrence wasn't sure if he was being mocked or not.

Harry leaned in with another spoonful. "I mean it."

"Thank you," Terrence replied with a mouthful of pretty pink salad.

"Your son, Chris…. He's a good fella. Him and Jordan are getting along very well."

"Chris likes everyone," Terrence began, then, catching himself, he added, "but your son certainly seems to have made friends with him faster than most."

"Can I offer some advice? Maybe you should put a little more into the games. I'm sure he'd appreciate it. I would too. Most of these guys here—the dads—I can beat with my hands tied behind my back. It would be nice to have some real competition." He winked and shoveled another spoonful into Terrence's mouth. "Some of those guys are so… dull."

"So blah," Terrence agreed, though he was becoming hard to understand.

"So straight."


WHEN the Sacred Band of Thebes burst through the doors of JR's at four o'clock in the afternoon for commencement of their victory party, it nearly scared the few straight patrons there senseless. The three alcoholic businessmen and the one career alcoholic were nearly stunned sober.

"What the hell is this?" the career alcoholic shouted and slurred, rubbing the gray stubble on his chin.

"This, sir," Seth yelled, "is the Sacred Band of Thebes. You no doubt have heard of us. Bow to us, for we are victorious, and we will have beer!"

"The Sacred—what-the-hell-ever! This is my quiet time, young fella."

"If you're not with us, you're against us!" Seth shouted playfully, approaching the man, every bit as intimidating in his jeans and polo as he was in his rugby gear.

"All right, all right," the old boozer said, holding up his hands. "Just asking is all. A man's got a right to know who's pissin' in his drink."

"Very good! That would be us. We are the pissers." The other players cheered in agreement. "Bring us beer, pizza, and hot ass!"

The young waitress on call gave a lusty grin. "Yes, sir!"

Seth looked at her. "On second thought, beer and pizza will do." Grabbing another player by the arm, pulling him near and squeezing his ass, he said, "I've got all the ass I want right here."

Manly cheers all around as the players dispersed to pool, darts, and tables.

Rick and James arrived a couple hours later. Seth had called James's cell and landline every ten minutes since he and the rest of the team had arrived at JR's. ("Where are you, man? You're missing the party!") But the calls were ignored, for during that time, James was emptying out the rest of his pent-up ferocity into and over Rick, much to Rick's delight. They fucked and wrestled over every inch of the house, reminding Rick of their very first sexual encounter more than a year earlier. Windows had face-prints, potted plants lay decimated, and condoms littered the floor.

"This is disgusting."

"Clean it up later. I've still got some man-juice for you. Bend over."

"First, put on those army shorts. Let's role-play again."

In the end, Rick was more than satisfied and deliciously sore. It was somewhere around six o'clock that he finally reluctantly agreed to rise from lying on James's chest so they could head to JR's.

"Now I see it," Rick said on the way to the bar.

"See what?"

"The allure of sports."

They entered the bar to a whir of activity and noise. The team and their significant others were there, most of them drunk and sure to keep the taxi services on their toes for the night. An old grizzled alcoholic sang karaoke with Will, the token straight guy, on the stage, and through the smoky air, pool balls could be heard knocking. The members of the opposing team were beginning to show up as well, all of them jovial; their loss was now a thing of the past in the name of good sportsmanship. There were only a few patrons who had nothing at all to do with the rugby game there, but they kept to themselves at tables in the back near the restrooms.

"Finally!" Seth shouted as James and Rick walked in. Seth had been drinking hard. Two hours in and he was already way too loud for Rick's taste. Of course, a whisper from Seth was too loud for Rick's taste. "What took you so long?" He gave Rick a fleeting but pointed look.

James wrapped an arm around Rick's waist. "We were having a little game of our own." He kissed Rick gently on the forehead.

Rick wrapped his own arm around James, giving him a kiss on the lips and tugging ever so slightly on the lower one, just enough for Seth to see.

A grin swept across Seth's face. "And I bet you won, didn't you?" he barked at James. "With those guns, who could stand against you? Let me see 'em!"

"What?" James laughed.

"Lemme see those guns. Come on! Flex."

James unhooked himself from Rick's waist and flexed his bicep. Instantly, Seth took hold of the arm and dragged his drunken tongue over the length of it in some strange, worshipful motion. The teammates watching laughed uproariously.

"Watch out, Rick! He's gonna steal your man."

Rick was too angry to immediately respond. Seth had only just realized what he had done, and instead of looking at James, he flashed confused eyes upon Rick.

James was the only one with any clarity running through his head, it not being clouded by liquor or rage. "Come on," he said, grabbing Rick by the hand and pulling him to one of the tables. "Let's get some drinks."

Seth still sat at the bar stunned for a moment, but then, roused by his teammates, returned his attention to the frivolity of the victory party.

"Let's not even talk about it right now," James said, seeing Rick on the verge of saying something. "I just want to have a good time. Can we do that? Please?"

Rick nodded. "I'll need a drink. Not beer—a real drink."

"You bet. Waitress!"

WHEN Jefferson had told Vera that he was taking her to JR's for their date, she was relieved. He tried to assuage any disappointment she might have had by saying he had very little money and this was all he could afford, but she was fine with heading to a seedy, loud, smelly bar with the little man. The less romantic the situation, the better. Any other man and Vera would have ended the date right there. She was a lady, after all. Ladies didn't head to dens of sordid debauchery—at least not on the first date. But the fact was Vera did not view this as a date at all. This was a fact-finding mission. She needed to get close to Jefferson Bloom to learn what his plans were in regard to Cassie. So far, she hadn't been too successful in her quest. She shivered at the idea that she might actually have to sleep with the little gnome.

So, walking into JR's, where the Sacred Band of Thebes' victory party was in full swing, Vera breathed a sigh of relief. At seeing the drunken rugby players, Jefferson, already a sweating, nervous disaster, tried to persuade her that they could head somewhere else.

"Dairy Queen or McDonald's?"

"Absolutely not!" Vera said with as best a smile as she could manage. "I know a lot of these boys. It will be fine."

Vera practically pushed Jefferson ahead of her into the bar, greeting some of the players, waving across the crowd at James and Rick at a booth, and Melinda and her new prospect Malcolm at another. Good, she thought. There were plenty of familiar faces around if she needed rescuing from Jefferson, though she doubted very much he would make a move on her in such a public place.

The only booth still available was in the very back, and it hadn't been open for long. It was still littered with peanut shells and condensation rings. Vera made certain she was facing the crowd in case she needed to catch Melinda's eye. They ordered drinks and a couple of slices of limp pizza. Jefferson ate his ferociously, but Vera let hers sit. It was a sorry-looking slice, peering up at her with two large pepperonis for eyes as if it could whimper at its state and hers.

"It sure is nice to have something to think about other than Cassie Bloom," Jefferson said, wiping his mouth with his sleeve.

"Well, I'm glad I can be of service," Vera replied over the crowd. "And how's that going? Your search?"

"Good. It's going real good." Nothing more. He drank down his beer without taking a breath. Was she supposed to drive his sorry ass home if he got drunk?

"You don't want to share any juicy tidbits?" She was going to scream if she didn't learn something soon. "Or don't you trust me?"

Jefferson changed his tune immediately. "I trust you!" he said, very rushed, reaching across the table to touch her manicured hands. "I do trust you. It's just... not here. I'll tell you sometime, but not here; not now."

"Okay, then. Sometime soon. I'm just so curious."

"I know, my dear," he said as he rubbed the back of her hand with his thumb. "I know you're dying to get away from her. I'll free you."

Who did he think he was? Some fairy tale prince? Vera searched her mind for the myriad of Disney prince's names. Who would he be? Prince Charming, Prince Eric... Shrek?

Jefferson hunched over the table at her, leaning in for a kiss. She was so disconcerted by the sudden movement, however, she first thought he was attacking her, and almost assaulted him. That was her cue to get help. "Melinda!" she yelled, giving her friend across the way a look that pleaded for aid. Melinda, though startled, rose at once, bringing her date with her.

"This must be Malcolm," Vera said. *Good, kind Melinda*, Vera thought. *Always there to help out her friends. God love her!* She introduced them to Jeff, who now sat back in his seat, defeated. He never once looked at Melinda, so she was able to study him without pause.

"So, is this your... a date?" Melinda asked, her eyes conveying that Vera could do so much better.

"Yes, he's moved in down the street."

Awkward silence, a space where any normal man would say something, but Jefferson remained quiet.

"How's Patrick?" Vera asked to keep Melinda around for a bit longer.

"He's well. He's coming home for a visit sometime soon. I don't know exactly when. Surprises, surprises." She laughed self-consciously.

"Well, you tell him to stop in and see his Auntie Vera."

"Oh, I will. I will."

"Would you like to join us?" Vera gestured elegantly at the booth.

"Actually, we're headed out," Melinda replied.

"We are?" Malcolm seemed surprised.

"We are." Melinda kept her eyes on Vera, smiling, but Vera swore she saw her neighbor nudge the wrestling coach as if to say "Hush." "It was nice to meet you," she said to Jeff as she hurried Malcolm away from the uncomfortable air around the booth.

*Damn you, Melinda!*

"Nice to meet you, Coach Nipple!" Vera screamed over the crowd.

Melinda glanced back at her in horror, her mouth cursing Becky as she and Malcolm escaped the loud cradle of filth that was JR's.

BEFORE Keiko's Alero had pulled into the driveway, eliciting, as it always did, a smile from Asha, the neighborhood had emptied for the evening. People went on their ways to parties or dinners or various other important engagements. The houses on Jasper Lane looked as if they were asleep as the streetlamps and security lights cast shadows on them. Asha only saw two other people all evening as she watched out the window: the writer who had married the gay porn star and the somewhat chubby speed-walker. With dour, thoughtful expressions, both of them had made their ways to the cul-de-sac that crowned the street. Soon after that the lights of that grand old place all mysteriously blinked off. Asha could wonder what was happening up there; she could investigate. But instead, she preferred to stay where she was and wait for Keiko to arrive home. They could eat that cheesecake that sweet Sandy Jones had brought them, the homemaker with the porn king husband. At least Jasper Lane wasn't boring. There could never be any danger of that. No, in fact, everyone was very peculiar. Not in a bad way. Well, except for the man across the street. He was creepy in a bad way. But the rest of them, those who had introduced themselves to Asha and Keiko, were quite nice.

"It's great to have another loving couple on the street," the writer, David, had said to her and Keiko when he and his husband Cliff had stopped by. Cliff had made them a peach cobbler. "We've got quite the caring community around here. We're family. Welcome."

As always, Asha was suspicious, but Keiko had invited the two in and in no time Asha too was comfortable with them. She could see why Sandy and Cliff were such good friends now that she had met her too. They must trade recipes or something, she thought.

The rest of the street's inhabitants were charming in their own ways too. Cassie Bloom was somewhat nosy, but she acted in such a nurturing, motherly way that it didn't matter.

"I think I'm going to feel at home here very soon," Keiko had told her after Cassie had taken her leave.

Still, and Asha had mentioned this to Keiko, why did everyone here look like a model? It was a matter of fiction to have so many great-looking people in such close proximity. Were they living on some kind of film set?

When Keiko walked in the door, tired from the day's shoot at Mattress Mania, unfulfilled by its complete lack of artistic opportunity, Asha gave her a kiss and then helped her settle in before handing her a plate of cheesecake.

"Before you say anything: No, I did not make it. So you're safe."

"Thank God!" Keiko teased, taking a taste of the treat and rolling her eyes back in satisfaction. "Delicious. Who made it?"

"Sandy Jones. That nice young mother down the street." They sat on the couch, Keiko kicking off her shoes and resting her feet on Asha's legs.

"I love these 'Welcome to the neighborhood' treats. We should move somewhere every week."

"Well, not everywhere might have as good cooks. I think we've just been lucky with our peppy housewife and her muscle-bound best friend."

"He is a big fella, isn't he?" Keiko stretched, reaching her hands in the air and unfurling them to their limits. Her cell phone rang in her pocket and, looking at the ID, Asha could tell she didn't recognize the number. Within a few seconds, Asha knew it was Steve Jones. He didn't waste any time, did he?

# Suburbilicious: Vignettes from Jasper Lane

Keiko's face held an expression of interest and uncertainty throughout the conversation. Keiko always did things believing that the end product would be worth the trouble; that it would turn out right. Asha was amazed at how resilient Keiko was even after dreams were smashed or projects were not quite what she had hoped they would be. But that was Keiko's area: hope. It wasn't like Keiko was an overly cheerful person; Asha wouldn't have been able to stand her if she were. Keiko was just cautiously optimistic, and it was strange how that optimism leveled Asha out, made her feel better about the world; that maybe it wasn't such a bad place after all. At least, as long as Keiko was in the room with her.

Keiko put down the cell on the end table and turned to Asha. "Steve Jones, from down the street. He wants to talk to me," she said, her eyes collecting the sparse light in the room. The TV was muted.

"About what?" Asha acted unaware.

"He's heard I'm a director. Somewhere, from someone, he's heard I'm a very good one. He wants to talk to me about directing a film."

"Porn? Gay porn?"

"Uh-huh. If it's a problem I won't even—"

"Are you kidding? Go for it. Sounds like a great opportunity!"

Asha could see ideas already going through Keiko's mind. Set designs and situations.

"He says he has a script, and it's like no porn that's ever been filmed before. I mean, it's not something to go on the CV, but it's more than I've got at the moment, right?"

"A real movie!" Asha beamed.

"Well, a porn. But hey, everyone has to start somewhere."

LIGHTS out. Every last one save Jason's bedroom. Cassie was stealthy and watchful in her glamorous fatigues. She had told Jason that David and Becky would be coming over to catch fireflies. She knew Jason thought that was the most ridiculous thing he had ever heard, but it was all she could come up with. It didn't matter, though. She just needed to give him a reason, some reason. He seemed to appreciate the effort and understand.

"I'll be upstairs," he said. "Things to do. People to chat with on the computer." He took a pint of Guinness with him, only looking over his shoulder once, and not with an expression of suspicion or anger. His was more a look of partnership, of abetment.

Cassie waited for her friends to arrive, watching for them on the front deck as she sipped on a martini, for once not accosted by spying eyes. The sun set slowly, and the houses of Jasper Lane emptied one by one. Each house now stood silent, every one of them like a big, pretty box of secrets. Cassie was relieved that she now had a semblance of truth with Jason. Nothing had been said; there was no outright confession. Yet the truth hung in the air of the house, wanting desperately to be spoken aloud. But that might never happen. The cul-de-sac was the largest box of secrets on the street. The secrets hidden in its basement by Jackson would drown her and Jason both if they ever knew them all. More than once she had thought of destroying the basement altogether, taking a torch to it like they do in those movies where the only way an ugly alien can be vanquished is by a flamethrower that just happens to be hanging on the wall of the alien's lair or in its pod or its stinking cave.

David and Becky came separately so as not to attract attention. They dressed in grays and blacks. Cassie, ever the hostess, had a drink ready for them before they retrieved the shovels and needed equipment from the basement. Then they turned off the lights.

"I bet this house looks downright creepy from Jasper Lane with all the lights off," Cassie mused as she led her friends to the side yard where the digging would commence. "You can call me Morticia for the night, darlings."

"Well, if we're making a game of it," David said, "I'll be the Wolfman. I've always had a werewolf fetish."

"I'm Else Lancester, the Bride of Frankenstein," Becky joined in.

The three of them stood silent and still for a moment, readying their nerves to attack the long-dead-and-buried Jackson Bloom. They glanced at each other and around the yard and gardens. "Let's do this and be done with it," Cassie finally said, taking a healthy swallow from her drink.

And their night began.

Cassie refused to not have a good time as she rummaged through the dirt and manure for her dead husband. He would not crowd festivity from her life, not even now. In between the found metacarpals and wrist bones, she prepared drinks for Becky and David from a cart she had wheeled out filled with liquor and ice. Maybe it was disrespectful, but Jackson did not deserve her respect.

They deposited the bones they located into a burlap sack. ("How original! How daring!" Cassie commented.) It soon occurred to them that it was going to take more than one night to remember and recover Jackson's various resting places. Cassie kept her eye on her son's room throughout, and was relieved when the light went out. She never saw a shadow by the window and so hoped he had ignored the temptation to look down upon them. David would occasionally walk around to the front of the house to make certain Jefferson and Vera had not yet returned. Of course, Vera knew to give them a call of warning, but still, better safe than… not safe.

"Look at this," David said to Cassie as he continued to dig. He held in his palm a little blue plastic ring, the kind children got in cereal boxes. David cleared the dirt that was caked around it.

"Must be one of Jason's." Cassie smiled, taking the ring, her eyes full of nostalgia. "It's a Wonder Woman ring. Jason's favorite. He was always acting like Wonder Woman when he was little. He had a crown, a whip, the whole kit. He loved being Wonder Woman."

"Who didn't?" David admitted.

"I didn't," Becky answered. "I was all about Smurfette."

"And I bet you were fierce!" David nudged her.

Cassie closed her hand over the ring.

"Maybe you should keep that." David rested his chin on the handle of his shovel.

"I will," Cassie said, glancing up to her son's room. She took a deep breath. "Anyone want another drink? We should probably call our un-undertaking quits for the evening just in case Vera comes back early, in case she can't take any more of that man."

"Good idea," Becky agreed. "Same time tomorrow?"

"We'll see. I'll have to find out if Miss Vera was able to find out anything this evening."

"Well, I think we've done well for ourselves tonight," David offered. "We've found both of the arms, and the pelvic bone."

They all silently contemplated the bizarre occurrences that had led to that statement.

"I'm buzzed," David said. "But I just realized something: I need to get drunk. Very, very drunk."

"Come on into Chez Cassie, my love. I've got what you need. Don't forget to bring the ol' bag of bones with you."

JASON watched them in the dark from his window after he had turned out his light, standing so that the moonlight would not shine on his naked skin. Every so often his mother would peer up, and he thought she might have seen him. But then she would return to her digging, to her exhuming of something that didn't necessarily need to be exhumed but did need to be removed. Jason saw his father's angry, contemptuous ghost everywhere, and he was tired of it. He was tired of even having had a father. Those memories from childhood, which at the time had seemed so wonderful, were now bitter. They were like a spoiled cake covered by perfect icing.

During his time in Europe and his trips elsewhere, Jason had begun to wonder if his mother had been right. Had Jackson not been the man he claimed to be? Had he not loved Jason at all? She had said nothing more than that by way of explanation. Jason returned to the States early, earlier than he let on. He investigated certain things, certain people, places, and events from Jackson's past. And he had discovered things that had disturbed him to the point that Jason felt himself slipping.

He now kept a watchful eye on his mother, a mother who he now knew cared for him more than his father ever had. Jason was going to make certain Cassie would not be brought to some corrupt idea of justice for killing a man who needed to be killed. She had done it all for him.

"You'll be gone soon," Jason mumbled over his shoulder to the silent ghost of his father. "We'll have a bonfire with your bones."

Of course, Jason realized he alone saw Jackson. He also knew somewhere inside that there was no ghost in the house. But he was also quite aware that he was a little insane, a last gift from his father.

"Mother killed you; I'll destroy you." A love of dramatics, a gift from his mother.

He watched until his mother and her friends went inside, and then he backed away from the window and crawled between the bed sheets. He'd been lonely for a while now. Only his anger and investigations kept him company. Staring at the ghost by the window, he knew that someday he would be happy again; he would have a lover, a new life. And that day was approaching. But first Jackson had to vanish altogether. Everything associated with him must be wiped out. Then his ghost would disappear with the remains. Jackson might have had a ghost, but Jason was certain that his father was absent a soul.

TERRENCE and Harry sat on the dock of the moonlit lake, their feet dipped into the water. The night air was fragrant with the scent of the forest—pine and wildflowers. An orchestra of night critters serenaded them. Terrence swatted at the night bugs that came too near his face. He wasn't deathly scared of the little critters, but he didn't want them all up in his business either. Their singing was great, but multi-legged molestation was out of the question. He was not averse to screeching over the sight of a spider on the hand or a daddy longlegs on the shirt.

When Harry had recommended that they ditch the other fathers for a bit and head to the lake (their sons were spending a night away from the dads at another campsite), Terrence had imagined skinny-dipping in the twilight. Amazingly, even to him, he had never done that, and he wanted to experience that particular clichéd thrill, especially with someone like Harry. But once they had settled down on the dock, Terrence's thoughts of frivolity and hot sex were replaced by, strangely, even more exciting thoughts of romance. He blamed the moon for that. He was moonstruck; he was Cher. They sat quite comfortably in their shorts and T-shirts, talking of any little thing that popped into their heads. It was easy conversation. And Terrence found that he didn't mind that they weren't making out like teenagers or re-creating underwater scenes from *Tarzan and His Mate*. The evening was actually pretty close to perfect. Well, except for the bugs.

"I knew it the moment I saw you," Terrence spoke.

"Knew what?" Harry sat beside him, only their little fingers touching on the deck.

"I knew you were one of the family. I knew you were gay. I could tell right then at sign-in. You send out very strong vibes; you should know that."

"Well, it would be odd if I weren't gay here, don't you think?"

"I don't know what that means, but I do know that it's damn lucky there's another gay man here with me. I don't feel so alone now." He kicked his feet in the water, content and in love with the evening.

Harry stared at him with a disbelieving grin. "Terrence, you do realize this is a retreat for gay fathers and their sons, right?"

*"It is not!"* His voice silenced the bugs and frogs.

Harry laughed. "I promise you, it is. Chris didn't explain that to you?"

"No. His mother set this up for us… as a gift."

"Good woman. You should marry her," Harry joked.

"Oh, my God! You mean this whole time…?"

"Yep."

"But everyone else is so… straight-looking. I mean, come on: Garlic Man?"

"His name's Reggie. And not every gay man on the planet looks the same. There's variety everywhere. Not all of us go to dance clubs or stay on top of the latest trends."

"Well, now I just feel awful about bad-mouthing Chris's mother." He kept his eyes locked to Harry's, still in shock. "A gay, Christian father/son camp. Really?"

"For real. Now that you know the truth, will you interact more with the rest of the group?"

"I don't know. Now it's almost worse. I mean, Garlic Man is gay? That's just bad advertising."

Harry laughed again. Terrence liked Harry's laugh; it was strong, hefty, reassuring. It almost seemed that Terrence would get a kiss out of the situation, but Harry settled down again.

"Look at what we got here," Harry said, reaching to Terrence's T-shirt. He lifted his index finger to Terrence's eyes. Crawling along that very sexy index finger was a lightning bug. It could have been a romantic moment between the two of them, but at once, Terrence shivered and knocked Harry's hand away, screaming like he had been bitten by a tarantula. In his shaky attempt to rise to his feet, he fell into the lake and flailed about even more there, unsure what creatures lay in the depths of campground lakes at night.

In between guffaws Harry pulled off his shirt and dove in after Terrence, calming him down immediately with his touch. They treaded the water, gazing into each other's eyes.

"Here's a perfect moment for us," Harry said quietly. "Let's not waste it, huh?"

Then they kissed. And for once, Terrence's life actually bested any of the films he had ever swooned over. "I don't suppose you'd want to skinny-dip?" he asked afterward.

RICK lay in bed listening to James's heavy breathing. When James drank to the level he had the night before at JR's, he always breathed with more pronounced huffs and puffs as he slept. It was like sleeping next to a bulldog.

The morning light was not a disturbance to either of them; the sky was overcast. The threat of rain had been forecast for the entire day, and unfortunately, the cloudy mood outside matched Rick's thoughts. No matter how hard he tried, he couldn't get the searing image of Seth licking James's bicep out of his mind. James, on the other hand, had seemed to think very little of it. Maybe that was a good sign. Rick wasn't sure. He wanted to talk about it when they had returned home, but James's mind was rambling drunk, his talk often incoherent. Once Rick got the intoxicated rugby hero out of the cab and to their room, James had fallen asleep the moment his head hit the headboard; he missed the pillow altogether.

Rick had to rearrange his large ex-army fellow on the bed, which was not an easy task. He took off James's shoes but left him more or less dressed otherwise. Though Rick wasn't as inebriated as James, he was still in no condition to do anything that required even a modicum of skill or real attention. He did well to undress himself and crawl into the bed beside James.

Rick thought that he would surely wake up with a hangover, but he hadn't. He had even scheduled it so that he wouldn't need to head to the gym until later just so he could sober up. But upon waking his head was clear, allowing thoughts of Seth's big ol' tongue to slobber all over his jealousies and insecurities.

James groaned. "I feel like shit. Did someone beat me over the head?"

"Yeah, his name was Jack Daniels."

"Who?" James mumbled into the pillow. He still lay on top of the bedcover in his clothes, which smelled of JR's.

"Never mind. You had fun, that's all that matters."

"And now I'm paying for it. Maybe we shouldn't win so much in the future."

"Not if you're going to keep drinking like you did."

James turned his head so that he faced Rick. "What's wrong with you? There's a twinge in your voice. Are you angry?"

"I don't get angry."

"Liar. You get angry all the time. You just don't show it. Normal people show it. If you're not careful, that hidden anger will fester inside you and become some deadly cold. Maybe you should take up a sport. It will get some of that aggression out."

"So, I'm not normal now? I bet Seth is normal." Did he sound bitter? More bitter than usual?

"Is that what this is about?" James tried to rise so that he would face Rick but collapsed in defeat once his head started throbbing. "You're pissed about what Seth did last night? Still?"

Rick didn't say anything. He didn't even look at James. The ceiling was much less judgmental.

"Listen," James said. "You saw the look on his face afterward. He didn't even realize what he was doing. He was drunk."

"The truth comes out easier when you drink. You know that. He was being honest about how he feels about you."

"This is ridiculous, Rick."

"What's ridiculous is that you refuse to see that he wants you. I see it all too well. He wants you bad."

"So what if he does? I'm with you. Didn't I show you how much you mean to me yesterday after the game?"

Rick had to admit that was a particularly strong argument in his favor. They had done some truly spectacular sexual feats. "So you're just going to shrug his tonguing off? You're not going to do anything?"

"Like what? You want me not to be friends with the guy because he's crushing on me? You can't ask me to do that, Ricky. That's not right."

Rick knew James had a point. He also knew he was yet again being over-possessive. But in his defense, he had never had someone like James before, someone he actually felt as strongly about. It was love, even if he never said the word. Why shouldn't he be a little possessive?

James moaned again. "I'll say something to Seth, okay? But first, can you go get me something for my head? How 'bout that? Wanna play nurse to me this morning, big man?"

Rick lightened up a little. He adored caring for James when James wasn't feeling well. "I'll be right back," he said, rising from the bed in his boxer shorts. "We'll get you fixed up."

Rick knew one thing for certain. Seth could never take care of James the way he did.

JASON walked around the exterior of the house. The clouds warned that it might rain at any moment, but he was not concerned with that. Most of the very bad weather was due far south of their region. Besides, he had spent many an afternoon on the streets of Paris and Vienna walking in the rain. It was always a relaxing activity for him.

## Suburbilicious: Vignettes from Jasper Lane

Cassie's morning gossip with Becky, Vera, and Melinda had been canceled because Cassie had some other matter to attend to. Becky and Vera knew what that other matter entailed. Melinda was the only one left out of the loop; Cassie had to come up with some lie to tell her. Jason didn't know what Cassie had told Melinda, but as he wandered about the freshly dug ground amidst the roses and bushes, he soon found out.

"Hi there, Jason." Melinda stood over him as he examined the dirt. His thoughts had been elsewhere, and he hadn't noticed her coming toward the cul-de-sac. A long white bone mischievously sticking up out of the earth had caught his attention; Jackson Bloom pointing fingers. Jason snatched it up quickly, sliding it into his back pocket, and then stood to greet Melinda.

"Good morning, Mrs. Gold. Didn't my mother tell you she had to do something else this morning so she wouldn't be able to have coffee?" He had collected himself flawlessly from the start Melinda had caused. There wasn't one stutter or suspicious pause.

"Yes, she did. And you know me. I couldn't help but stop by and see for myself."

"See what?"

"The new landscaping, of course. I adore a beautifully landscaped home." She looked at the dirt and frowned. "It doesn't seem they've done a very good job. Is she certain she's hired good people? I know a lovely group of Mexicans I can refer her to."

"They had to leave." Jason was making up stories. "Yeah, they just got started early this morning."

"I thought they started last night?"

"They did. I mean, they brought their equipment over last night, and I think did a little digging." He watched Melinda to make sure his story was jiving with what she had been told by Cassie. "But they were set to really begin this morning."

"But they had to leave?"

"Yeah, well, Mother thought that since it is going to rain it might be best to put it off for a day, just until the sky is clear. They had already started when she told them. That's why it's such a mess."

Melinda seemed to accept this without qualm. "Well, I hope they get it all figured out. Is your mother around?" She moved toward the front of the house.

"She's asleep!" Jason shouted, making Melinda jump.

"Is she ill?" She had an expression of true concern on her face. This touched Jason. Despite Melinda Gold's demeanor, her stuffiness, Jason could tell she was a good person.

"She's just... uh, tired. Insomnia."

Melinda shook her head as if she understood completely. "I've had bouts myself," she commiserated. "Especially lately. Well, then I'll just stop by some other time. I'd love to hear what she plans to do with it."

"With what?"

"With the landscaping, silly." She smiled. "Oh, and I wanted to tell you, Patrick is coming home for a visit sometime soon. Maybe the two of you could get together. I know you never got together before, but that's my fault. I'd really like to see the two of you as friends. We could do things together, Patrick and me, you and your mother. Picnics and the like. Doesn't that sound fun?"

"Sounds perfect," Jason replied, and the truth was, he meant it a bit.

"Good. I'll see you. Don't forget to tell Cassie I stopped by."

"I won't." He waved as she walked away. It began to sprinkle a little, causing Melinda to quicken her pace down the hill toward her own house.

She wasn't so bad, really. And his mother was right. Melinda had changed a lot since that old lady was gone. Jason remembered how Cassie detested Nanna. That woman was a member of every ultra-conservative hate group parading as religion in the tri-state area. It was amazing that Patrick had turned out to be sane at all. Jason envied Patrick's strength, and he didn't even know the guy. To not snap under that much pressure—that was a feat. One that Jason had not accomplished.

He felt the bone in his pocket. He'd take it inside and place it on the table beside the door to the basement. His mother would see it when she came back up.


CASSIE didn't know why there was a powerful incinerator in her basement. She had discovered it only after Jackson had been killed; she was never allowed down there when he drew breath. It creeped her out, honestly; it would anyone. She didn't want to think what horror show Jackson had used it for, but she imagined it might have been very close to what she was doing at that very moment: stoking the fires with bones.

When had her life on Jasper Lane turned into an Edgar Allan Poe story?

The answer: When she had decided to take control, to survive. His death was justified; that was something she had to keep reminding herself. Jackson would have certainly killed her if Vera had not intervened. Then Jason would have been left alone with a father who didn't care to have a gay son. Jackson would have sent Jason to a camp where he would have been treated with all sorts of tortures. Or worse still, Jackson might have administered his own brand of torture in the basement. Either way Jason would not have survived intact. Certain things needed to be done in order to survive even if they fell beyond the realm of some third party's idea of justice. Third parties, Cassie reasoned, are nearsighted anyway.

Cassie pitched the bones into the massive incinerator. There would be more of them later. It made her sick to her stomach if she thought too hard about what she was doing. It made her angry to think she even had to do it. If only Jefferson had stayed away. Jackson's family never bothered with him before. Why were they showing up now? Was Jefferson the only one snooping around? Was it possible that Jackson's mother, too, was investigating Cassie?

She was sweating through her cotton T-shirt as she stepped out of the chamber into the long hallway that lay beneath the house lined with other dark rooms and secrets. The silence echoed around her. Wiping her forehead, Cassie leaned against the wall. This was worth it. It was all worth it if it gave Jason some peace. She saw the trouble in his eyes every time she looked at him; she heard the crack in his voice when he spoke. She would find every last particle of Jackson, every skin cell he left behind if she had to, and destroy them all. She would burn the boxes of pictures next and then the suits.

Still, could every bit of the odious man be accounted for assuredly?

That morning, as Cassie went out at dawn to make sure the neighborhood dogs hadn't turned up the fresh dirt and exposed a forgotten bone or two, something rather frightening had been discovered. She had knelt to the spot where Jackson's head, his skull, lay buried and noticed that the soil had been disturbed, yet not freshly as had the soil under the rosebushes. No, this soil looked as if it was settling once again. It had been at least a week since the ground over the head had been dug at. Cassie at once dug into the dirt with her hands. The mud came up easily, but she went for a shovel all the same.

She breathed heavily, panicked. The skull was gone. Somebody knew. Somebody on Jasper Lane knew.

IT WAS a morning of spectacular planning. Steve had never been this excited about a project before, and Sandy was right there to bolster his excitement. The night before, Steve had called Keiko to ascertain if she might be interested in directing a film. He was worried that she would turn him down. In fact, he was sure she would after she learned it was a gay porn, but instead she seemed very excited about the idea. Keiko, Cliff, Steve, and Sandy sat at a round table in the GetchyaSome! offices. Cliff, as the writer of the piece, was ecstatic to finally have his vision filmed.

"*Manwhore of the Ages*. It's an epic," he said excitedly. "Think Conan the Barbarian filled with amazing sex and not a woman in sight."

"Except for me," chimed in Keiko.

"And me," said Sandy. "I can visit the set, right? I want to visit the set."

"Well, of course, you," Steve said. "You're a producer now."

Keiko nodded with casual acceptance of the matter.

Sandy was dazzled by this. "My name will be on the credits as a producer? Elizabeth will have a heart attack."

"What we're looking at is porn filmmaking on a massive scale never quite done before," Steve continued. "I'm putting all the company's efforts and money into this. We need to put any other upcoming productions on hold for a bit. I've already told the rest of the company. Keiko, you just tell me what you need and it's yours. Location shoots, new lighting, anything."

"I'll read the script today," she said. "I'll have some ideas to you first thing tomorrow, if not later tonight."

"It's a good script, real good," Steve told her, looking at Cliff, who smiled with pride. "We'll need costumes, sets, effects. We're not holding anything back."

"That could get very expensive, very fast," Keiko warned.

"I know. This is going to be a make-it-or-break-it deal. We're taking a huge risk here. But I think it will pay off."

"We'll make every penny back," Sandy assured him. "You'll see."

"And then some," Cliff agreed. "I promise you, this is the porn every gay man and every gay porn wife in America has been waiting for. If we can make that tentacle scene come to life…."

"We can do it," Keiko said. "It'll take work, but you don't need CGI to make a film with good effects."

"This is porn," Cliff joked. "Any special effects are good special effects. Slo-mo cum shots are considered good special effects."

"I'm going to make you a promise, Steve." Keiko smiled with determination. "In the 1970s porn went briefly into the mainstream. *Deep Throat* played in regular theaters in some areas of the country. I'm going to do that with *Manwhore*. And every gay man and housewife will want a copy on DVD and Blu-ray."

"I like the way you think," Steve said.

Sandy and Cliff beamed at each other, almost too giddy for words.

"We've got a hell of a lot of work ahead of us," Steve reminded them. "Fun work, but work all the same."

JAMES was almost hoping Seth wouldn't be at the gym when he walked in with Rick. But there he was, stretching his tree trunk legs, ready for their usual routine. Rick gave a low grumble and then walked to the office. James had had enough of the jealousy. He really wanted Rick to like Seth. Yet the only way that was going to happen was if they were forced to share some space together. A dinner, maybe. Seth had already told James how cool he thought Rick was, so there would be no difficulty in persuading him to come over.

"What do you think?" James asked as he and Seth loaded a bar with weight.

"I'd love to come for dinner. When?"

"I don't know. How about tomorrow night?"

Seth paused. "Do you think Rick will have a problem with it? I mean, he didn't exactly look happy with me last night. I remembered that when I woke up this morning to that anvil in my head."

"Seth, you licked my arm." James laughed. "It was just a little strange. Rick thinks you have a thing for me. That's the honest truth."

"What? Really?"

"Yeah. But that's the whole point behind getting the two of you together." He studied Seth. The big guy had looked a bit jittery when

James had mentioned Rick's suspicions. "I want to assure him that that's not the case. It isn't, is it? You're not in love with me or anything, are you?"

"Huh…. No…. No. Absolutely not!"

James thought he sounded too sincere.

"You're not my type. Not at all," Seth assured him. "You're too beefy."

"Yeah, that's what I thought."

They stared at each other momentarily over the weight bench as a disco tune sang at them from the speakers.

"Okay." James broke the awkward crawl of the moment. "Let's get our pump on!"

"Let's do it!" Slapping palms together, scattering chalk, ignoring discomfort. Men, straight or gay, were masters of that.

From behind the front desk across the gym, Rick kept his eye on the two of them. Only when a new patron or gym member bothered him did he lose track of what was happening at the weight bench. Even as he did his rounds about the fitness center, cleaning and racking weights, he kept them in view. Seth spotted him once but refused to make eye contact with him after that.

As the day wore on, a few of the other rugby players stumbled in, some still hung over from the previous night's celebrations. They descended upon the heavy weights like bulky vultures. Rick found it harder to watch James because of all of the thick bodies that refused to stay stationary for very long and continually obstructed his view.

"You're right to watch him," Rick heard a voice from behind him say. It was Token Straight Guy. Rick could never remember his name, which was strange since he was the only het on the team. One would have thought that would have made him stand out in the mind more so than the others.

"Excuse me?" Rick said.

"Seth." Token Straight Guy nodded in James's and Seth's direction. "He's a player. A complete slut. Gives you gay guys a bad name."

"You know him?"

"I hear him talk." He picked up some dumbbells for shrugs. "He's like one of those guys in the locker rooms. You know the type."

"You mean the kind of het that gives you straight guys a bad name?"

Token Straight Guy accepted the jab. "Point taken," he said. "All men are dogs, gay or straight. Anyway, you're right to keep your eye on him. Not that I think that James would ever think about cheating on you."

"You think Seth is going to make a move on James?"

"I didn't say that."

"Then what are you saying? Why tell me anything if you have no reason to back your suspicions up?" Rick couldn't help being confrontational. He needed to take his pent-up frustration out on someone.

"Listen," the guy said defensively, putting down the weights. "I'm just offering my two cents. Sorry if I've overstepped. James is a good guy. Forget I said anything."

*Fuck you*, Rick thought as he turned back around to watch James. But they were gone now, slipped off to some other part of the fitness center.

"Is it that obvious?" Rick asked Token Straight Guy.

"That you're concerned about Seth? I can tell, and I'm a breeder."

At that moment Rick was rather annoyed with himself. He had become that creepy girl who followed her boyfriend around, who obsessed over his every move, who was so self-conscious about losing her guy that she lost her mind. The thing was, though, Rick now understood why a girl like that would do what she did. He was sympathetic to the symphony of losers, because he had identified himself as one of them for so long.

TERRENCE always loved those scenes in a film where a bitter or wayward character would at last lighten up and a montage of funny yet poignant shots would convey the whole transformation set to some cutesy Rachel Portman score. This was that part of the film for Terrence, and Chris was recording it happily with his mini-cam. He thought that he might even make a little film for Terrence once they had arrived back at Jasper Lane. Maybe open it with the theme song to *The Facts of Life*, complete with cheesy grins and poses.

There was Terrence and Harry at breakfast singing a melody of their favorite cereal jingles.

The potato bag race, which no one won because of the pileup caused by Terrence swerving unjustifiably into another lane to avoid a dragonfly.

Terrence giving the "Oh no you didn't!" look to Garlic Man as he stole the last chicken leg.

Terrence tackling said thief while the pastor tried to restrain him, and Harry and Chris did nothing but laugh.

Terrence jumping out of the lake, screeching and swearing until he was blue that there was something in the water.

Harry calming Terrence with a quick kiss when they thought no one was watching.

Terrence catching butterflies as the other fathers watched him wave about his humongous catching net in disbelief.

Terrence flinging the net down when another of those pesky dragonflies got caught in it.

Chris captured enough great footage in one day to last ten birthdays' worth of embarrassing video montage gifts. He was having fun with Terrence at last, and Terrence seemed to be having fun as well. Thank God someone had enlightened him as to the point and function of the camp. Terrence had even started showing up at the daily prayer meetings, though he still crinkled his nose at the more archaic and ridiculous parts of the services. And truthfully Chris doubted if Terrence even listened to what Father Donaghan was saying. He was too busy flirting with Harry, who always saved Terrence a seat right beside him. More than once bursts of giggles interrupted the silence of the prayer. But this time it was Terrence making Harry laugh with some campy and absurd face.

No, Terrence would never be religious. Of that much Chris was certain. But at least he was becoming more tolerant. After all, some of Chris's best friends were religious, and Terrence would just have to learn to accept that no matter how abnormal it was.

TO CELEBRATE the impending production of the porn epic *Manwhore of the Ages*, Sandy and Cliff immediately drove to the local expensive natural foods store after the production meeting. There they could find all the finest wines they wanted and toast to the film's assured success. Sandy had wine aplenty at home, of course, but this was a special occasion. It called for something directly from one of the local vineyards, and Trader Mo's had every kind of fine wine produced in the area.

They pushed their cart full of wines and cheeses up and down the aisles, giggling with delight. Cliff was still elated his script was actually going to be made into a film; Sandy was delighted that she might have a chance against Elizabeth Trump as the GPWC's new president after all. Aside from that, it was just fun for both of them to be working on something together.

She wouldn't have to wait long to talk to Elizabeth, to tell her the news, or rather, to rub it in her Botoxed-to-marble face, for as Cliff and Sandy rounded the natural laxative aisle, there were Elizabeth and Eddie Licious. All of their faces registered the same expression of shock and displeasure. They faced one another down, the enemies they were, each turning with their carts in a slow, clockwise manner. Workers and shoppers stopped around them, sensing something was about to go down.

"Showdown in aisle five!" boomed a voice over the loudspeaker.

Cliff popped his neck; Eddie raised an eyebrow. Elizabeth raised her nose; Sandy put her hands on her hips. Elizabeth and Eddie would have been outnumbered if Sandy had had Amy, but Amy was with Steve at the office. Cliff was practically three men put together anyway. If there was a rumble, Cliff could break Eddie in two without even breaking one jar of pickles on the sales rack. It would be that quick.

"Elizabeth," Sandy said in a warning style of greeting.

"Sandra," Elizabeth warned back.

"It's Sandy."

Elizabeth ignored her, still looking every bit the drag queen à la Evita. "I would think that the prices here are a little out of your league with the way you usually dress. Though, lately you do look better. Tell me, will that change once I beat you?"

Cliff growled. Eddie flinched.

"Nothing will change. I'll still be loved, and you'll still be a bitter, liquored-up has-been who refuses to see the winds of change."

"My dear, I'm not the one with a cart full of alcohol."

"No, because you store it up that tight sphincter, you enema-obsessed bitch!" Cliff battled. Sandy put her hand on his shoulder to calm him.

"Hey!" Eddie barked. He couldn't really do too much more than that. As muscular as he was, he was still a yappy poodle against Cliff's Great Dane.

"It's all right, sweetheart," Elizabeth said to her husband. "Once I win the election again, I'm going to make certain Sandra here is ousted from the Gay Porn Wives Club for good, and her husband's company will never make another dime. And you," she said, looking at Cliff, "all that muscle will amount to nothing because no one will want to hire you after the rumors I start spreading."

Sandy laughed cinematically here. It caught everyone, including Elizabeth, off guard. Sandy had never thought she was capable of one of those condescending laughs, but there it was.

"What's so funny?" Elizabeth growled.

"Nothing, really. Well, yes. Actually, it is something. I'm set to be the producer on the biggest, most expensive porn ever made—gay or straight or anywhere in between. Me, Elizabeth! This film is going to be so huge it will be considered a classic in less than a year. In fact, that's where Cliff and I just came from. We're celebrating, you see? That's what all this wine is for."

Elizabeth's face fell. Eddie looked suddenly very uncomfortable. "What is it?" Elizabeth demanded. "What's the story?"

"We're not going to tell you that," Cliff replied, crossing his arms over his chest.

"Cliff here wrote it, and we've got a top-notch director. Not a porn director either. We've found someone from outside the porn community and brought them in. This is major league, Trump."

"She went to film school, has directed on the stage," Cliff offered.

The little color Elizabeth had to her face was draining. She was gripping her cart tightly, her knuckles white. "Well," she finally spoke, "I'm going to be *in* a porn!"

Even Eddie seemed taken aback by this. "You are?"

"Yes. Don't you remember, darling? You asked me… last night?"

"Y—yes…. Of course. I asked you last night."

If Elizabeth could make that happen, things might swing back in her favor. Sandy realized she should have kept her mouth shut about the film and waited until the last minute to reveal her fantastic news.

"Good luck with that," Sandy said.

"You as well." Elizabeth was composed again. "Good day," she said as she began to walk away with her cart.

Eddie followed but quickly dashed back for a moment to Cliff's side where he asked, "Do you think there might be a part for me in your film?"

"Get out of here!" Cliff grumbled.

"Eddie!" Elizabeth yelled.

FOR their second "date," Vera politely recommended they go somewhere a bit less conspicuous. She did this under the guise of wanting to be alone with Jefferson, but the truth was she would have folded over dead if any of her friends or, God forbid, employees saw her out and about with Jefferson. He was a tacky, classless man. He sneezed into his hands and wiped it onto his slacks, for Christ's sake! It was bad enough that people Vera didn't even know had to see them. What a couple they must have seemed! A short, overweight, pocked white man walking around with a true fashionista, a fierce Amazon princess as black and beautiful as had ever lived. Of course, even in Vera's mind that thought read as a bit snooty, but she could not make herself feel bad for thinking it.

There was a city garden park a few miles from the downtown area. The park land twisted and turned over acres of serenity: trees, ponds, hills. It was big enough so that one didn't run into too many other people. It was a lovely place to sit and think, or read and relax, or make out with a lover. Vera, unfortunately, was there to do none of those things. She was there to investigate this strange little man and to hope that Jefferson's refusal to give her any solid answers didn't turn her into a serial killer on the spot. She could see it now:

"TRANNY KILLER TARGETS MEN NAMED FOR DEAD PRESIDENTS!"

They walked beneath a canopy of trees. The sky was still overcast and gray, but the sprinkling had ceased. Jefferson tried to reach for Vera's hand a few times, but she avoided his grasp, feigning a sneeze or an itch. She was prepared to drop-kick the asshole if she had to.

"I've had such a good time with you the last couple of days," Jefferson relayed with a sniff. He was allergic to pollen. Oops. "But you're keeping me away from my reason for being on Jasper Lane."

"From Cassie Bloom? Am I?" (Well, there was something good anyway.)

"Yes. I think I'll have to stay longer than I had originally planned. You know, to get all the information I need. I can't afford to keep renting that house, though. Sure would be nice to stay somewhere where there was someone to come home to after a hard day's investigating. Investigating is hard, lonely work."

*That wasn't a very subtle hint, Slick.*

"You wouldn't like my place. I don't live anywhere near Jasper Lane," Vera said.

"I can drive there every day."

"With gas prices the way they are? No, sir."

"Well, then you can drop me off there every day."

"I live above a nightclub. You'd hate it. I hate it."

"We take what we can get. I can't be choosy."

"A gay nightclub."

"Well...."

Vera took this lull to change the subject. "What have you found out about Cas—Miss Bloom?"

He created a long pause in the conversation and then said, "I don't know if I should say."

"You don't trust me!" Vera acted upset. And she was, but not for the reason Jefferson thought. "You told me you'd tell me, but you don't trust me. You'll never trust me!" She ran with dramatic pantomime to the nearest tree and cried into its bark.

"That's not true! I trust you. I really do." He was pleading desperately as he raced to her. "Please don't cry." He sniffed, sneezed, and then touched Vera with his sniffly, sneezy hands. She almost threw up.

Vera turned to face him. "So you'll tell me? I have to know how much longer I am to be under her control."

Jefferson relaxed his expression. "It won't be for too much longer, my dear. That wicked woman…. She'll be gone before month's end, her and her putrid son!"

Jefferson laid his hand on Vera's fine jaw and twittled with her earlobe. She was feeling nauseous.

"I know she killed my brother. He's buried somewhere on his property. I just have to wait until she's gone to search it for myself—but she never leaves!"

"How do you know she killed him?" Vera asked as they now continued walking through the gardens. She let him hold her hand. It was worth it if it enabled her to get more information from him.

"A brother knows. A mother knows. Mom's the one who told me to come here. She always thought that there was something fishy about Cassie. Never liked her. Jackson was her favorite. She thought Cassie was beneath him. I always wanted to be just like him; Mom always wanted me to be just like him too."

"Were you close to Jackson?"

"When we were kids, I think we were. But I haven't spoken to him in years. He cut ties with us after he married Cassie and got that government job. Then Mom moved away, got a new family of her own. This was the first I heard from her in a while. She said I owed it to her and Jackson."

"If he was in the government, why haven't they opened up an investigation into his disappearance?" This was something Vera always wondered about.

Jefferson leaned into her and said very secretly, "He did things... bad things for the government. That's what I think anyway. They just wanted to get rid of him. They didn't care how he was gotten rid of."

"I see," Vera said, extremely disturbed.

She feared Jefferson's proximity to her face might require she kiss him. He had, after all, just divulged some useful information... finally. But she saw some orange tiger lilies ahead where a young girl was standing, admiring them.

"I do love tiger lilies!" she exclaimed, avoiding Jefferson's gaze. "Isn't that a beautiful orange? I just adore orange."

At once, Jefferson walked to the flowers. The young girl was about to pick a particularly large and delicate blossom, but Jefferson reached in and grabbed it first. The girl stared after him, completely destroyed. She began to cry as he brought the flower to Vera.

"Here you go, my sweet," he said with an uncomfortable grin.

Vera took the flower from him, horrified. She acted pleased, but as they passed the young, weeping girl Vera handed the flower to her on the sly and picked another. Jefferson didn't notice the tradeoff.

CASSIE had never barred Jason from setting foot in the basement. What good would that have done? Restrictions only make a person more curious about what they are being kept away from. She just assumed Jason would know to steer clear of it. As a child he had been warned away by his father. Then it was locked. Jason never saw his father or mother use the door to the basement. He had never seen it opened in his life, not until he came back from Europe. When he was young he had heard it, though. Jackson worked in the basement at night when Cassie was long since passed out from alcohol and unhappiness and Jason was locked in his room. When Jackson shut the door to the basement, it shook the house and a draft of unease spread through the hallways. Even as a child Jason understood something terrifying went on below him.

When he had come home at last after his travels abroad and the door to the basement was unlocked, he couldn't resist it. He was no longer the young boy who stared at the basement door all hours of the day, hiding behind a piece of elegant furniture, fearing what lay beyond the lock, believing that the basement door might be the gate to hell and convincing himself that his father went down there every night to battle demons. No, Jason was now a young man determined. He needed to see, to know the truth.

In those first few weeks, while Cassie was lounging around on the deck with her friends, Jason took that time to investigate. It wasn't as if Cassie would stop him from getting to the truth, but he knew that she didn't truly want him down there in the basement either. He knew she feared what had happened in the basement, the horrors she never truly understood, somehow still hung in the air waiting to attach themselves to whomever descended the steps. Cassie feared for her son's sanity. He didn't have the heart to tell her his mind was already slipping away. Maybe he should seek therapy. But not now. Not until after he had all the answers. Then he would get better. And he'd let his mother care for him. She would love that.

When he entered the basement for the first time upon returning home, he could feel more than his father's ghost behind him; he could feel the tortured souls of others. He tried to restrain them, though. He tried to keep them from invading his space as he walked the long hallway and peered into the strange, dark rooms. It was hard that first time. He couldn't stay down there too long. But each time after that it got a little easier.

Finally he was able to stay in the basement for a good while; he was able to research and discover information about his father. He knew Jackson's work was of the horror movie variety; he could ascertain that much from Jackson's stoic ghost. That's not what he was looking for. He was searching for the truth about his own questions.

What were his father's intentions toward him? Was he truly planning to send him away to some camp?

It was in a tattered box of old notes by the large incinerator that he found a curious link. Underneath piles of strange letters and envelopes with familiar addresses lay a single pamphlet. On the cover was a photo of a group of well-dressed and deliriously happy-looking young people, some of them not even teenagers. Their faces were pleasant but forced, as if they smiled out of fear. Behind them stood two older people who did not smile. They did not frown either. In fact, they looked too passive. Like mannequins. Their eyes were faded and drained. Above the picture it read "Straight to the Heart: Through God's Love We Cure."

Jason's heart sank as he realized his mother had been telling him the truth, though, somewhere inside he had known it all along. He swallowed and refused the tears. Jason looked for an address on the pamphlet but couldn't find one. He did see a Web site, however, and made a note of it.

Before he made his way quietly upstairs, Jason tucked the pamphlet in the back pocket of his faded jeans, along with one of the letters sent from that familiar address. Frank Gold, Jasper Lane. Melinda's ex-husband. That was the name on the envelope. But the letter inside was written by another hand: Nanna's.

*You need to send him away at once!* read the angry letter. *He's been infected. It's an illness. I can get him in. I know people at that camp. Just you leave it to me.*

It was dated the day before Jackson disappeared. Why was Jackson Bloom talking to Nanna? Jason could never remember seeing them so much as within two yards of each other.

When Cassie, David, and Becky were excavating Jackson's remains that first night, Jason was online as he told his mother he would be. But he was not chatting with any friends. He didn't have any of those at the moment. Instead, he was researching the Straight to the Heart Web site and getting more vengeful by the minute.

# Suburbilicious: Vignettes from Jasper Lane

AS EVENING descended on the campgrounds, a bullying storm started to roll in. It was the same front that had teased Jasper Lane all day but never truly threatened. The campers rushed about securing items, making certain their tents were strong enough to make it through the gusts of wind and rain. The activities and prayer meetings for the evening had been canceled. At four in the afternoon it looked like dusk; at five it looked like midnight and the rain had begun to fall in earnest. Terrence didn't like the shaking of the tent, the howling he heard outside.

"It'll be okay, Dad," Chris assured him as they huddled together beneath blankets. Chris had given up trying to listen to the pocket radio. The pouring rain was drowning the sound out. "It's highly unlikely we'll be struck by lightning. I mean, lightning strikes aren't too common, are they?"

"Really?"

A crack and a flash disputed Chris's assurance.

"To the minivan!" Terrence jumped up. "Let's get to the minivan right now!"

Another crack of lightning and he collapsed to the tent floor again, hiding beneath the blankets.

"Dad," Chris yelled above the storm. "I'm glad we came. I'm glad the two of us could spend this time together, away from everyone else. I just wanted to tell you that."

Terrence peaked out from beneath the covers. "Me too," he mumbled.

"What?"

"I said me too!" Terrence let go of his death grip on the blanket and watched his son. Whether Chris wanted it or not, Terrence was going to give him a hug.

Chris chuckled. "Let's have it then," he said, opening his arms.

"You're not upset with me?" Terrence asked in his son's ear.

"Of course not! You wouldn't be you without a little drama. I know that. I knew you were going to be a handful when I first saw you that day in the airport when we met face-to-face for the first time."

The rain let up just enough for Terrence and Chris to hear someone struggling to open their tent flap.

"Who is it?" Chris called. But there was no way whoever it was could hear above the rain pelting the tent.

Terrence leaned forward and quickly unzipped the flap. Harry poked his head in, drenched and smiling. "You got room for us?" he asked.

"How dare you even ask!" Terrence declared, sliding over immediately to make room for Harry beside him.

Harry and Jordan piled quickly into the tent with blankets and food. "It seems we have a leak in our tent," Harry explained. "We'd sleep in the Jeep, but—"

"And be uncomfortable?" Terrence objected. "I think not. Sleeping in vehicles is gauche."

"Dad, you were just thinking about sleeping in the minivan," Chris reminded him.

"The little one must be silent," Terrence hummed to his son as Harry brought out a thermos of hot chocolate. Harry drew close to Terrence, shoulder to shoulder. Even with the lightning and thunder, Terrence didn't so much as jump now.

"How's the camp look?" Chris asked.

"It's a mess," Harry replied. "Reggie—Garlic Man—he stepped out of his tent for a minute, leaving his poor son inside, that little stick figure of a boy. Well, the tent must not have been fastened to the ground too well, because a gust of wind came along and the tent went a rolling, occupant and all." Terrence started laughing along with Harry. "The kid was a screaming, hysterical mess when we finally caught the cartwheeling tent."

"It was kind of hard not to laugh at," Jordan interjected.

Harry, Terrence, and Jordan had a difficult time trying to drink their hot chocolate in between bursts of laughter.

"You're all heartless," Chris said with a grin.

"Not true," Terrence objected. "I would never laugh if that happened to you."

"So we're in here for a while together." Harry leaned close to Terrence. "What are our plans? Ghost stories?"

"Dad will scream." Chris looked at his father with a wink.

"I will not!"

"I'll be here," Harry whispered into his ear. "I'll be here all night."

"Make it a good one," Terrence demanded as he slid up to Harry's chest. The two boys rolled their eyes.

"I CAN'T believe I'm doing this," Melinda said under her breath as she zipped up the knee-high leather boots in Malcolm's bathroom.

"Change here, in front of me," he'd asked.

Fat chance! She didn't want to try on the slick, glossy dominatrix outfit in the first place; she certainly wasn't going to slide into the unforgiving costume in front of him. It had taken him a while to convince her, anyway. There was a fair bit of pleading and begging from him, groveling even. She had never seen someone want something so bad—until she remembered how bad she wanted to be the grand dame of Jasper Lane at one time. Then she felt for him.

Still, this was a rather odd thing to be so obsessed about, wasn't it? Leather, a whip, and a mask.

The costume was just as uncomfortable as it looked. Though, she had to admit, when she glanced in the mirror, she did look striking. All that speed-walking with Becky was paying off. Not that she was ever overweight, but as a woman ages it does become harder to keep those few extra pounds from sneaking up on her. Melinda felt a bit like a superhero in the outfit, like Catwoman. Especially with the mask on and her hair pulled back from her face. Her skin was so pale against the leather.

"Meow!" she growled playfully into the mirror.

"What?" Malcolm called from the bedroom.

"Nothing!" she answered, jolted that he had even heard her. She studied the whip. It was a long, mean-looking thing. Who would use this on another person for sexual satisfaction? She snapped it once, just like she had seen in the movies. The tail knocked a sports poster off the wall, and it crashed to the floor.

"Sorry!" she screeched.

"Save that aggression for me, baby! Yow!"

*What a strange man!* She would not be using the whip on him, no matter how much he begged, but as an affectation she would carry it out with her. It *was* part of the costume.

"Am I dating a pervert?" she asked herself with some concern.

*No, Melinda. That's the old you talking. Just enjoy it. This is your new life. He's just an ordinary man with an ordinary sex drive. Well, maybe not ordinary. Heightened.*

"I'm ready!" Malcolm called for her.

Here goes, she thought as she opened the bathroom door and walked out cautiously into the dimly lit bedroom. It took her a few seconds to find Malcolm on his hands and knees on the floor at the foot of the bed. As her eyes adjusted she saw he was naked but for a harness and… what was that?

Melinda walked around to his rear end. There was something—

"Yeah, Momma! How you like that?" Malcolm growled through the harness as he shook his ass at her. An ass that now gripped tightly to a fake horse tail lodged in the anus.

Melinda stumbled backward and dropped the whip. *"Pervert!"* she blurted out before she could stop herself.

# Suburbilicious: Vignettes from Jasper Lane

SANDY sat with Joyce, the VP of the Gay Porn Wives Club, over a couple cups of coffee in her backyard. The drizzle and gray of the previous day had disappeared, and the morning sun shone bright and cheery. Amy toddled about in the yard, playing with butterflies and dandelions.

"Just don't eat them, honey," Sandy said to her daughter. "The flowers either."

"You have to watch her closely?" Joyce asked.

"Constantly. She's an eater, that one." She turned her attention back to what Joyce had been saying. "Neck and neck, you say?"

Joyce swallowed a taste of coffee, nodding her head. "It's very exciting. It's the first time the club has ever had a real fight for president. We honestly can't tell who will win. Loyalties aren't as strong as Elizabeth had hoped." Joyce's own husband had been a major porn star at one time; now he only acted occasionally. Joyce and he had settled into a calm suburban existence. They looked like the everyday couple, quite content in being plain and ordinary. They had even started resembling each other: short black hair and pleasant expressions.

"From what I could tell," Sandy noted, "Elizabeth doesn't seem to be very well-liked."

"She's not. But she gets the job done." Joyce paused. "Plus, look at her. She's Brunhilda scary. No one else wants to take on that."

"Why haven't you tried for the position? You're VP. Surely you've thought about president."

"I have, before I had kids and other priorities. Once upon a time when my husband and I were first married and he was a big star, I wanted to run, but—"

"Elizabeth scared you away from it, didn't she?" Sandy knew Elizabeth would stop at nothing to secure her title. "She's already threatened both Cliff and I with deadly rumors."

"She's already started spreading them, honey," Joyce informed her. "But don't worry. There's a group of us stamping those rumors out just as soon as she fans them. I don't know how successful we'll be, though."

Amy ran to her mother, giggling, holding a fistful of grass and clovers as a gift. Sandy thanked her, and Amy ran out onto the lawn once more.

"There is something you need to ask yourself before you take on this mantle, though," Joyce said more seriously. "Can you do this? It's a heavy responsibility, and while Elizabeth is a major bitch, she gets the job done. Can you do that same job along with all your other priorities?"

Sandy wanted to scream, *It's gay porn, for God's sake! Lighten the hell up!* But she refrained from saying anything.

"I can do this, Joyce," she reassured her guest. "I've been going nuts here at home. I love Amy; I love Steve. But being at home every hour of the day—it's driving me crazy. I need this. I can do this."

Joyce relaxed with a smile. "That's all I needed to hear. You've got my vote."

"Who are you running against for the office of VP?"

"No one. I've been the VP for a little longer than Elizabeth has been president. Nobody really runs. That's why everyone is so excited about your contention in the race."

"You mean, this is the first election, real election, you've had?"

"In a while," Joyce said. "I mean, who has the time? If it were easier, if Elizabeth wasn't such a hard-ass with the rules and who she wanted in her cabinet, then maybe some others would run. There's a platform for you."

"Promise positions of power for votes?" Sandy chuckled. "Sounds like something a sleazy governor from Kentucky or Tennessee would do."

"Sleazy governors get elected and they never pay for what they've done." Joyce winked.

Sandy watched Amy chasing a butterfly. Such innocence; she was intent on catching it as if it were the only thing that mattered in all the world. And here Sandy was thinking about buying votes for the presidency of the Gay Porn Wives Club. Perspective really was everything. Oh, the importance of life's trivialities. How they continuously changed.

VERA had explained to Cassie the night before that they needed to get into a fight—a heavy-duty argument—the next morning at coffee on the deck for Jefferson's benefit. He still seemed a bit reticent about letting Vera into the house he rented; he still didn't fully trust her. Maybe he wasn't such a fool after all. Vera reasoned that if the two of them could get into a little sparring match when Jefferson was sure to be watching through his binoculars on the straining branches of some poor tree then she could get into his rented house without committing a felony. He would invite her in to comfort her. Cassie agreed with the idea.

Becky, of course, was told of the plan so that she wouldn't think her friends had gone totally insane. She admitted, however, that it would be virtually impossible for her to keep a straight face through it all.

"I'm not an actor! I work in the porn industry. What do I know about acting?"

So she giggled her way absent of the occasion, wishing she could be there to see Melinda's clueless face when it all went down. There was no way Melinda could be told. To tell her anything would draw suspicion and curiosity. Soon she would be dragged into their little world of creepy undoings, and it might very well drive her virgin mind insane. Poor Melinda. She was like the kid at a slumber party who everyone had to comfort after a ghost story because she was too easily prone to nightmares.

Melinda sat in between Vera and Cassie. She sipped at her coffee anxiously. The night before with Malcolm had been somewhat unnerving, and now Cassie and Vera seemed to be acting rather strange, very cool to each other. Melinda felt like she had walked in on the middle of an argument. Vera gave Cassie a death glare; Cassie returned the stare with ferocity.

"So," Cassie finally spoke, and very loudly too, by Melinda's estimation. Cassie nearly yelled across the table at Vera. "That's it then, huh?"

"That's right," Vera responded just as verbose.

Melinda hid behind the rim of her coffee mug. *What's it?*, she wanted to ask.

"After all these years, after all we've been through, you're just going to stab me in the back?" Cassie inquired viciously.

"Don't kid yourself, darling! You've seen this coming for some time."

Melinda shrunk in her seat as if to avoid any poisoned darts that might be brought out of pocket and flung about. What was happening? Where was Jason? He was usually out on the deck painting in the morning.

"You hid your true self well, you conniving, manipulating bitch! My husband was right about you."

"You're a vile, soul-sucking old hag who's just jealous!"

"Jealous of what? Of your lack of style? Your whorish ways? Why don't you head on back to that place you call a club and leave the rest of us humans alone!"

"Ladies!" Melinda finally interrupted. "What's gotten into you? What's the meaning of all of this?"

Cassie still eyed Vera. "Well, I guess there is one person you haven't told all my secrets to."

"She'll know soon enough!"

## Suburbilicious: Vignettes from Jasper Lane

Cassie stood abruptly and slammed her coffee mug to the ground, where it shattered. Melinda jumped to her feet with a squeal. Vera almost started laughing, nearly spoiled the whole routine. Instead, she rose as well. Jefferson was getting quite a show, and Melinda was playing her part to perfection.

"I'll ruin you, Vera!" Cassie hissed. "I still have my clout in this town. We'll run you and your club out of the state, out of the country!"

"Do your worst, Cassie Bloom! How did I ever think of you as a friend?"

"You didn't. You thought of me as your meal ticket."

Melinda didn't know what to think. Her coffees in the morning with Vera, Cassie, and Becky had been one of the few constants in her life for the past year, ever since Jasper Lane had opened its arms to her, forgiven her for being a less-than-neighborly neighbor. But as she listened to the two of them, those mornings, that constant, was slipping away.

"Can't we talk about this?" Melinda asked. "Get things out in the open? I'm sure it's not as bad as either of you think. Misunderstandings happen all the time between friends."

"Oh, no, my dear. It's much worse than I thought!" *Meh*, Cassie shrugged on the inside. *A predictable line but it worked.* Melinda gasped discontentedly.

"Harpie!"

"Hag!"

"Two-faced bitch!"

"Big-assed whore!"

"Wretched, wretched, cum-guzzling slut!"

Vera threw her mug against the side of the house just as Jason came outside to see what all the fuss was about. She gave Cassie a dramatic raised eyebrow that would have put Joan Crawford to shame. "You've not heard the last of me, Cassie Bloom!" she cried before she marched down the hill past the small crowd of onlookers toward her car.

"You're through!" Cassie exclaimed as she turned on her heels old Hollywood-style (she wore her most flowing morning robe for the effect) and walked past Jason and into the house.

Melinda was left stunned, still holding her coffee and staring at the crowd that had gathered.

"Something wrong?" Jason asked dryly.

Melinda turned to him and shook her head, bewildered.

RICK woke up from a nightmare and decided he was going to let it all go. He wasn't going to let James's friendship with Seth—and that's all it was, he kept reminding himself in mantra: a friendship—bother him any longer. In his dream, James had left him. Not because there was another man, or, God forbid, a woman (*Ew!*), but because Rick had been such an unbearable nuisance about Seth.

"You've rattled the love I had for you right out of me," James said without the slightest hint of feeling in the dream. Then he walked out of the house, which had at some time during the nightmare become Tara from *Gone with the Wind*, and Rick and James were playing out the final scene between Scarlett and Rhett. Rick hated *Gone with the Wind*.

When Rick woke, he got dressed, went downstairs, and made James a big breakfast: eggs, toast, bacon, sausage… the American coronary special. He set it out on the kitchen table beside a glass vase of dandelions and daisies he had picked. He wouldn't be there to watch James eat because he needed to get to work, but he wanted to show James he was going to try a new outlook on things. He was going to change. There was no need for James to leave him in a melodramatic huff.

Rick walked to the car. The sky was beautiful. The birds were singing. What a beautiful morning! He would let nothing dampen his mood today.

Driving to work, passengers in other cars smiled and waved. He waved back, which was very odd for him. He still didn't smile, but he was working on that. Maybe by the time he reached the gym he would be able to eke out a smile.

The other drivers' manners were pristine. "You go ahead," one car seemed to be saying politely to another at a four-way stop.

"No, you. I insist!" said another.

The employees in the gym didn't know what to think of Rick when he walked in. He was cheerful. Not that Rick was ever really depressed; he just looked it. But he actually smiled today, and this caught all the employees off guard. Why, he looked as if he might break out whistling at any moment!

Rick greeted every patron with a strong "Hello" and his shocking facial expression. When they tried to talk to him, he actually stood there and listened, looking them in the eyes. This new Rick had become a hit within an hour. The entire mood of the place was lifted from bummed obligation (Who wanted to work out?) to a sense of well-being. People were absolutely jovial.

Even Rick's work didn't seem as monotonous and boring to him now. He did everything efficiently and quickly, always willing to help out a gym-goer in need. This was easy, he thought. No problem at all. As long as he reminded himself that James and Seth were just friends, that Seth was not on some secretive mission to come between them, Rick could concentrate much better. Sure, it was a façade over his fears. But it would keep him from driving James away. So smile, Rick. Smile.

His cell phone vibrated in his jeans pocket. It was James. How perfect! "Hey, baby," Rick answered cheerfully.

It took James a bit to respond. "Rick?" he said incredulously.

"Of course, it's me." Rick laughed. Jeez, his face was hurting. "Who else would it be? You dialed my number, didn't you?"

"I did. It's just…." Pause. "You sound so… happy."

"I am. I am happy. I have you. Why wouldn't I be happy? No one on Jasper Lane has more of a right to be happy than me." Gym patrons smiled and greeted Rick as he talked on his phone at the front desk.

"Well, okay. Thank you for the breakfast, hon. That was very sweet." Another pause. "Is something the matter?"

"What? Why? No. Just thought I'd make you breakfast. Just a whim."

"Uh-huh." James didn't sound convinced. "Thanks. Um, listen... can you stop by the store on your way home and pick up a couple of bottles of white wine?"

"Are we having pasta tonight? A romantic dinner?"

"We are having pasta, but we're entertaining tonight. Sorry. No romance until later." Something in James's voice told Rick there was something he was not too keen on telling him.

"We're entertaining tonight? Who?"

"Now, don't freak out," James pleaded. "Promise me you won't freak out."

"Seth. You invited Seth," Rick said. Smile. Just smile.

"Yes. I invited Seth. I thought if I could get you two together... if I could let you see how he acts around me when we're not at the gym or when he's not drinking...."

Rick was quiet. Perfectly still. He stopped responding to the gym patrons when they greeted him, though his painful smile remained.

"Rick? Say something. Are you angry?"

Calm, Rick. Think of Rhett Butler. "No," he lied. "Absolutely not."

Shocked silence. "Seriously?"

"Seriously. I think that's a great idea. Two bottles of white coming right up." *God, this job was tedious! So monotonous.*

"That… that's great, Rick! I'm so glad you're okay with this. I'll see you later, babe. Thanks for breakfast. You're the best!"

"No. You are." *Stupid gym members! Why do they keep smiling at me?*

"Love you, baby!"

"You too." Click.

Keep smiling. Just remember they're just friends. Don't let anything get you down. Not even the roidtard over there who's probably going to throw his back out by doing all that weight or the Oprahlite who's not even using that machine correctly. Don't let any of these sweet, kind, moronic bastards get you down.

"Rick." It was David talking to him. He'd just walked in for his morning workout, his baggy workout clothes doing nothing to hide his physique. "What's with the weird, toothy grin? Buddy, you pretending to be happy is *not* the first thing I want to see in the morning."


TERRENCE couldn't ever remember waking up with such a feeling of contentment. The ground was hard even with his extra-padded sleeping bag and blankets; he shouldn't have been as comfortable as he had been all night long. But he hadn't woken up in discomfort once, and it wasn't because of the Aquaman sleeping bag. It was the large arms that were wrapped around him all night, the breathing on his neck, the feel of strength behind him. He had been spooned and held by Harry the whole night through, and it was wonderful. What was happening to him? Unlike every other morning when Terrence had met a new day with another man, this time he didn't want to quickly escape from the situation. He wanted to lay there forever.

Finally, he gulped in anxiety. Was this love? The thought seemed ludicrous but frightening and possible at the same time. He was calmed down almost immediately, though, as Harry snuggled into his shoulders.

*So what if it was love?* Terrence grinned lazily. That was such a deep thought. Too deep for early morning... in a tent... at a religious camp... in a superhero sleeping bag.

He watched Chris and Jordan stir on the opposite side of the tent. Thank God this was a big tent. Not that Harry and he had done anything or ever would with the boys in there, but still, it was nice that there could be some space between them.

The boys were awake. Terrence heard them whispering, but he couldn't understand what they were saying. It was all hushed *esses* from where he lay. Finally, Chris sat up. Terrence shut his eyes, but not completely; just so that he could see Chris, yet Chris would still think he was sleeping. Chris smiled at his father and yawned as he scratched his morning head. He nudged Jordan and the other sat up at once.

"Let's let them sleep some more," Chris said.

Terrence shut his eyes tighter as the boys rustled and fidgeted their ways into clothes and out of the tent. Terrence was proud of the son he had. Proud of what kind of person he had become.

"They leave us alone?" Harry asked into Terrence's ear. He stretched and made morning sighs.

"Yeah. They're good guys, huh? We've got great sons."

"Hell, yeah, we do." He squeezed Terrence. "I like this. This was nice. We should do it again sometime."

"Or we could just stay here and enjoy what we have now for a little while longer," Terrence proposed.

"I'd love to. But if we're going to do anything I still need to get rid of my morning breath," Harry joked.

The fact that that statement did nothing to deter Terrence's usually picky attractions was a surefire sign that Harry was unlike anyone he had ever met. He had never been so attracted to a man in his life. And they hadn't even had sex.

"Just a few more minutes?" Terrence pleaded. Was this how Steve felt every morning with Cliff? How Rick felt wrapped up with

James? And Sandy in Steve's embrace? Suddenly, Terrence was jealous of all the time he had missed out on. All the mornings he had not woken up just like this.

"Okay," Harry agreed. "Just a bit more." And he nuzzled again into Terrence's neck.

MANWHORE was defenseless and vulnerable. He lay prone, chained to the large boulder, his meaty ass stripped of his magical protective loincloth. The evil Trolls of Cumland had at last captured him and stood about, waiting for their leader to take his rightful first fuck before they could ravage the unfortunate hero en masse.

"You fool," spoke Rimrod, the King of the Trolls. "You fell into my trap, and now I shall have your sexual power as my own." He held in his hand the Golden Cock of Power. "With your huge, sinewy ass out of the way, I will rule the land."

Manwhore knew if he was fucked by the huge piece of golden meat, if he survived it, he would lose all of his strength; it would be emptied out of him and into the giant golden phallus with each hungry thrust.

Manwhore struggled against the chains. "You can't win, Rimrod!" he shouted angrily at the king. "You may get rid of me, but there are others who will stand up against your sexual tyranny."

"But none with such a mighty weapon as this," the king said as he caressed Manwhore's ass with the gold dildo's tip. "Now you will feel its true power!" he sneered.

With that, he parted Manwhore's ass dumplings and positioned the golden cock head at the ready for intrusion. The crowd of muscular trolls cheered in victory, each already priming their dicks for the evening's feast. Manwhore knew for certain he would not survive the night....

"*Cut!*" Keiko called out. The lights went up over the barren desert set, and the actors relaxed. A small battalion of fluffers rushed onto the set to keep the actors hard. "Let's get Cliff ready for the golden dildo fuck scene."

Cliff rose from the fake boulder and chains, and was handed his robe.

"Good scene," said Dom Bottom, the actor playing the troll king. "You've really got some kind of classic with this film."

"Thanks," Cliff said. "Nice makeup effects they have on you guys." Cliff nodded at the penis-shaped horns protruding from Dom's head. And it *was* well-done. In fact, it was the production Cliff had always dreamed of, right down to the lighting and effects. Keiko had contacted a makeup artist friend of hers she had worked with before, and Dom and his fellow erect trolls were colored a sexy shade of muscle-defining gray.

"Good job, Cliff," Keiko said as she approached and put her arms around Cliff's shoulder—well, as best her arms would reach around his shoulder. There was so much of him, after all. "Is it feeling right to you? Your script?"

"You've no idea," Cliff replied excitedly as he tied the belt on his robe. "This is an absolute dream. I never thought it would happen. How's my performance?"

"Very nice. You're acting your heart out, hon. Go take a break. I think Sandy's waiting for you in your changing room." The next scene to be filmed did not require Cliff. Strictly troll-on-troll action.

Cliff had just set foot in his room when Sandy jumped him, squealing in delight. "We're doing it!" she cried. "We're actually doing it!"

"You bet we are." He held onto her as her legs were wrapped tight around him. "This wouldn't have happened without you," he said. "Thank you for letting me realize my dream."

"No, thank you, baby," she said, climbing down. "I don't know why beating Elizabeth is so important to me, but—"

"You need something to do."

"Desperately. I need to feel important. Not that Steve doesn't...." She stopped. She was hitting on something, a fact that she didn't want to acknowledge about her relationship with her husband. Not just yet. "Anyway," she said, shaking the worrisome thoughts away. "This is a good day. A great day. Nothing can go wrong today. The first day of filming."

Cliff had sensed something had been strained in Steve and Sandy's relationship since the birth of Amy, but until Sandy was ready to talk about it, Cliff was not going to push her. Perhaps David had noticed a similar oddness with Steve. He'd have to ask him about it when he got home that night.

As far as a perfect day for filming, that was almost true. Cliff decided not to tell Sandy about his altercation that morning. He had been getting a pump out back near the pool, so he would look swollen for the first scene, when he noticed movement out of the corner of his eye. One of the tall wood boards of the fence that surrounded the pool area had been loosened, and it seemed someone was peering through it. Cliff carefully strolled nearer the loose plank, and, when the moment was right, he pounced. He leaped at the fence, knocking it down. The spy grunted and hollered. Cliff stood up at once and saw Eddie Licious running for his car—and for his life. He had a camera.

Naked and unconcerned with being naked, Cliff took off after Eddie. Eddie was in the locked car by the time Cliff reached him. Eddie couldn't help but stare at the sweaty, meaty behemoth as he frantically tried to start his car. Cliff yelled and banged on the roof, and then he jumped on the hood of the car with his bare ass, leaving a dent. Eddie screamed. Screamed, as in, like a little girl. At once, Cliff's rage dissipated, and he started laughing at the shrill shriek that had come from the man. He jumped off the hood and, with a condescending showman's gesture, let Eddie drive away. Eddie squealed his tires and was out of sight before Cliff could stop laughing.

"Cliff?" A porn page poked his head into the room where Cliff and Sandy were talking. "Steve says not to worry about the fence. He's just going to put it in with the production costs."

"What happened to the fence?" Sandy asked. "Was there a particularly rough sex scene? Could the wood not take your wood?" She thought she was being very clever.

"Uh, yeah," Cliff lied. "Sometimes being this big is a curse. I'm like Colossus or something."

IT WAS the human wheelbarrow race that finally ended Chris and Terrence's stay at the campgrounds. Everything had started out innocent enough, and afterward Terrence was quick to tell everyone present that no alcohol had been involved. But he was also quick—very quick—to tell them that he was not in the least bit sorry about what had occurred. He had, in fact, enjoyed it very much. Maybe a bit too much for some of the more conservative fathers' tastes. Terrence was typecast, after all; a fact that he rather enjoyed. He knew he was the Hollywood stereotype of a gay man, and he relished in it. Most of the others at the camp save Harry just couldn't warm up to that fact.

There were seven teams competing in the human wheelbarrow race. The fathers would be held by the ankles by their sons and race along the grass with their hands to a designated finishing line, in this case a line of pine trees near the edge of the campsite. Terrence and Harry were right next to each other in the race. Frivolity was in the air. When Father Donaghan gave the shout for the racing to commence, two of the heavier-set fathers were down for the count almost immediately. The other three were keeping up a decent pace, but it was clear this was going to be a race between Terrence and Harry. They shouted playful insults at each other as they grabbed frantically at the grass in front of them.

"Fruitcake!"

"Pillow-biter!"

"Grow up, guys," Chris interjected.

Terrence shouted back to his son. "Quiet, Chris! This is grown-up talk. Daddy needs to concentrate."

146

It wasn't long before the other three fathers had completely and hopelessly fallen behind. Terrence and Harry were, quite literally, neck and neck. Harry reached over and joyfully swatted at Terrence's wrist, hoping to bring him down.

"You obnoxious, cheating whore!" Terrence cried, swatting back.

"Language!" one of the other fathers shouted as they watched now from the sidelines. It was probably goddamned Garlic Man, Terrence thought.

Harry swatted again at Terrence's wrist, and Terrence lost some ground but quickly regained it as he tugged on Harry's pant leg, causing Harry to stumble.

"Play fair, gentlemen," the pastor reminded them from the side.

"I am so taking you out," Harry grunted in between breaths.

"What?" Terrence snickered. "Can't take a little competition? See you at the pines." With that he sped up.

"Oh, no you don't!" Harry said.

He slipped from his son's grasp and pounced on Terrence, who let out a delighted vocal spasm. Now Terrence was free of Chris as well, and both he and Harry went rolling around on the ground. This was odd since there was no hill. They were clearly propelling themselves, and the fathers and sons just watched.

Terrence and Harry giggled and laughed, forgetting where they were. They pinched and slapped each other. Terrence grabbed Harry's ass with both hands, and they began kissing uncontrollably. Garlic Man gasped and covered his son's eyes.

Terrence had never been kissed so thoroughly, so… perfectly. He reached past Harry's belt buckle and into his jeans and would most certainly have gone further if Chris hadn't stopped him.

"Dad!" Chris shouted. "Think of the children!"

Terrence and Harry looked up from their wrestling, remembering they were not alone. The campers watched them, mouths agape.

147

"Well, at least you're finally having a good time," Chris said to his father.

"You two are in so much trouble!" Jordan commented.

THE tension lay over the dinner table thicker than the pasta and wine. James had tried to spark a conversation between Rick and Seth; he wanted this dinner to resemble a gathering of friends. But nothing worked, nothing seemed to catch between them, so now they all sat, not eating, counting breaths. Rick knew James was becoming agitated with him, but he had tried. He really had. He had tried to welcome Seth cordially into their home. They had sat through drinks in the living room together, and though Rick hadn't said very much, he had smiled, dammit! He had even smiled all the way through dinner. He was smiling still. He sincerely feared his face might be stuck forever that way. He didn't realize that his efforts were only adding to the awkwardness of the night. It was an odd play of eyes. James stared at Rick; Rick stared and smiled at Seth; Seth stared at his plate of hardly touched food.

James sighed angrily, fed up at last. "Rick! For God's sake, stop staring at him."

"I'm being nice. I'm doing my best."

"You're being an ass!"

The smile fell right off Rick's face, and he shot a glance over at James. "I'm making him feel comfortable, just like you wanted."

"I wanted you to be civil, not weird." James was gritting through his teeth. "It's like you're trying your best not to be you. What is it with that grin? You never show all those teeth."

"I appreciate it, Rick. I do," Seth spoke, at last looking up from the plate. "It can't be easy, I mean, with James, it can't be...." He paused. "I don't know how to finish that sentence." Once again he poured an abnormal amount of attention on his food, slightly embarrassed.

"There's no need to try and make him feel better, Seth. Rick's just being a baby. When I talked with him on the phone—"

"You gave me no choice!" Rick exclaimed. "Why would you ask him to dinner when you know how I feel? He's in love with you, James!"

Seth's neck jerked up in surprise, his face growing pinker by the second.

"Can we not talk about this now?" James growled.

"You started this conversation. Not me."

Seth fidgeted, pushing his chair back. "I think I should leave. This was a bad idea. Clearly, there are some things—"

"You are not leaving." James pounded the table. Seth stayed still.

"James is right, Seth. You're not leaving." Rick rose to his feet, throwing his napkin on his plate. He stormed out of the room without another word.

"Rick!" James yelled. His voice shook the room and rattled the glass.

The front door slammed, and James ran to the living room window in time to see Rick drive off.

"Sorry, Jimmy," Seth said, coming up from behind. "I should have guessed something like this would happen."

"Don't apologize." James waved Seth's statement off as he continued to watch out the window. "Rick overreacts. He overreacts to everything. I don't understand him sometimes."

"Actually, there is something I want to talk to you about," Seth began. "Maybe it's good that he left. It makes it somewhat easier."

"Can it wait?" James asked, thoroughly uninterested in anything at the moment. "I'm exhausted."

"S-sure. We can talk about it later. I'll help you clean up. Then I'll go."

BACK at JR's yet again (it was the only place Jefferson could afford, and he found he rather liked the smoky, shady atmosphere), Vera had turned on the waterworks. Her tear ducts had been quite busy the past few days. Thank the heavens for waterproof mascara! She had cried so many fake tears she wondered if she could cry real ones if the time ever came. JR's wasn't too busy this night. Only a handful of regulars were there. Some sad sap bawled at the jukebox as it played "Don't Cry Out Loud."

Sitting at a quiet and secluded booth, Jefferson had explained to Vera that he had seen the argument from his position high in the limbs of a tree, every last hateful gesture Cassie Bloom had made toward Vera, and it infuriated him. He hadn't heard exactly what was being shouted, but he knew anger when he saw it. He folded his hands around Vera's on the table, and she did her best not to flinch. It was everything he could do, he said, to stop himself from climbing out of the tree, marching up to the house, and exposing her on the spot.

"You have what you need then? To expose her?" Vera asked, unnerved by his statement.

"Not yet," he replied. "But I have some good, solid stuff. I think it's safe to show you now. Let's head back to my place."

Vera's heart leaped. She was finally going to be let into his lair. If she could find what both she and Cassie needed, this torture would soon be over.

"Let me just go freshen up first," Vera said as she excused herself from the table, pulling her hand out from underneath Jefferson's rather heavy paw. He ogled her as she walked away, his eyes playing dirty little ideas with her rear end.

"Vera," said a voice from the bar as she passed it on her way to the ladies' room. She ignored it at first, but then the voice called again.

She turned and saw Jason Bloom on a barstool, hunched over a bowl of pretzels and nuts.

"Jason? What are you doing here?" She sauntered up beside him, watching to make sure she couldn't be seen by Jefferson. Smoke and dimness obscured eyesight all around.

"I'm taking Mother's advice," he answered. "I'm getting out of the house." He reached for a handful of nuts, but Vera pushed the bowl away from him.

"You don't want to eat that, honey. Who knows who's stuck their filthy hands in there? It's probably riddled with viruses."

"Is that the man from down the street?" Jason asked, nodding in the direction of Jefferson.

Vera wondered how much Jason knew. "It is," she replied with caution.

"Investigating, huh?" He watched the expression change slightly on her face. "I know more than you or Mother think I do. I know a bit about investigating."

"What do you know?" She set her purse down on the bar.

"I know that you of all people would never date somebody like that. I know there are reasons that aren't apparent to everyone. Reasons…." He trailed off, staring into nothingness.

Vera touched his arm. "Baby, are you all right?"

"Getting there," he said, still zoned out.

"Maybe you should head on home. I'll get you a cab." She reached into her purse for her cell phone.

"No, thanks. But I do need to ask you a question."

She waited patiently, checking every now and then to make certain the wall of haze that separated her from Jefferson was still there.

"You know the Golds? Melinda and Frank?" he asked.

"Of course."

"Did Father know Nanna? Did they ever talk?"

Vera had never once heard Jason refer to Nanna. Vera herself didn't know Nanna existed until a year earlier. Jason must have seen her before the old crone had her fall, before she had moved in for a short time with the Golds.

"I don't think he knew her, no. Why, baby?"

"Investigations," he said.

"Well, you be careful with your investigations." She would have to tell Cassie about this little exchange. "Listen, you get home," she said. "You get right on home. You don't seem yourself. You haven't seemed yourself since you came home, if you don't mind my saying."

"You're right. 'Myself' has long since disappeared." He rose from the stool. "And Vera," he said. "Be careful with your own investigation as well. That man's not right."

He turned and left, leaving Vera to ponder the words spoken. She walked back to Jefferson without heading to the restroom.

"Ready to go?" she asked pleasantly.


RICK normally wouldn't have frequented JR's alone, certainly not of his own will. But tonight he didn't care. It was the first bar he saw, so he stopped in.

He was still shaking from rage and disappointment. Rage that James couldn't see why he was so upset and disappointment in himself for not sticking to the notion of the New Rick.

He found the joint to be pretty dismal and managed to locate an empty, lonely stool at the end of the bar. Ordering a beer, he hunkered down for an evening of solitude and self-pity. He wondered at times if he liked being miserable; he was certainly well-acquainted with misery. Maybe subconsciously he sought it out.

He didn't know if he would go home after JR's. Maybe he would get a hotel room; maybe he would just stay right where he was, drunk and disorderly. The bar owner would call the cops who would haul Rick off to jail, and then he wouldn't need to get a hotel room.

He grasped the beer that was slid in front of him and drank it down greedily, looking for a respite for his nerves. The more he drank, the less agitated he would feel. He could see the allure of the alcoholic. A bar like this, a night like this, Rick could definitely see where not knowing his own name and not caring about ever knowing it again would be desirable.

Rick tilted his head and listened to the piano chords that struggled to emerge from the jukebox above the noise of the crowd. Was that Joni Mitchell? Was that "The Last Time I Saw Richard"? How appropriate, he thought. And how odd. Didn't bars like this usually play AC/DC and Led Zeppelin?

Rick felt a shadow over him; someone standing behind him. If it was James, Rick thought he would just die. He had no more fight left in him for the night, and he couldn't get over his fears and his jealousies. He swiveled in his stool to try to face things only to find that it was not James at all who stood there. Yet it was someone he knew.

"Hey, Ricky," said the nervous voice. "Still wearing the patch, huh?" Coby motioned to Rick's eye patch.

Coby, the former boyfriend who was the cause of Rick having but one eye, was the very last thing Rick needed. He definitely needed to drink more if he was going to be dealing with this. He slammed his glass on the bar to get the attention of the man behind it. Rick didn't say a word to Coby. He didn't need to. His expression said it all.

"I've changed, Rick," Coby finally said after a long pause. "I really have. I got my life back in order, I'm off the drugs, I don't gamble. I mean, I'm no angel, but…."

"What do you want, Coby?" He wanted to give Coby the thrashing he deserved, the thrashing Coby never received after causing so much trouble.

"I wanted to find you to apologize." Rick noticed that Coby did in fact look much better than he had. There were no longer dark rings under his eyes, and his hair was short and trimmed, not greasy and unkempt. He was even wearing a nice button-up shirt and slacks. He looked like a Mormon.

"Well, you've done that. You've apologized. Now go, before my gratitude is no longer able to control my rage." Rick swiveled back around to the bar top just in time to meet his beer as the bartender placed it in front of him.

"I want you back, Ricky," Coby said in his nervous, unsure manner. "I think—"

"You think?" He took a long gulp. "Go away. I'm with someone. I'm happy."

"Pardon me for saying it, but you don't look happy." Coby sat down at the bar, leaving a stool between them, a buffer zone.

Rick gave him the full impact of his one useful, angry eye. "You don't know shit, Coby."

"Sorry. You're right." He played with the bowl of peanuts. "So tell me what I should know. I want to know, Ricky. I want to know you again. I don't want you to be angry with me anymore. I want you to be happy with me. Can you see it? Me and you, happy together?"

MELINDA had rather hoped for a night off. She and Malcolm had been spending every night together for a while now, and it was beginning to make her feel a bit suffocated. She desperately wanted some "Melinda time," but she wasn't sure how to break that to Malcolm. What she had wanted to say, if honesty were to be respected, was "I'm tired of all the kinky sex, Malcolm. I just want a night alone. That leather really chafed me the other night, and, to be honest, I'm a little freaked out by your predilection for bondage and spanking. It was fun for one, maybe two, nights, but not all of the time, darling!"

What she actually said was, "I think I'd like to curl up on the sofa tonight and watch a movie."

"Sounds great!" Malcolm responded right away. "Just the two of us watching scary movies and cuddling."

She pinched herself for not making the statement more "Melinda Wants to Be Alone" oriented. She smiled and said, "Goody!"

She was already tiring of him. But why? He was a great guy. A real catch, anyone would think so. Anyone who was into nipple clamps and butt plugs. (*Honestly! What woman would consent to a butt plug?*) She nearly fainted when Malcolm surprised her with that little delight.

The plain fact, though, was that her attraction to him was waning, and it had nothing to do with how he treated her or how handsome he was. It was the fact that his sexual dalliances and fantasies were to her so extreme. Or maybe it was because hers were so normal. Either way, being with him was beginning to make her uncomfortable. She had promised herself that when she started dating again she would take it slow, as in baby steps. A leather harness or Mean-Principal-Gives-Coach-A-Good-Talking-To was definitely not baby steps. That was all the way at the finish line of a city marathon.

Melinda sat curled on her couch with Malcolm's arm hugging her close to his chest. She could barely hear the film for his chewing, chomping, and churning of the spicy popcorn he had brought. Melinda hated popcorn. Anyone concerned for their teeth would. Maybe she should date a dentist. She'd have to give that deeper thought later. There were probably some nice single dentists out there.

They had argued over what movie to watch. Well, to Melinda it was an argument; to Malcolm it was a light tussle where he finally gave in to her. She explained to him that there was no way she was going to sit through a scare fest that would keep her up all night.

"It's not even that scary. It was made in the seventies," Malcolm reasoned.

"Malcolm, it's *The Exorcist*! I won't be able to sit through it. We're watching *The Notebook*, and that's final." She still had prejudices about *The Exorcist*. Nanna had told her it was a film that invited demons into the home. Of course, to Nanna, *Saturday Night Fever* did the same thing.

"Yes, ma'am!"

*Oh, good Lord! He's excited. Maybe a romantic film wasn't the best choice after all.*

But he controlled himself, content to eat his popcorn and watch the chick flick. Throughout the movie, though, Melinda's mind was still on the morning's upheaval at Cassie's. She wished Becky had been there to calm things down. What could have happened between Vera and Cassie to make them so evil toward each other? She'd just have to find a way to get them back together. After all, the Joneses' Fourth of July party was just a few weeks away. What was the Fourth on Jasper Lane without those two coming together in their most outlandish costumes and hogging the spotlight?

Melinda sighed with her head on the coach's chest. "There, there," he said, thinking she was becoming overcome by the sentimentality of the film. "I'm here. Your Coach Nipple is here."

THE pool lights were on again, making dazzling, electric displays all around. Cassie, David, and Becky lounged on the chairs, still in their digging clothes and soaking up the moonlight, drinks in hand. The sound of the night could be heard in the trees and hills that lay just behind the Bloom place. Cassie had gone in and put an on Ella Fitzgerald record as they rested and let the sweet sound play low on the speakers.

"Well, that's it," David said, clearly relieved that the ghoulish chore was done. "We've found every bone in the anatomy charts."

"All but one," Cassie reminded him. Jackson's skull was still unaccounted for.

"It will turn up," Becky assured her. "If Jefferson somehow had hold of it, we'd all be in a lot of trouble right now, and if some dog has dug it up…. Well, then he's probably buried it somewhere else."

"Hopefully somewhere far, far away," David said.

"How did we end up here?" Cassie wondered aloud. "I was fine in my old life, before I met Jackson. Then I went and married him. Granted, that gave me my treasure, my love, Jason, but that one action has also caused so much turmoil and trouble in the lives of those around me."

"You couldn't have foreseen any of this," David comforted her.

"No, I know. But it still doesn't keep the 'what ifs' away. If I had never met Jackson my last year in college, none of this would have happened. We wouldn't be sitting here. I wouldn't have gone through years of abuse, Vera wouldn't have killed the sick bastard, and Jason…." She paused, swallowing her hurt. "Jason would be happy being someone else, having some other mother."

"You're the best mother he could have had, Cassie Bloom!" Becky chided her. "You're his mother because you're who is supposed to be his mother. Jason was going to have it rough in this life. Somewhere, some powerful entity knew that, and that same entity also knew you would be the best mother for him. That you'd do anything to protect him, to keep him alive. That's how I look at it."

Cassie glanced at Becky lovingly. "Sweet girl."

"To mothers." David raised his glass in a toast.

"To mothers," the ladies repeated, raising theirs.

"Tomorrow I'll burn the last of the bones. Jackson will be gone, and not a moment too soon." Cassie hated the idea of setting foot in the basement again, but it needed to be done. The purging needed to happen. Maybe she could have the basement filled in after that.

There was a sound from inside the house; Jason coming back from a night out. Soon after, the sliding door to the pool area opened and Jason walked out in his flip-flops to join them. He stood near to where his mother sat at the edge of the pool. His hands were in his pockets, and he stared up into the night sky.

"What have you been up to, darling?" Cassie asked, reaching for her son's hand. His grasp was tight, needy.

"Just went out. Drove around."

"See anyone? Any of your friends?"

"No. I've got no friends here anymore." Cassie hated the sound of that. "I saw Vera, though. She was out with some man. Not her type. Not at all."

"I know the man."

"Is that what the fight was about? The scene this afternoon? The play?" He shot her a glance and a grin.

Cassie returned a lopsided smile. "Yes. That's what it was about."

"Poor Melinda!" Becky broke in laughing.

"You'll have to make up with Vera, you know," Jason said. "Melinda's world would crumble without the stability you bring to her."

"You see quite a lot, don't you?" David inquired.

"I really do," Jason admitted. He turned to them. "I'll… uh… I'll get out here in the early morning and do some more landscaping. It looks awkward. You should fire those landscapers you hired. They look like they had something else on their minds entirely."

Cassie bit her lip. "I think they're all done, sweetheart. I believe it's almost over."

Jason turned to go back inside, his flip-flops shuffling and slapping along the concrete. "That's good," he said.

WALKING into Jefferson's rented home, Vera saw that it looked exactly how she thought it might. There wasn't much in the way of furniture and design. What little there was were remnants of the house's former occupants. Pizza and takeout boxes littered the floor. Vera thought that it had probably looked nice once before, when Cock Ring Girl (What *was* her name?) and her husband had lived there, but it was in a wretched state now, and it smelled of dream decay.

Vera stepped over a pile of mail lying unopened on the floor as Jefferson hurried in front of her to the living room. She assumed he meant her to follow him.

"Sorry the place is such a mess," he shouted from the living room as she carefully found her way there. "I've just been so busy with…." He raised a handful of notes and photographs from the rumpled old couch he intended them to sit on.

"Is that what you have against Miss Bloom?" Vera asked, smiling as she approached, her purse pressed tightly to her side by her elbow. "May I see?"

"It's nothing too big," Jefferson replied. "Nothing too big yet." But instead of handing the photographs and notes to Vera, he took them in the direction of the kitchen.

Vera took the time to look around the living room, scoping about for any scraps he might have left behind. She looked behind the couch, under the cushions, but nothing. She heard him shuffling his way back toward her and quickly sat down on the raggedy couch. A scratched coffee table was positioned in front of the couch, and across from it, on the floor, sat a small TV. The lighting in the room was dim due to the fact that only one overhead light hadn't blown. Jefferson didn't seem to even have enough money to afford new light bulbs.

"So," Jefferson said leadingly as he sat beside Vera on the couch. He was very close, and she could guess he was only going to get closer. He held a cheap bottle of wine and two streaked wineglasses, which he had brought from the kitchen. "Shall we drink to our developing… friendship?"

"How sweet," Vera said, taking the offered wineglass by the sticky stem.

"I know it's your fault," Jefferson said, a dreamy look on his face as he stared at Vera in the eyes, his head resting on his hand, his elbow on the back of the couch.

Vera was momentarily frightened. Had he discovered the truth? "How do you mean?" she asked, ready to bolt.

"I know you're the reason Cassie isn't locked up yet. If it wasn't for you, she'd already be in jail. But you see, you've sidetracked me. Your beauty has distracted me from my plans." He gave his best romantic-lead grin; it was like a train wreck. Vera couldn't look away.

"Oh, that," Vera said, relieved. "Well, it can't be helped, can it?"

"That beauty of yours is a curse."

"I'm beginning to think so."

"I'd put on some music, but…."

"No CD player?" Vera asked. "No worries. Music can get in the way sometimes. I'd rather see what you've dug up—" *Oops! Wrong choice of words,* "—on Miss Bloom."

Glancing at him, she saw he was leaning into her, his face sliding off his hand, his eyes closing. He was headed in for a kiss! He was going to try to get her in bed. Vera jumped up immediately.

"I am not that type of woman, Jefferson!" Vera exclaimed. "I'm not sleeping with you tonight. Can't we take it slower?" (Like glacial?)

She then realized that he wasn't leaning in to kiss her at all. He had passed out. "Jefferson?" She shook him gently.

He had been so awake all night. How could he just pass out?

Vera gasped as she came upon the answer to her question. "Try to drug me, you twitching asshole!" She swatted him with her purse. But then she laughed at the notion that he had been so inept at his plans of seduction as to mix their drinks up.

Since his plan had so thoroughly backfired, Vera took the opportunity to head to the kitchen to look for the notes and photos. She didn't know how long Jefferson would be out, but she could at least use the allotted time for some good. She searched through the cabinetry and the refrigerator quickly. Most everything was empty. There were a few boxes of utensils piled atop the counters, but nothing of any interest to Vera. The refrigerator looked and smelled as if it hadn't been used since Cock Ring Girl had left. Vera was becoming frustrated at the whole predicament until she found one cabinet that would not open. No matter how hard Vera pulled on it, the thing would not give. She knew whatever it was she was searching for had to be in there. She was about to pull a knife from the box of utensils when she heard a loud waking snore from the living room.

"Dammit!" she hissed.

Not wanting to get caught and definitely not wanting to spend the night with Walrus Man of the Ugly People in there on the couch, Vera quickly and quietly departed the house through the back door.

The night had not been a failure, though. There was progress made. She had definitive answers now, or if not, she knew in which kitchen cabinet those answers were kept.

CLIFF was reading the next day's script in bed when David returned home from Cassie's. He wandered about for a bit in the kitchen then trudged up the stairs. Cliff had taken to reading historical romances of late when he wasn't working on the script for *Manwhore*. Great literature, no. But they were always sexy and entertaining and had inspired a few of the scenes in his film. He read naked with the summer sheets pulled over his lap and his thin-rimmed glasses set low on the bridge of his nose. Cliff liked his glasses. He had always hated contacts and dreaded the idea of ever having eye surgery. Besides, David liked him in his glasses as well. He had told him once that he thought they were sexy and distinguished.

David entered the bedroom, stripping his way to the bed. "Hello, lover," he said, clearly fatigued.

"You're not going to shower?" Cliff inquired, not glancing up from the script.

"I'm too tired." David crawled into bed, and they kissed as married folk do. "How was your day?" David asked, getting under the covers and nuzzling underneath Cliff's arm. One finger gently played with Cliff's left nipple; strangely, his left nipple was always more sensitive to touch than the one on the right.

"Uh… fine," Cliff replied, looking down at David with a gentle smile. "Same ol' thing. Nothing special. The day comes, the day goes." No need to go into details about leaving an ass print on the hood of a car or being gang-raped by a band of trolls. "And yours?"

"Fine," David responded, kissing the hulking side of Cliff's left tit. "Some ol' thing. Nothing special." No need to go into details about digging up the remains of a murdered government official.

"That's good."

"Yeah. It's nice to have such ordinary lives."

Cliff closed the script, dog-earing it first so that he would not lose his place. (David hated dog-eared pages. "Just get a scrap of paper and use it as a bookmark." "Why? This works just as well." "It's ugly!") He set his glasses on the script on the nightstand and turned off the light before rolling over and covering David with his mass. Cliff liked to feel David at all times while he slept. It was both an issue of security and possession. David loved this about Cliff.

"Has Steve said anything to you lately?" Cliff asked. "About him and Sandy, I mean?"

David replied but his words were muffled by Cliff's pectorals. This had become something of a nightly ritual between them for the five years they'd been together: Cliff would ask a question and would get an inaudible reply from a mouthful of man-boob.

"What?" Cliff drew back.

"Not really," David repeated. "And the fact that he hasn't said anything about them is a little strange. He used to talk about Sandy all the time." Pause. "Why? Do you know something? Has Sandy said something?"

"No. She's just been acting strange, is all. Especially whenever her and Steve's relationship is brought up in conversation."

"You don't think they're going to split, do you?" David was horrified by the thought.

"I hope not. Should we say something to them?"

David thought for a moment. "Better not yet. Let's wait until the right moment presents itself. But we will; we have to."

Cliff pressed into David again.

"Baby," David mumbled beneath pounds of muscle. "I can't breathe."

Cliff loosened his grip, and David turned around so that his back now faced Cliff. Cliff secured his arms around his husband.

After a bit, Cliff spoke again. "You know what I think, baby?"

"What's that, Hot Pocket?"

"I think you and I are the most normal couple on this street."

David smiled. "I think you may be right."

"Good night, sweetheart."

"Good night."

Soon Cliff was asleep, breathing into David's hair.

BOTH had decided that they would be stalwart and furious with each other.

Rick had been driving all night, refusing to stop in at home even to take a shower and clean up before his morning shift at the fitness center. He had chatted with Coby for a while. Or more accurately, Coby had continued to expound upon his new virtues, how he was now a changed man, and that Rick might also find that change in himself and take Coby back. Rick listened as long as he could, fighting off the urge to buy himself something else to drink so he could be completely intoxicated, until the bar closed at three a.m. When it finally became clear to Coby that Rick was not going to invite him back to his place, the defeated one skulked away into the morning haze of the hillbilly parking lot. Rick was soon driving the nearly empty streets of town, deep in thought. He pulled into Wal-Mart and then quickly left, realizing it just might be the scariest place in the world at five o'clock in the morning.

Rick only wanted to be alone and stew in his righteous bitterness. He couldn't go home and talk about things, though he knew James was probably there waiting up. He would drive into work when it opened, see James working out with Seth, and then, finally, give them both a royal working over.

While this was happening, James had decided during his night of restless sleep that he would go straight to the fitness center in the morning before it even opened and stand directly on Rick's employee parking space. When Rick pulled up he would demand to know where Rick had been, what he had been up to, and what he thought he was doing making his partner worry himself sick all night long. It was time to get everything out in the open; let the drama loose onto the unsuspecting world. He hadn't slept, so James was definitely ready to stir some trouble.

And that's exactly what happened... to a point.

For when Rick pulled into his parking space and saw James standing there hero-like, arms crossed, scowling in his tight army shirt and shorts, he melted. His anger went from a scream to a whisper. His plans were foiled by a pretty face, the beginning of many a civilization's downfall.

And when James saw Rick pull into the space right up to his knee cap he almost began to whimper like a puppy lost from home. His questions and accusations, however baseless he knew they were in the first place, evaporated. He wasn't the wall he thought he was.

164

Rick jumped out of the car and ran right into James's arms. "I'm so sorry," he sobbed.

James's shoulders sagged as he let Rick hold on to him. "Me too. It was all stupid. I'll stop speaking to Seth if you want. Just look at me. One night without you and I turn into a whiny little bitch. I can't have this happening again."

And so, the words that the moment called for—that clichéd, hackneyed phrase—issued forth from Rick's mouth. He just couldn't help himself. "Let's never fight again!" he exclaimed. He'd have to remember to hit himself in the balls later for saying that.

From the sidewalk, walking into the gym, was a mother holding the hand of her daughter. "Look, Mommy! They're BFFs!"

Then, behind them and playfully mocking the reunited Rick and James, a cooing couple in the form of David and Steven. "Ah, look! The girls done made up."


BECKY couldn't wait to tell Cassie the news of what Vera had found the previous night on her sour date with Jefferson Bloom. Things were stealthy and on the down-low now. Vera and Cassie couldn't take any chances being seen talking to each other. There was to be no obvious interaction between them, no matter how much they missed each other. Becky was their lifeline. She sent information to and from, and she loved it. She felt like a spy, like a secret government liaison. She even spoke in hushed tones as if Jefferson might have the technology to detect what they were saying wherever they were. To be safe, Cassie had made certain there were no bugs or hidden recorders around the house or lying about on the deck. She knew, of course, that there wouldn't be. Jefferson hadn't the money for high-tech, and plus, he was too scared to come that close. Whether he was scared of her or the house itself, Cassie could not tell.

Becky waited until the morning coffee gossip was over and Melinda left the two of them on the deck. Melinda was not her usual innocently prying self that day either. It was a strange, awkward, gossip-free morning, a bit depressing really. She had commented that she was glad to see Cassie had fired the landscapers, but that was it. Something was going on between Melinda and Coach Nipple. That much was very apparent. Becky would have to find out what had happened later on their daily speed-walk. *Oh, the gossip was just so ripe this summer!*

Once Melinda was gone, Becky lowered her voice and her brow and explained everything Vera had told her, from the messy layout of the house to the attempted drugging to the locked kitchen cabinet.

"He drugged himself?" Cassie exclaimed. "Well, now I'm definitely not too worried about him. What a terrible, tacky man!" She swilled the coffee and Kahlua in her mouth.

"Do you think it could be a trick?" Becky asked.

"You mean, could he be playing dumb? I don't think so. I think he might be the real bird. The last dodo just waiting to bump himself off. Still, it doesn't mean he's harmless."

"What do we do?"

Cassie thought, staring out over the lawns of Jasper Lane. "We invite him over for brunch."

"Yes, we…. Wait! Why do we do that?"

"Because he'll never keep his eyes off this house. He's just waiting for me to leave it so he can waddle on in. If I invite him over, I can keep my eyes on him." She looked at Becky with a twinkle in her eyes. "*We* can keep an eye on him."

Becky chirped in excitement, jumping in her seat. "How fun!"

"Yes, it will be. We'll let him see what he thinks he wants to see. We might even get Melinda over here as well for a little touch of realism just in case one of us hams it up too much."

"I don't think he'd be able to tell."

"No, from what Vera says he enjoys the dramatics." She stood from the table and paced to the edge of the deck. "And while we're up here, entertaining and beguiling our neighborhood intruder—giving him the show of his life—Vera can be searching through that house, getting into that cabinet."

"Do you think he has pictures?" Becky's voice became serious. Well, serious for her. There was always too much of a squeak in it for it to be thought of as anything more cryptic than Snow White. Becky gasped as she thought of something else. "Do you think he has…?"

"Jackson's skull? I've been thinking about that. But if he had found it, that would be all the evidence he would need to put both Vera and I away, or at least under suspicion."

"Maybe he really is in love with Vera," Becky posited.

Cassie looked back at her friend, smiling. "Well, of course he is. Vera's the finest thing to grace his path… *ever*." She sat back down at the table. "Now tell me what she said about seeing Jason at the bar. He was acting strange? How?"

THERE was an audience gathered outside check-in. Everyone was sure there would be fireworks from within, and they didn't want to miss them.

Chris sat on an old wooden bench with Jordan, ready to defend Terrence's flamboyant ramblings, if need be. Everyone was quiet, straining to hear any talk at all from the pastor and the two fathers inside the little structure. Terrence and Harry were being admonished. Lustful open display at a Christian camp! And during a game too! What would Jesus do?

But the great combustion that the other fathers and sons were waiting on, that which would surely blow down the walls of the check-in, never occurred. Instead the door opened quite normally and both Terrence and Harry strode out looking quite pleasant. They were followed by Father Donaghan. A sigh of disappointment could be heard from the others.

The boys looked at each other and shrugged.

Terrence made his way to Chris. Harry stood still, his own son coming to him. "You coming, sunshine?" Terrence asked Chris, nodding in the direction of their tent.

Chris followed, past the fathers and their judgmental glares. "So?" he said quietly. "What happened in there?"

Terrence walked nonchalantly, an oddity for him, his hands in his pockets, admiring the day around him. "We were told that it was best if we keep away from each other for the duration of the retreat. They want you and me to pitch our tent a bit farther from Harry's. I think they're planning to shun me."

Chris was stunned. "What? That's not right. They can't do that!" He was shouting now so that the others could hear him. "They've got no right. Why didn't you stand up for yourselves? Didn't you say anything?"

Terrence shrugged and continued walking.

"Where's the father I know who would have screamed and ranted and told that pastor to fuck off? Where's the Terrence who would have then come out and rightfully berated these sorry excuses for fathers as being even sorrier excuses for gay men?"

"There's no need," Terrence said calmly.

"What the hell did that pastor do to you in there?" Chris was becoming very concerned. This was becoming apparent to Terrence because Chris hardly ever used cuss words. But he had never seen Terrence so subdued. It reminded him of the creepy religious zealots his mother sometimes introduced him to.

"Nothing. I actually don't remember too much of what the old man said. I was still so enthralled by what had happened right before Father Donaghan began to speak." He swung his arms backward around a tree they had come upon and swooned dreamily into the sky.

Chris breathed a sigh of relief. Words like "enthralled" and actions like swooning, those were definite Terrence-isms.

"He asked me out," Terrence explained. "When we leave, after the retreat is over, we're going to go out. It will be the best date ever! Ever, ever, ever!"

"He asked you out on a date right before you were about to be chastised by a minister for groping openly in the meadow?"

"Yep. Romantic, huh?"

"I guess." Chris looked back at the check-in. The other fathers and sons were dispersing now, making their ways back to their own tents. They still watched Terrence with jealousy thinly disguised as righteous indignation. Chris couldn't find Harry and Jordan in the group, though. "We can go, you know. It's totally okay with me if we leave," Chris said.

"What?"

"We can leave now if you want. I'm bored here. These aren't our friends. These fathers and sons, they're boring. They're not like me and you. I'd rather hang out with David and Cliff and Rick and Cassie Bloom."

"But there's still two more weeks. Are you sure you don't want to stay?" Terrence couldn't hide the excitement in his voice. It's not like he and Harry would be able to do anything anyway. They'd be watched as if they were animals in a cage. If he and Chris left early, he could get back, go to the gym, and be all prettified when he and Harry had their first legitimate date.

"I'm absolutely certain, Dad. This place blows bible scrolls."

JASON BLOOM treaded barefoot across the pristine lawns of the residents of Jasper Lane on his way to the most pristine of them all: Melinda Gold's. He looked somewhat out of place here in his torn T-shirt and faded, baggy jeans. Gayhound panted happily alongside him. Jason had passed beneath Jefferson—rather beneath the tree Jefferson had chosen as his watchtower for the day—and glanced upward with a nod. Jefferson didn't acknowledge him; he remained still, as if by doing so Jason wouldn't notice the two-hundred-pound man in a suit holding binoculars in the tree. Gayhound barked once but then continued following Jason.

Jason liked the dog. David was watching Gayhound while Terrence was away; he let him out every day, and Gayhound always returned in the evening to Terrence's backyard. During the day, though, he was becoming something of an only friend to Jason. He would even show up at the cul-de-sac, wait for Jason to come out on the deck, and then sit and watch him paint. He was a dog in search of a pack.

Melinda seemed distracted when she answered the door. Jason had expected to be politely scolded about traipsing across other people's lawns, with a dog no less, but Melinda said nothing. She came out on the porch with Jason, closing the door tightly behind her as if there were something inside she'd rather he didn't see. Jason assumed she hadn't dusted yet or something equally unimportant. She smiled with some effort, even as Gayhound growled at her. (The two still didn't get along; she was constantly having to remind Terrence to keep him off her lawn.)

"Jason," she said. "What can I do for you?"

"Hi, Miss Bloom. I hope I didn't get you at a bad time."

"Bad time? Don't be silly. There's a…. I just have something out back I need to tend to." Gayhound barked. Melinda jumped.

"I'll be quick," Jason promised. She gave him an expression that agreed that hastiness was a good thing in this situation. "It's about my father."

"Jackson?"

"Yeah…. Um, how well did he and Nanna know one another?"

"Jason, if they knew one another at all, it would be news to me. I never saw Nanna anywhere near Jackson. Excuse me for saying, but she never really cared for him."

"Or my mother."

170

Melinda nodded embarrassingly. "Or your mother."

"So they never had any correspondence that you know of? No phone calls? No letters?"

"No." Melinda became concerned. "Jason, what's this about?"

"I'm not sure yet," he replied. "Where does Nanna live now?"

"After I kicked her out of here, she got a small apartment at an old folks' condo. Sweet Homes, I think it's called. I don't talk to her much anymore. I could try and find her number for you later." She was urging him gently to wrap up his line of questioning.

"No, thanks," he said. "You've been very helpful. Thank you."

Melinda opened the door a bit, ready to retreat to whatever pressing matter called to her. "Nanna hasn't caused more problems, has she?" she asked. "Is everything okay with you and your mother?"

He stared at her for a moment. "I'm not sure," he said again. "Come on, Gayhound." He turned about, snapping his fingers at the dog as they made their way down the driveway and back onto the sidewalk. Melinda did not watch him go; the door was already closed.


MELINDA closed the door and raced to the bureau, finding the gold scissors where she kept them, beneath her elegant stationery and antique pens. She headed directly for the backyard with them.

This was not how she had pictured her morning. She had assumed that upon leaving for her morning chat at Cassie's, Malcolm, too, would up and leave, but he hadn't. There was a strange quality to her morning coffee with Cassie and Becky. The chill of Cassie's fight with Vera still hung in the air, and Melinda was convinced she wasn't being told everything, so she left a bit earlier than usual. She didn't like how things always seemed to be in a state of change around her lately. She was hoping something familiar would save the morning once she got back to her own house and could spend some time alone, perhaps going through her recipes or seeing to her lawn. But on arriving home she saw that Malcolm's Hummer was still sprawled out in the drive. Her heart sank. Yet upon going into the house, she couldn't find him anywhere. He wasn't in the bedroom, the living room, any of the bathrooms, or the kitchen. It wasn't until she looked in the backyard that she found him.

*Thank God she had high fences!* What she saw nearly floored her.

Malcolm was naked in the rope hammock, facing the ground. "Surprise!" he said. He was twisted and tangled to the point that his face was scrunched. He strained to look at her. His ass looked like roped meat and his erect penis, poking out and strangled between the rope, was turning a lovely shade of dark purple.

"What are you doing?" Melinda gasped in hushed horror, rushing to his side.

"I was wanting to play around a bit before I left," Malcolm explained. "A surprise for you when you got back. I saw this hammock and knew this would be the perfect 'good morning'."

"Hammock bondage?"

"Cool idea, huh?" He spoke with a calmness Melinda thought completely inappropriate for the situation. "But I got a little carried away with the twisting. I'm afraid I'm going to have to ask you to destroy your hammock. It's cutting off the circulation to my dick."

Melinda bent down and took a look at his dangling, suffocating member.

"Hurry, please," Malcolm pleaded.

"Oh, Jesus!" Melinda hightailed it to the house for the scissors, and that was when Jason rang the doorbell.

Now, worried that she might not make it back to Malcolm before his penis fell off (which would only serve him right!), Melinda disregarded the adage concerning running with scissors and sprinted across her lawn in her heels and skirt. "There was someone at the door," she said by way of an excuse. Malcolm said nothing; his eyes were beginning to tear up. "What would you have done if I had decided to go on my Avon route without coming back home first?" She didn't really expect an answer.

Melinda slid on her back in the grass beneath the hammock, realizing she would definitely have to scrub some stains from her lovely blouse, and carefully wedged the scissor blade between the rope and Malcolm's scrotum. She felt like a character in one of those ridiculous spy movies about to clip a wire and hoping it was the right one. Of course, in those films it was *always* the right one.

*What are you doing thinking about action films? A man's penis is at stake here! God, vaginas are so much easier. So much less of a hazard. Penises are always getting caught in the most awful predicaments!*

She readied herself for the task at hand.

*Please don't let me cut it off*, she prayed to herself. *And if I do, please don't let it poke me in the eye!*

She clinched her teeth and clipped. Malcolm's pleading, strangled penis moved closer to her face in relief, and Malcolm gave a muffled sigh of elation. "Thank you, thank you, thank you," he sobbed.

Melinda stared eye to eye with his member. She was relieved, horrified, and angry, and was about to say so when something else got her attention.

"Mom?" a third-party voice said.

Melinda's eyes grew wide, and her blood went cold. She tilted her head slightly on the grass so she could see the sliding-glass door where Patrick, home from college with his laundry bag, now stood.

"Hi, Patrick. Welcome home," she squeaked out, humiliated.

Patrick studied the cocooned figure above her. "Is that Coach Nipple?"

SANDY found herself drinking her morning coffee miles from Jasper Lane, on the expensive, ultra-modern veranda of Elizabeth Trump's expensive, ultra-modern home. The design of the home, the straight lines and angles, the whites and blacks, the unforgiving austerity, and art direction quality of it all fit right in with Elizabeth's rather harsh persona. Could anyone actually be that sterile? Elizabeth's design practically screamed that this was no place for children—which is why Sandy brought Amy, who sat quietly on her lap. Elizabeth's look of disdain could not be hidden.

"Do children drink coffee?" Elizabeth had asked.

Elizabeth now stood with her back to Sandy. She stared out onto the highway in front of the house. Her hair was pulled back tight, and she wore a gray jacket draped over her shoulders. "You're wondering why I asked you here," she finally said. She hadn't yet taken a drink from the coffee she held.

"I was thinking on that, yes. It seems strange that you would invite me over for a friendly little chat when we are clearly enemies."

"Enemies?" Elizabeth said with unconvincing innocence. She turned and walked back to Sandy. "Not enemies. We could be partners. In fact, I think I might have something that might interest you. A proposal."

"Some lie? Some fabrication you and your husband have cooked up?" Sandy all the while stroked Amy's hair, letting the little girl play with Elizabeth's expensive china until the host none-so-politely took the dishware away. Sandy studied Elizabeth's face. She had never seemed so masculine before. The morning light here on the veranda was not very kind to her. Sandy thought about mentioning this.

"I don't cook," Elizabeth spat. "I leave that for the help. No, what I have for you is something altogether better. Something that will help us both in the end. You'd do your best to accept it."

Sandy didn't say a thing.

"I have no fear about the outcome of this election," Elizabeth continued. "But I do think… now anyway, that you might be an asset to the organization."

"Just now? Why the change of mind?" Not "change of heart"; never "heart."

Elizabeth at last took a sip of her coffee. "It's Joyce I'm concerned about. As vice president she's grown static. Dull."

"You want to get rid of Joyce?"

"And have you take her place as vice president. See how marvelous that would be? With the two of us in charge, ours would be the most formidable porn organization around. No one could touch us."

"You're scared."

Elizabeth's face dropped. "What?" she exclaimed.

"You're afraid you're going to lose to me, so you're willing to sacrifice those who once supported you, like Joyce."

"I will not lose," Elizabeth assured Sandy. "And Joyce is a bore."

"I've heard the same of you. That the only reason you're in office is that you're safe and you get things done. Are you a bore, Elizabeth?"

Amy giggled, and Elizabeth shot the little girl a vicious glare. "I'm only offering you a much-needed boost, Sandra."

"You're tossing yourself a life preserver." Sandy rose with Amy, hoisting her on her hip. "I'll see you on the floor."

"You're prone to mistakes, aren't you?"

"I'll show myself out," Sandy replied. "Thank you for the invite." Sandy turned, all too ready to leave Elizabeth's ice castle.

"You're prone to mistakes!" Elizabeth repeated after her.

MELINDA found herself walking very quickly down Jasper Lane, head down, hands clutching elbows. She had lifted herself from beneath the hammock and its fleshy ornamentation and ran past her son so quickly it was all a blur now. She didn't even remember any of the words Patrick had said to her or what Malcolm was shouting at her as she pressed forth out the front door. She couldn't look at her son. She only wanted to escape the situation.

What must Patrick think of her? She wanted to burst into tears, and surely she would once the shock of the moment subsided and the reality settled in. For right now, though, she would just keep walking. Just walk. Past the houses that she knew, that she had competed against in lawn contests. Past every familiar mailbox and driveway. She might just keep walking farther still, past houses she no longer recognized as being inhabited by people she knew. Maybe she could sneak into one of them and take up a new identity.

How had she let things get this far? She was uncomfortable with Malcolm and should have ended it days ago.

*Oh, Patrick! Your mother's not a whore!*

Still in the throes of shock, Melinda didn't hear the rather large vehicle creeping alongside her as she walked. "Let's talk," Malcolm called from inside. Melinda glanced at him. He had dressed hurriedly. His shirt was unbuttoned, and his face still wore the pattern of the hammock rope.

"Leave me alone!" she cried, her voice very near to breaking.

"I can't," he replied. "I want to talk about this."

"There is nothing to talk about. Now go away. People are staring."

"They're staring at the Hummer, not at you," Malcolm tried to comfort her. "Patrick's a big boy. He can handle what he saw."

"He saw his mother with a man's… member pointed directly at her face. There will be therapy bills. Don't kid yourself!"

"Then I'll help pay."

"What if I just turned him gay?" She shot him a worried expression.

"Melinda, baby, if he's not gay by now from all your over-mothering…."

Her look changed from humiliation to one that warned him to tread very lightly. "How can I ever face him again?"

"Will you stop walking and get in? We can fix this."

Melinda turned to him and screamed, "How would you say we can fix this? Some kind of amnesia pill? For the both of us? Is there some wrestling move? Like a Vulcan neck pinch thing?"

"You're not going to at least talk to me?"

"We *are* talking!" she screamed. Then she calmed down and approached the window on the passenger's side. Though, it being a Hummer, all Malcolm could see was the top of her head. "I need some time…. Some time alone. I need to spend some time with my son."

"What about us?" Malcolm crawled over so he could see her face clearly.

She sighed and gave the most peaceful smile she could manage. "I need some time alone. I should have said so earlier, before things got this far."

"But what about us?" he repeated.

She knew what he was asking but was unprepared to give the answer just yet. "I'm going to keep walking," she said. "Just for a bit."

"I'll be waiting for that answer, Melinda."

Melinda backed away as he drove off. She couldn't think of anything else to say, so she watched him go. Why did things have to be so complicated? Why couldn't things be more normal? But then, Melinda knew her life had never truly been what was thought of as normal. What would normal be like?

"FUCKING Spunktube.com," Rick mumbled to himself.

This was the second time this week that he had to chase a group of horny assholes from the showers for filming a jack-off session. The Internet was rife with sites like YouTube and AssTube and SpunkTube. Get yourself on them and your crotch and sperm are uploaded and downloaded across the world. Rick never understood the draw of all of that. Where was the intimacy?

Thankfully there were some gym patrons who didn't like the idea of possibly winding up on the Internet as extras. "There are some kids wackin' it in the shower," a patron had kindly informed Rick. "And I think they have a camera."

So despite his high from having made up that morning with James, Rick charged into the shower area in full, uncompromising, irritable bastard mode. The kids (for that's what they were: nineteen at most) fled barefoot and in towels with Rick telling them their memberships were hitherto revoked and if they set foot in the gym again, he'd have the rugby team pound their asses.

Walking back into the locker area of the men's changing room after surveying the grounds of the shower for... evidence of foul play, Rick felt the looming presence of what could only be a rugby player in front of him. Standing there, his hands on his meaty hips, sweat-laden and grinning as if he wanted to share something that Rick would surely like, was Seth. Standing like he was, Seth reminded Rick of that cartoon vegetable giant—except naked and not green. Rick couldn't help but notice that between the giant's legs, swaying, was a rapidly engorging penis.

"Hello... Seth," Rick said carefully. Was there going to be a confrontation? Here? In the midst of steam and nudity and a very noticeable erection?

"Hey, Rick." He was nervous, but not the kind of nervous that presupposes a fight.

"Can I help you? Can you not get your locker open?"

"Um, no." There was a falter of the penis; a flinch. "I just wanted to talk. But I'm not very good at talking about things like this. So it's probably best if I just lay it all bare."

"Things like this?" Rick asked. "You mean about James." He sighed and sat down on a bench. "I thought it might come to this eventually."

"You did? Good." Seth sounded relieved, and his little pet even perked up, but his stance remained the same.

"If you want a fight for James, then you've got one," Rick said. "I'm not letting him go. I've spent my whole life looking for a guy like him, and to have him want me just as much... well, it's a miracle. Lord knows, I'm a lot to put up with."

Seth seemed to lose ground. Mr. Happy deflated, and Seth's shoulders lost some of their size, and he slumped.

"So?" Rick stood. "What's it to be? Fists? Kickboxing?" He hated the idea of fighting and knew he would be pulverized by Seth, but this was for James.

"What? No," Seth said. His arms fell to his sides abruptly. "You've got it all wrong."

"You don't expect me to silently step aside and just let you have him, do you?"

"But, Rick, I don't want him! I want *you*."

Rick looked around confused. Was this a joke for an Internet video? Maybe Punk'dTube or something? "You what?"

"Well, yeah. What did you think all this was about? Why did you think I always got so nervous around you?" He walked closer to Rick, his penis rising ever so slowly, the eager little dragon.

"I thought you were anxious about me catching you hitting on James."

"This has nothing to do with James. He's a great guy, but I've never felt anything more for him. I've been with guys like him all my life. But you're different. Why don't you leave him... for me?" Seth took Rick's hand. His big legs and their wide strides had already crossed the distance between the two of them. "I could make you happy."

"I am happy. Very happy."

"Happier. And besides," Seth glanced down at his large cock that was now beaming up at Rick, "no one in the city has a one-eyed monster this size." His face lost its color when he realized what he had just said.

Rick wasn't concerned with the statement. One-eyed monster? Who cares? He wrested his hand from Seth. "I'm already the happiest I could ever be," he said.

Seth stood humiliated by his own slip of the tongue. "I'm so stupid!" he admonished himself as Rick rose and walked away.

Rick smiled. All this time and there was nothing to be jealous about. Seth was not after James, but *him*. All that wasted energy worrying. Should he tell James? But then how would that make things better? It would certainly show James that Rick's jealousies were hibernating—at least until James's next great-looking guy friend came along. Other than that, though, it might only prove to make James more uncomfortable around his friends.

"Sorry, Rick!" Seth called. "About the one-eye thing."

TERRENCE sat at the wheel of the minivan soaking up the moment as he listened to the sad songs playing on the CD player. Harry leaned against the door with an elbow, his cowboy hat (Where had he gotten a cowboy hat?) tipped back and a concerned expression on his ruggedly handsome face. Terrence and Christian were all packed and had informed the camp they were leaving. There weren't many who objected. Father Donaghan bid them farewell, but other than that, only Harry and Jordan actually saw them off in a friendly manner. The other fathers and sons just watched from a respectable gawker's distance.

"When will I see you again?" Terrence asked, emotionally, cinematically. He leaned out the window as if he were going to crawl through it.

"We'll meet again," Harry said, placing his arm on Terrence's. "As sure as the wind blows, I'll be there. I'll find you." He found he liked Terrence's dramatics even more when he participated in them.

"Oh, Harry! I just can't leave you."

"But you must. It's the only way." They kissed delicately.

"Come on!" Chris objected from the passenger's seat. He turned off the CD Terrence had slipped in as they were setting to go, *Cinema's Greatest Sappy Scores.* "You're going to see each other in a week or two. Let's go home, Dad."

Terrence rolled his eyes. "I'm trying to create a mood!" he screamed.

"Call me tonight?" Harry asked, smiling at the little play he had just enjoyed and the thought of more of them. Jordan stood beside him and waved goodbye to Chris.

"Are you kidding? I'll be calling the moment we pull out of here." Terrence brought up his cell phone and jiggled it.

"Give me a chance to turn my cell back on." Harry winked. He slapped the van door the way all manly men do when saying an affectionate farewell and stepped away with a nod to Chris.

"You're going to spend all evening at the hotel chatting with him on the phone, huh?" Chris guessed as the minivan backed away.

Terrence nodded. "But until then, it's you, me, and my sing-along collection."

"Carly Simon's up first." Chris grabbed a CD and slid it in.

Terrence was distracted for a moment, however. He glared ahead at something, vicious intent in his eyes. "*Garlic Man!*" he hissed as he suddenly veered off the road toward his frightened-looking nemesis.

"Dad!"

"Sorry." Terrence said as he found the road again. "I just wanted to give that asshole one final scare before I left. We're going home, son. We're headed back to Jasper Lane." He smiled at Chris, and Chris beamed back, and they sang "Mockingbird" as they left camp.


MELINDA walked along Jasper Lane, back near her home after some serious sidewalk therapy, her mind still a mash of things. She was somewhat more settled than she had been earlier in the day when Patrick had witnessed... whatever that was. But that still didn't stave off the humiliation. How would she be able to face her son again? How would she explain?

Of course, what Patrick had seen in the backyard wasn't far from the truth of what Melinda had been doing with Malcolm. But that had all been done indoors! There was a difference. Somehow.

What of Malcolm? Melinda sighed. She liked him, but it seemed to her that he had a much deeper interest in her than she in him. That made her feel even worse. For all the walking she had done today, she was still nowhere near understanding what she should do about her newest uncomfortable circumstances. She decided that the problem was men. All of them: Malcolm, God, even her Patrick. If she didn't have to deal with men life might be perfect. *Maybe that's why some women are lesbians*, she thought.

It was in the midst of this thought that Melinda heard a thud and a smooshing sound come from the side of one of her neighbor's homes. It was the house that the strange new man was renting, the one Vera was dating.

Dusk was settling on Jasper Lane, so Melinda walked carefully through the yard to get a closer look, comfortable that her curiosity would be covered by the fading light. The TV was flickering rapidly inside the house, and it was loud enough to smother out the awkward thuds coming from outside. Melinda crept closer to the side of the house, her arms at her side, and saw there none other than Cassie

Bloom, pitching eggs. A container of two dozen large eggs was opened and half-empty; it lay on top of at least five other cartons.

"Good evening, Melinda," Cassie said as if she had been expecting her. She pitched an egg as if it were a softball at the house.

"Cassie! What are you doing?" Melinda exclaimed quietly. "He'll hear you."

"No, he won't. He's drunk out of his mind. Probably passed out by now, choking on his own vomit and tears. He asked Vera out, and she turned him down. He's drowning his sorrows."

The truth was that it was difficult for Vera not to beat the shit out of Jefferson when he asked her for another date. After all, he had tried to incapacitate her and take advantage. But Vera grinned and said politely she had other plans. So, Cassie, knowing the kind of man he was, waited until Jefferson was good and sauced (which didn't take long) and decided she would enact a little vengeance of her own for all the trouble Jefferson had caused.

"Martini?" Cassie paused her pitching and offered Melinda a drink from a canister she held.

"No, thank you."

"Egg?" Cassie asked, gesturing to the crates.

It wasn't as if Melinda decided "Yes. I'll throw an egg at this man's house. I don't know him, but I'll throw an egg." She just instinctively felt that it was something she needed to do. She immediately went to Cassie's side, picked up a large, white, fragile thing and tossed it at the house. The moment it hit Melinda felt a release, a surge of tension escape her body. And the sound of that egg cracking and splattering sounded just like a crowd yelling, in exasperated agreement, "MEN!"

As soon as the thought had come to her, Melinda began whaling on the house with the eggs, every shell breaking with a satisfying crunch and painting the house. She imagined Frank and Malcolm's face alternately as she played a game of whack-a-mole on Jefferson's home. Her giddy fury was only encouraged by Cassie's surprised laughter.

"Get him, girl!" Cassie cackled, drinking from her canister.

Melinda laughed and would have continued the fun if their loud frolicking had not caused other neighbors to step outdoors and turn on their lights to assess the situation. Fortunately, it was dimly lit where Cassie and Melinda stood, and Cassie, while slightly buzzed, still had the good sense to keep a lookout.

Cassie grabbed Melinda by the forearm as she readied to throw another egg. "We're busted!" Cassie said. "Run!"

Melinda was immediately pulled by Cassie, who still clung to her drink, across the back lawns of Jasper Lane.

"Your eggs," Melinda exclaimed as they left the cartons on the grass.

"He can have them. The man's starving anyway."

This was good enough for Melinda. She and Cassie fled like wayward schoolgirls away from the scene of the crime.


DAMN, he was sore!

That was James's first thought on waking to the new day. He rarely bottomed, but he had the previous night. It wasn't because he didn't like it or considered himself a die-hard top. Insertion never scared him. It was simply because he had a very tight asshole. This made it very painful for him to take anything.

But he was into it last night, and so was Rick. Since their reconciliation and understanding in the parking lot outside of the gym, things had been amazing. Rick was wanting sex as much as when their relationship had just begun.

So, Rick lubed James up real good, excessively maybe, and then used James's bum for his most carnal, wanton desires. They lasted until the early hours of morning before Rick tired out, and they both finally drifted off to sleep in each other's arms. Now, two hours later, James was awake again. And his bum hurt. He smiled, wondering if he'd be able to walk without a limp that day. Rick stirred next to him, pulling away and snuggling on the edge of the mattress.

James rose with an audible groan, then hushed himself, and quietly snickered, remembering some of the things Rick had done the night before.

"Who's my muscle-bitch?" Rick had screamed, deep inside James, ready to explode.

"I am, sir!" James had uncharacteristically yelled back.

James fled the bedroom to avoid waking Rick with his laughter. He headed to the kitchen, tying his robe along the way.

He started the coffee, making enough for him and Rick. He knew Rick would want some. Rick would smile victoriously over the steam at James. James would grin in return, a little embarrassed.

"You'll get yours tonight," James promised to say when this goofy morning confrontation happened whenever Rick woke up. "Don't get too cocky."

It was during his fantasy conversation that the front doorbell chimed. James thoughtlessly went to the door, still smiling and thinking of things that had happened, or things that would happen very soon. They'd probably end up back in the bedroom. At the door stood a well-dressed man in a white dress shirt and slacks. His expression of resoluteness turned to something like terror when he saw James.

"I have a god, thanks," James said, assuming the man was a Mormon or a Jehovah's Witness.

The man looked confused and then forced himself to speak. "I'm not…." He swallowed. "Is Rick here?"

"He's asleep. I'd rather not wake him."

The man stood there, staring blankly for a moment.

*Was this a stare-down?* James wondered. He raised his eyebrows impatiently to hurry the man along.

185

The man fidgeted, half-smiled, and then spoke hastily. "Would you tell him that Coby stopped by, and that it was good seeing him the other night?"

James knew that name. Coby was the dick-weasel who had cost Rick his eye. His expression informed Coby that James knew exactly who he was.

"The other night?" James asked. But Coby had already sprinted to his car and was driving off, staring fearfully back at James.

"Who was that?" came Rick's sleepy voice from behind James. He came nearer and wrapped his arms around James's waist, playfully bumping his rump.

"Nobody," James answered, staring out into the front yard.

*What was Rick doing with Coby? Had their argument driven him to do something stupid?*

*Damn, his ass was sore!*

THE morning was awkward for poor Melinda Gold as she sat with Patrick in the kitchen eating a hearty and nutritious breakfast. She had felt like a disobedient teenager the night before, sneaking back into the house after egging Jefferson's house with Cassie Bloom. She was terrified that she would run into Patrick and he would judge her for being a bad mother, for playing sexual games in the clear light of day. Her face had remained a shade of red since the incident had happened. The shade would relax or strengthen depending on whom she passed on her walk or what she thought about.

When Melinda finally returned to the house the previous night, out of breath from being dragged and then left there by Cassie, Patrick was in his room. She hurried to her own, undressed, and hopped into bed. After a bit, she heard the bedroom door creak open and Patrick whisper her name to see if she was awake, but she feigned exhaustion.

186

## Suburbilicious: Vignettes from Jasper Lane

Melinda was exhausted by herself and scared to death of the awkwardness around her.

But now, at the breakfast table, she knew she had to face her son. Well, not so much face as sit opposite him while staring at her sausage links and eggs. She wondered if the eggs on her plate were any relation to those she had splattered on that house. She would occasionally steal a glance upward to see if Patrick was looking at her, and he always was, but she could never tell if his glance was harsh or just confused. She was nervous. Her stomach hurt. Would this be the way of things from now on? Every time Patrick came home from college would there be nothing but awkward looks and no words? That could not be! She had just gotten to the point where they were actually forming a real mother/son relationship. She couldn't let a penis in a hammock come between them! She took a breath.

"Patrick," she forced herself to say, holding a death grip on her fork as if it would help her.

"Mom," he cut her off. She looked up to see his face. It was pleasant with a hint of a smile, not accusing at all. "I made a young mother cry," he said.

Melinda loosened her grip on the fork. "W-what?" She was puzzled. Was this some new phrase the kids were using?

"I stopped at this general store on my way home. It was in this small town; I don't know where. They all look the same after a while. I needed something to drink. Anyway, there was this young mother about my age in line in front of me when I went up to pay for things."

Melinda's face didn't change.

Patrick continued. "Her kid—a little girl... I think—was being really loud, really obnoxious. Not like I was raised at all."

This made Melinda feel better.

"The mother was having a hard time controlling her, and they had a lot of items. It was going to take forever. All I could see was the back of the kid's head at first, but then the little tyke turned around. And... Mom, it was the ugliest little thing I have ever seen."

Melinda gasped. "Patrick!"

"I'm not kidding, Mom. A troll. I swear she had three eyes. I flinched and made a sound. When that little freak turned to look at me it caught me off guard. Still gives me chills. Anyway, the mother saw. But I couldn't stop staring. All the while this snaggle-toothed monster-baby was growling at me, taking her bratty craziness out on me because I was the closest person to her. I should have stepped out of line, but I couldn't take my eyes off the little sock puppet. It's like it put me under a spell or something. Before I could stop myself I said 'That is one grotesque kid.' Just like that!"

Melinda dropped her fork and covered her mouth in shock. "What did the mother do?"

"She burst into tears. I felt awful, and the little brat started hitting me for making her mommy cry. Needless to say, I left without my drink."

Melinda stared at Patrick for a moment as he continued eating as if his story was simply ordinary conversation. He looked back up at her, and a smile crept across his face. "She better have one hell of a personality when she grows up," he said.

Melinda suddenly felt better than she had in days.


SANDY left Amy with the sitter. She was getting very nervous about the evening's Gay Porn Wives election. She needed reassurance and knew there was only one place to find it: on the set of her new epic gay porn. She dressed in her best casual yet elegant business suit and set off for the studio.

"I've got to see it for myself," Sandy said over the cell phone as she sped through the streets of town.

"It's going to be a masterpiece," Steve responded. "I promise you that you have nothing to worry about." Steve wasn't watching the filming of the picture as he usually did. Instead, he was in his office going over press and the dull business side of things.

"I'd still feel better seeing it myself." She veered sharply onto the studio's street.

Steve knew when he was licked and sighed. "I'll have Becky meet you in the lobby."

Once there, Sandy met Becky in the lobby of the large Victorian house that served as the studio.

"This is so exciting!" Becky said, taking Sandy's hand and leading her through the house to the barn studio out back, where the current scene was being filmed. "Now, you'll need to be quiet. They've been setting up a very impressive scene all day long, and I believe they're ready to film."

Becky opened the door quietly, and Sandy followed her into the hushed space. At first, Sandy couldn't see anything but crew members and the backs of crew members. But then, she saw it in an Emerald City-like revelation. She gasped, delighted.

Before her was a wall of rock and naked muscle. The scene was an orgy on Technicolor sets, lit perfect. Water was pumped through holes and ditches in the fake rocks as men dressed as warriors and trolls wriggled and writhed over one another. Yet it wasn't tawdry. To Sandy's eyes it was magnificent and high-class filmmaking. There was even a blue screen to add special effects to the scene. In the middle of all of this wonder was Cliff, being carefully hoisted up and down on a large golden dildo by four huge musclemen made up as trolls. His head, limp on his neck, his body convulsing and bucking to the rhythm. Sandy knew that Cliff was a porn actor famous (or infamous) for how much girth and width he could take up his bulbous bum, but this was astonishing!

"I mustn't give in to… *the pleasure*!" Cliff exclaimed in character. "Ugh!" he yelled barbarically as he erupted all over the set and the trolls. The music swelled.

*Magnificent! Magnificent!*

Sandy grabbed Becky's arm triumphantly. "I'm going to win!" she shouted.

IT WAS David who volunteered to act as Cassie's obsessive devotee and show up at Jefferson's home to invite him to the grand dame's cul-de-sac for brunch. He gave his best vacant-faced, cult member stare as he said, "Mrs. Bloom would love for you to come," and handed Jefferson a delicately written invitation.

A brick would have been shit on the spot, if that were at all possible. Jefferson's eyes immediately replied to David's invitation without him saying a word. At last, he would get close to Cassie. He salivated at the idea and snickered inwardly that she was bringing about her own downfall. Surely he would find something on her in the house. He would just need to be sneaky, stealthy, like he had been for a while now spying on her from the trees.

Jefferson took the invitation greedily and watched as David mechanically walked away. He wondered what to expect. What type of home did a dragon lady such as Cassie Bloom keep? Was his brother Jackson perhaps still alive after all, kept in some dark dungeon, beaten nightly with whips?

*Oh, the excitement!* Pearls of sweat brought on by anticipation formed above his mouth. This turn of events definitely made up for the mysterious egging his house had undergone the night before.

CASSIE wanted to give Jefferson a real show, not just a hint of her supposed malevolence, but the whole crazy, Norma Desmond shebang. She had David and Jason help her move things around: the front parlor was draped with dark, heavy curtains and cleared of most of its furniture; a large throne set-piece found in the attic was placed in the middle of the room; candles were lit to offer a creepy ambience; and an armoire was moved in front of the basement door, just in case Jefferson got nosy. It was unlikely he would get away from Cassie, but still.

As for Cassie, she dressed in a heavy, beaded costume she had used years before at one of the Joneses' Fourth of July costume parties. It was black, with a tremendous dip at the neck and cleavage, and dragged noisily along the floor behind her. She wore long, fake, black nails and an ostentatious matching headdress. For any reasonable, thoughtful person it would have been easily seen as the affectations of an act.

The door had been left wide open when Jefferson showed up and nervously peered in. Cassie noted that he hadn't even had the decency to bring flowers or a bottle of wine as any first-time guest should. "Hello," he called in a shaky voice as he stepped forward. His voice echoed through the now almost empty hall.

Cassie was at the top of the stairs that stood opposite the doorway, her eyes wide and accusatory as she massaged the banister with one hand and descended very slowly. "Come in at once!" she shouted. "And close the door behind you. I had to let a servant go this morning, and she left bawling and thoughtless. Can you imagine?" Becky had to work and so was unable to participate in the show as planned.

Jefferson was immediately terrified and bewildered.

"Close the door!" Cassie cried again.

Jefferson jumped and slammed the door in fear, at once looking at her for forgiveness. Finally, at the bottom of the stairs, she said, "Follow," and led him past the lit candles and darkened house to the front parlor. The room looked completely different from how it normally did. This was always the liveliest room in the house, with cocktail hours and gay porn parties, but Jefferson didn't know about those. He just saw the throne, and he tensed.

The beads of Cassie's gown dragged along the wood floor, sounding similar to fingernails, and she sat carefully on the throne. She had never sat on it before, and it was a very uncomfortable thing, but she hid that fact well.

191

"Have a seat," she commanded, gesturing fluidly to a small, wooden chair off in the corner. He took a seat and stared at her nervously, perspiring. Before Jason had left that morning (he said he was going out for a drive), he had told his mother not to overdo it. "This guy can't be that thickheaded."

She had feared the same for a second—half a second. But looking at him now, it was all going to be too easy. All she had to do was keep him occupied while Vera searched his cabinetry for any evidence against them that Jefferson might have collected.

"Why have you come here?" Cassie boomed, her voice echoing through the room.

"Because… you asked me to…."

"Not here, you fool! Why have you come to Jasper Lane?" She gave him an impatient glare.

"Well… you know…. You go where the job takes you."

"Indeed." She looked to a hidden corner of the room where there stood a table under flickering candlelight. "Would you like something to eat?" she asked.

He was up at once, munching on cookies and drinking lemonade as if he were dying of thirst. She just had to keep him interested for a bit: tell him some red herrings, show him significant insignificant things, or feed him. Cassie noticed a protrusion in the side pocket of his jacket, a camera no doubt. Jefferson had come prepared, but when he got back home he would be very disappointed.

VERA got into Jefferson's house easily. She shouldn't have even bothered. She thought to herself that burning the whole place down was no less than he deserved. Then whatever evidence he had acquired would be up in smoke with whatever trinkets and sordidness he called a life.

Vera was bitter.

"Asshole try and take advantage of me!" she said under her breath as she broke into the kitchen cabinet, easily laying waste to it with a crack. Her daddy was a strong man and had passed that strength on to her.

Inside the cabinet was a metal strong box. "Locked, of course."

Not knowing exactly how things were going with Cassie or how long she would be able to keep Jefferson occupied, Vera quickly gathered the strong box beneath her arm and fled out the back door. She bounded—ladylike—across lawns. She had a taxi waiting for her two houses down. It was safer that way, just in case Jefferson did return. He knew what she drove, after all, and she couldn't hide if he saw her car in the driveway. She had assured the taxi driver she wouldn't be long.

"It's your money," he had said. "You're the boss."

"You know it, baby," she said as she slid out of the backseat.

Now, she had successfully accomplished her mission and slid back into her seat. "Thank you, driver," she said. "Let's get the hell out of here."

The taxi sped off, no questions asked. Good ol' taxi drivers.

Vera sighed in relief as they drove away. She held tight to the metal box, pondering its contents. What did Jefferson have against them? She suddenly didn't know if she wanted to see what the box held, but she did know there was no turning back now. Besides, Cassie would be there with her when she opened it. They could cringe together.

Aside from the contents of the box, there was one other thing that was bothering Vera. As she got back into the taxi, so careful to distance herself from her actual crime scene, she noticed Asha Fields staring directly at her from across the street. Had she been there the whole time? It didn't register until now, but Vera was beginning to think she was being watched.

"YOU'RE kicking me to the curb," said Malcolm with his arms crossed over his chest. Melinda stood opposite him in the large school gym as his wrestlers straddled and practiced the homoerotic game behind him. "I could tell it by your voice on the phone when you called saying we had to talk. I can see it in your eyes now. You're kicking me to the freaking curb."

"There's no kicking. I don't kick," Melinda defended, trying to make things as amiable as possible.

"Oh, you've kicked." He winked, making her recall one of his many strange bedroom requests.

Melinda blushed. "Please don't be hurt." She tried to continue, unwaveringly. She couldn't look Malcolm in the eyes, though. If she was breaking his heart, she didn't want to see it. Patrick had given her strength by being so understanding about the Hammock Incident, but he hadn't given her *that* much strength. "I just can't do this right now. What we had was fun, but it was… it was too much for me."

"Don't act like that. You're not a prude."

"I am!" she exclaimed, making eye contact. "I really am."

"Melinda, you loved the things we did. At least, some of them. Give me that."

"It was interesting."

"It was fun. Admit it. You were able to let your inner freak out, and you loved it."

Melinda gasped. "I haven't got an inner freak!"

"No. You're right. It's not 'inner' anymore. She's out in the world now with the rest of us. There's no hiding now, baby." He smiled. He was enjoying this. Finally, seeing that Melinda would not be able to gather herself from the charge of outward freakiness anytime soon, Malcolm relaxed his arms. "I had a great time with you, babe. Truth is, I knew it wouldn't last. There was a small hope that it might, though, so I pushed it and introduced you to my sister. I think that scared you."

"Yes," was all she could say. She watched the boys wrestling behind him; their grappling wasn't even embarrassing her. She might have been seeing them, but she wasn't observing them.

"Maybe in the future we could pick things up again?" Malcolm asked.

Melinda finally assumed a gentler expression and looked at him. "Maybe," she said doubtfully. "But right now, we're just not good for each other."

"You mean I'm not good for you."

"No," she corrected him. "I meant exactly what I said. You need someone who can give you what you want without qualms. That's not me. I need something gentler at the moment. I'm afraid to say it, but I need someone who isn't as exciting."

"Someone as dull as Frank? But you hated being with him."

"Well, hopefully someone a little more exciting than him. Maybe a priest, or a science teacher, or a librarian."

"Librarians are kinky," Malcolm teased.

She leaned in and kissed him on the cheek. The wrestling team flipped and flopped on rubber mats, but she wasn't flustered by them. "It has been fun," she admitted.

"I knew it!"

"Can I ask a favor?" she asked.

"What's that?"

"Keep your sister away from me. I don't want to be killed when she finds out we broke up."

Malcolm laughed.

"Goodbye, Malcolm."

"Can I ask you something now?" he asked as she began walking away. "What can I do different next time, just in case you decide to give me another shot?"

From behind him came the beckoning shout from one of the wrestlers "Nipple!"

Melinda cringed. "Change your name!"

THE old woman's apartment in the religious old folks' home was bare but for a few necessary items of furniture—an uncomfortable pair of chairs, a kitchen table—and a small wooden cross on the wall. Directly in front of the chairs sat a TV loudly playing an old movie. The natural light of the day was sufficient for the old woman apparently; there wasn't a light on anywhere. The room smelled of a strange odor, which Jason could not and did not want to identify.

Nanna looked him up and down as Jason sat across from her. She squinted at him with large, judging eyes. He had tried to clean himself up before he came to see her: he shaved, clipped his hair shorter, and even wore a tie over an untucked dress shirt. But he still wore his jeans and sandals. She pointed these out disapprovingly.

"Jesus wore sandals," he explained.

"You're not Jesus!"

The TV was so loud that Jason had to ask that it be turned down before they could talk. Nanna complied with a huff, still watching him as if he were going to jump her or turn into a demon before her very eyes. He didn't realize that she viewed everyone she met with that gaze.

"You say you're a recent college graduate?" she spoke at last. "I never cared for these worldly schools they have nowadays. Nests of sin, if you ask me. It wouldn't surprise me if they're the first institutions to feel God's wrath come judgment day."

"Well, that's why I'm here. I agree wholeheartedly."

Nanna's face lifted somewhat. "You do?"

"Yes! I was disgusted with the college I attended, ma'am. Everywhere a person looks, there's sinning going on. Sin! Sin! Sin! It's one sin in particular I've come to seek your help with. I've heard you know of a camp that can turn a boy or a girl onto the straight and narrow, if you get my drift."

"Are you a homosexual?" she shouted accusingly. Jason wasn't surprised she didn't recognize who he was. They had never met, and Jackson had probably never shown her any photos. Her only view of Jackson's little homosexual son (who he was trying to "fix") was from afar.

"I *was*. But now the Lord has made me see the error of my lustful habits." Jason sat perfectly still, boiling on the inside from what he was saying.

Nanna calmed down. "Good for you!" she said forcefully. She even leaned forward and patted his knee. His skin crawled. "What can I do for you?" She was much more obliging in tone now, if still suspicious.

"I would like to be in touch with this camp. In fact, I would like to work for them." Jason saw his father standing behind Nanna, stoic and dead.

"They do need all the help they can get in this battle, and you would be a great inspiration. To have come out of the darkness like you have. The things you must have done in college!"

Jason watched as her eyes left him for a moment and wandered over sexual acts he himself could probably never imagine. "It's a detestable world," he said. "There are things I could tell you...." He shivered in play, becoming just as good an actor as his own mother, Cassie Bloom.

"What things?" Nanna inquired greedily. She fondled the remote in her hands but then got hold of herself. "Never mind. Never mind. You just leave it to me." She touched his leg again. "I'll put in a word for you. You'll be hearing from them soon, I should think. That camp works, I tell you. I wish there were more young men like you."

"Me too," Jason agreed with a smirk.

"I have a grandson named Patrick. There are quite a few things amiss with him. He and his mother have both been ensnared by the

197

world. I wouldn't be surprised if he came out of college a homosexual." She remembered the incident at Cassie Bloom's gay porn party where Nanna, outside with a camera, had seen Patrick dancing on top of a dinner table with a muscle-bound heathen. "He most likely already is," she seethed.

"If only he were more like me," Jason consoled.

"From your mouth to God's ears."

"NOW that we have taken roll, this special election-night meeting of the Gay Porn Wives Club shall come to order."

A hush fell over the small crowd of mostly women as Joyce acted as chairperson for the event. Everyone there was extremely anxious to see how things would turn out. This was better than a soap opera. Sandy Jones and Elizabeth Trump sat on opposite sides of the room, ready to cast their votes for president. The tension was intoxicating to everyone there. Beside each of them sat their male allies in the fight, Cliff and Eddie, respectively.

Joyce continued, "I will ask both Mrs. Jones and President Trump to come up momentarily to cast their votes. After which the rest of us will then form a line and cast our own ballots. Any questions?"

There wasn't a sound.

"Mrs. Jones and President Trump, please come and cast your votes."

Both women rose and approached the ballot box on the table as Joyce seated herself. Cliff eyed Eddie Licious, who was still somewhat shaken by his previous run-in with the top-rated porn star. Both women stood on either side of the ballot box as they cast their votes by writing their names on a small piece of paper.

"I hope you can survive the loss you're about to suffer," Elizabeth said quietly as she dropped her vote into the box.

"No talking!" Joyce reminded them.

# Suburbilicious: Vignettes from Jasper Lane

Sandy was silent as she cast her ballot. Elizabeth wouldn't get a show out of her, not here. There was a good chance she would lose, but she could as well win if she had succeeded in stirring an uprising and impressing the other women with her epic porn. She would only have to wait until the results were announced tomorrow night to know for certain. She didn't know why it was going to take so long to count the votes. There wouldn't be that many of them. She supposed, like anything, it was all more or less for show.

The other members of the club formed a line as Sandy seated herself again beside Cliff. She sighed nervously. "Well, if I don't win at least I still have the best-looking date." Cliff squeezed his best friend's hand reassuringly as the voting got under way.

JEFFERSON patted his pocket where he had kept his camera hidden from Cassie while he was in her house. He had a profound sense of accomplishment. Soon, with all the evidence that he had collected against Cassie Bloom, she would be rotting in jail. Then maybe they'd electrocute her for killing Jackson. His mother would be so proud of him. Maybe he could even get them tickets so they could watch! He would at last be his mother's favorite son. And the best part was Cassie had been the unwitting accomplice to her own downfall.

He chuckled as he unlocked his front door and made his way into the house. Cassie had led him thoughtlessly around her house, showing him this and that, her back always turned just long enough for Jefferson to snap a picture or make a note. He was sure there was evidence in these new photos somewhere. He would just need to go through them meticulously. Right now, though, he would put the camera with the rest of the photos that were already developed in the—

Jefferson choked and sputtered. His heart shook, then sank. In the kitchen, the cabinetry had been shattered. But not just any cabinet. The very one that held the strong box and the emerging cache of evidence.

"No! No! No!" Jefferson shouted, sliding his grasping claws over the empty cabinet shelf as if the strong box had become invisible momentarily and would simply reappear if he felt for it.

His face turned bitter and angry as he hit the shelving. This had to be Cassie Bloom's work. *But how?* She was with him all day. He had been in her creepy company and hadn't let her out of his sight, not once.

Jefferson paced around the kitchen, his heart pounding in rage and his mind racing in bewilderment. Cassie had servants. Maybe she had persuaded one of them to do this. It wouldn't be hard, considering her glare. Jefferson sat down and held his head, trying to squeeze the answer out of his temples.

"Just think. Just think and breathe," he chided himself. "Who could it be?" Taking a deep breath, he closed his eyes and tried to gain some control of the situation. All his life situations had always controlled him. This was why his mother was so often disgusted by him. "Be a man, Jefferson!" he said, his words taking on a semblance of his mother's angry voice. "Get a hold of yourself and think."

It was then that Jefferson smelled the slightest hint of a familiar and enchanting perfume. If it was an honest sensory perception or just a memory he could not say, but it gave him the answer he needed.

*Vera!*


AT THAT very moment, in the incinerator room of the Bloom basement, a gunshot shattered the lock on Jefferson's stolen strong box.

"I forgot how interesting that feels," Cassie said as she lowered the revolver. She had kept a gun in the house, thinking she might be thankful for it on the off chance someone broke into her home one day. "I haven't used a gun in a while." She studied the thing in her hands. "My feelings haven't changed. I still hate them."

Vera was standing eagerly over the strong box now. "Let's see what my ex-honey has against us," she said as she tipped the defunct metal lid up.

Inside were scraps of paper with scratchy handwriting. "He's taken lots of notes on you," Vera noted as she read through them quickly. "Your comings and goings."

Cassie dug past the papers to the photos beneath them. "You'd think he'd invest in a digital camera," she mumbled as she flipped through the pictures. There were a few rolls of undeveloped film underneath the "evidence." "He's been watching me for a while."

"Anything interesting?"

Cassie began to laugh. "Good Lord! He went to town when I disrobed on the front deck. It's like a modeling shoot. And Vera, look! Here's you. Remember? This was when I had that get-together last month and Gayhound wouldn't let Melinda come up onto the front deck."

"And she fell covered in egg salad. Poor Melinda."

"Vera, there's nothing here. Absolutely nothing he could use against us. It's like a photo box of old memories and insignificant ramblings." She laughed again and pointed at another photo. Vera joined in the merriment.

They decided not to destroy the photos—at least not right away. Instead, they went upstairs to the front parlor, fixed some drinks, and laughed over the recent memories frozen in someone else's pictures.

"We need to hire him again the next time we have a party. These aren't that bad at all," Cassie commented.

WHEN Rick woke up he could tell it was going to be one of those days usually reserved for fiction, where everything conspires to be wrapped up for good or bad in a neat little bow, and not just for the lead character. Clouds hung over Jasper Lane waiting to either be scattered by sunlight or burst open with rain.

James was already up. He had a game and was preparing a good breakfast before the slaughter. Rick decided to take the day off from the gym so that he could go and watch. Seth was over for breakfast. James had told Rick they were driving to the pitch together. James was stunned when Rick had said that was completely fine. Rick, though, was a little uneasy about being around Seth for reasons James was not aware of, that being Seth's big, gay crush on Rick.

When Rick sat at the dining room table, he felt Seth's eyes on him, molesting him. James was still in the kitchen scrambling eggs and grilling steak.

"How are you?" Seth said quietly from across the table.

Rick looked at him and gave a polite nod. "I'm fine."

"Gloomy morning, huh?"

Thankfully, Rick was saved from further awkward conversation by James entering the room with arms filled with breakfast. For the most part, Seth's attention was drawn to James as they talked about rugby, about how they were set to squash the day's opponents. They joked and imagined their enemies' bodies trampled easily underfoot as they hollered a victorious Theban yell.

Every so often, however, Seth would sneak a flirting glimpse at Rick. James didn't seem to notice. Or perhaps he did and he assumed it was playfulness or that the two were finally beginning to warm up to each other. Rick felt violated at his very own breakfast table. Well, at James's breakfast table. Technically, at James's uncle's breakfast table. Rick shook his head of its meandering thoughts about the ownership of the table and took a huge forkful of steak into his mouth. Maybe he should bring up his one eye; sort of nudge at Seth's locker room impropriety and subsequent misspeak. He wondered if that would shoo Seth away any sooner.

That was the longest breakfast Rick could ever remember having even though he ate as quickly as he could, and he rose at once, saying he would clean the table. "You should get going," he said, rather excitedly for his nature.

James looked at him playfully and explained to Seth, "Baby wants me to win 'cause he knows when I win, he wins."

"That's right," Rick said, not at all in James's leading tone as he collected plates that weren't yet empty. "Now get your butt out there and win."

"Butts," James said.

"What?"

"Butts. There are two of us. You want Seth's butt to do well, too, don't you? You want his butt to win too."

Seth was grinning mischievously.

"Of course," Rick backtracked. "More power to Seth's victorious butt."


"HE'S watching us again." Cassie said the words without amusement but rather with a drab annoyance. She and Vera sat once more on the front deck having coffee without restrictions now that their investigations had been completed. They hadn't yet informed Becky or Melinda that things were to return to normal in regard to their morning ritual.

Vera looked down the hill, and, sure enough, saw the unmistakable shake and fuss of a man in a tree. "So what," she said, taking a sip of her cappuccino. "We're watching him too."

"Why do you think he's still here? Do you suppose he has some actual evidence that we didn't find?"

"I think he doesn't know when he's beat. He's starting all over again." Vera stood up impatiently. "Get on, now! Get on outta that tree, Jefferson Bloom," she shouted. "Damn fool!"

"We'll need to tell David about this," Cassie said as Vera sat down. "He can help us keep watch. I think we've rid the house of everything pertaining to Jackson, but one never knows. I don't want Jefferson stepping one foot on my grass again."

"We need to get rid of Jefferson Bloom for good. He's just going to keep coming after us. Even if he never finds a thing, it's still one hell of an annoyance."

"How? We can't force him to leave." Cassie was quiet for a few seconds. "We need to get something against him. He's a Bloom; he's got to have a past that simply reeks." She leaned back in her chair. "What about when you saw Asha as you came out of his place with the box? Did she look suspicious?"

"She certainly looked as if she knew something. Maybe Jefferson isn't the one we should be cautious around anymore."

"I should invite Asha and Keiko over sometime. Get to know them better. They don't seem the dangerous sort, but who can tell?"

Vera decided to change the subject. All this talk about Jefferson had brought Jackson's gory death to mind, and that was something she did not relish to think on for too long. "How's Jason doing? Is he adapting to Jasper Lane again?"

"He's better, I suppose. He seems to be at least filling his days with things. Though he left early again this morning. Much earlier than yesterday. It was still dark out. I would ask him about it, but…."

Vera nodded. "It's a forest of secrets around here, isn't it?"

"With a spy in every tree." Cassie arched her eyebrow.

Vera smiled, stood, walked to a large, antique flower pot filled with small stones, and hurled a rock down the hill at the tree wherein spied Jefferson. Though the rock didn't hit him, it certainly scared him enough that he fell out of the tree. Then, collecting himself, he ran back to his own house, occasionally glancing hatefully over his shoulder at the cul-de-sac.

"One less spy," Vera proclaimed.

# Suburbilicious: Vignettes from Jasper Lane

JASON had indeed risen from bed and left early that morning. He hadn't told Cassie exactly why, and he knew she wouldn't ask. He was grateful for that. She'd find out soon enough, as soon as he had finished his task anyway. Her not knowing right away was for the best. Jason was fixin' to stir up some trouble.

Lives would be changed forever by what he was setting out to do. But this was merely the first step on a long journey.

He picked up some coffee at a mini-mart to keep him awake on the drive. Jackson sat like a stone in the backseat. Jason could see him over his shoulder in the mirror; he could sense his cold stare on the back of his head.

Nanna had been quick on her promise. She'd talked to someone at the Straight to the Heart asylum the moment Jason had left her condo. He was all set up for an interview to be a counselor. He printed out the directions that he had already saved on his computer and was now on his way to become the most beloved counselor at that prison.

Oh, yes! They would love him plenty. His story, his diligence, his praise to their angry god. They would adore him, right up to the point that the rubber band that had been wound so tight all these years finally snapped right in front of them.

THERE were dirty looks even before the rugby game began. Rick noticed them straight away. And they weren't the game-player faces of opposing teams trying to knock down the other team's confidence. These dirty looks went from teammate to teammate, more accurately from James to Seth. Seth avoided James's gaze by eyeing down, a bit unsuccessfully, an opponent.

Rick realized what had happened just as the thunder clapped overhead and it began to rain over the pitch. The game commenced. Things were going to get very dirty, very fast.

Rick watched anxiously, getting wet without an umbrella. "Just get through the game without ripping his head off, James," he whispered. "Remember, he's on your team."

James seemed to be doing well at first. He put all his anger into attacking the other team. But Rick noticed he was getting more and more ferocious and leering hatefully at Seth whenever he had the chance. Like everyone in the game, he was quickly being covered in mud, and there was a pervasive fear from the other team. It was as if they were aware of a maniac in their midst, and not the good kind.

James's own team was stoked by the rage, all except Seth, who was withdrawing bit by bit from his Theban persona. He was too busy watching James.

Finally, Seth looked to the sidelines at Rick as if asking for help. Rick knew instantly that had been a huge mistake. A great growl broke up the game, and Seth soon lay flattened in the mud with James atop him, beating him. Their teammates soon came to the fight, trying their best to pull the growling, testosterone-charged warrior off Seth.

Rick couldn't see anything for a few minutes. A crowd of players, both mates and opponents, surrounded the two, yelling this and that. The rain fell harder now, thunder roared, and spectators either fled for cover or watched awestruck from under their useless umbrellas.

At last, when Rick did see James again, it was like a scene from an old film, a B movie. With an angry roar James burst free of the crowd trying to restrain him. His clothes had been torn away, and he stood naked, muddy, and wet over a whimpering Seth.

"You have got to be kidding me," Rick mumbled, a little scared and excited at once.

# Suburbilicious: Vignettes from Jasper Lane

"FREE food."

That was Patrick's response when he was asked by his mother why he had dragged her to the Gay Porn Wives Club electoral banquet. They sat at a table, Melinda nervously fidgeting. She had never been near so many people associated with the sex industry.

"Patrick, I could have fixed you something to eat at home. We're not poor."

"I didn't say we were." He pointed to the paper plate in front of him filled with buffalo wings, mac and cheese, cheese sticks, and various other sundry, unhealthy items. "But come on! Look at this spread."

She gasped. "You're going to have a coronary at the age of twenty. Sometimes I wish you *were* gay; you'd take better care of your body."

"That's a stereotype, Mom," he said with his mouth full.

"A very healthy one! Be gay, Patrick. Be gay now."

"Let him eat what he wants while he's still got the metabolism to do it." Steve and Becky sat with them at the table, amused by the mother/son banter. Sandy and Cliff were schmoozing about the room with other members and assorted porn stars who had shown up out of curiosity. "Sandy really appreciates you being here, Melinda."

"I always support my friends' endeavors," Melinda replied with a gracious smile.

"Did you hear?" Becky asked Melinda. "Vera and Cassie have made up. Coffee is back on in the mornings."

"I'm so relieved. I was very concerned. Have they ever fought like that before?"

"I can honestly say never."

"Well, I'm happy it's over. I thrive on stability. I don't know if you know that about me, Becky." Melinda watched Patrick with motherly disgust as he cleaned his plate.

"How are things with the coach?" Becky asked innocently. She made an effort not to say the coach's last name.

"Unstable," Melinda replied.

Outside the storm was whipping the rain against the windows. The lights flickered momentarily, causing a stir from those at the electoral banquet. People were seating themselves. Sandy and Cliff rejoined their table. It was apparent by the sudden lowering of voices that Joyce was about to read the results of the polling.

"Ladies and guests," she began from the podium. After that it was hard to tell who was really listening. Joyce talked a bit about the history of the club, what they did, what the original intent was, but mostly everyone just wanted her to get to the results. And the results of the results were what were even more eagerly anticipated. Would there be blood drawn if Elizabeth lost?

There were those in the room who didn't care one way or the other, though. Not really. Patrick was more concerned with his delicious buffalo wings; Becky was casting flirtatious glances at a pretty bi porn star at another table; and Melinda was surveying the room to see who she was more refined than. Only Sandy, Steve, and Cliff listened from their table, both men holding onto one of Sandy's hands.

Finally, the moment had arrived. Joyce brought forth an envelope from an ornate wooden box and took her time opening it.

"Tension is never funny," Sandy whispered to her men. "Everyone thinks it's funny, but it's not."

Joyce deflated before she read, and Sandy knew then that she had lost. "Elizabeth Trump."

There was a small triumphant cry from a portion of the crowd. Elizabeth stood and walked to the podium with Eddie Licious close behind. Steve and Cliff consoled Sandy with gentle touches. She sat stoic under the waiting, watchful eyes of the other club members. They wanted their fight. They wanted Sandy to get up and throttle Elizabeth and then parade around with her head on a stick.

# Suburbilicious: Vignettes from Jasper Lane

Elizabeth gave a long speech, milking every bit she could out of her supposed hardships the past few days and how much she deserved the win. She shot a cold stare back at Sandy more than once. The storm roared on without letup outside. By the end of the speech, most people had zoned out. Patrick was even starting to fall asleep due to all the food he had eaten.

"And now," Elizabeth said in conclusion, "I shall offer my hand in reconciliation to my former rival in hopes we may be friends."

All heads turned once again to Sandy as Elizabeth left the podium and began walking toward her. Sandy knew what "reconciliation" meant to Elizabeth. She was going to be kicked out of the club as soon as Elizabeth had the chance to act.

Elizabeth took her time, walking with steady, elegant steps so the guests at the banquet might stare longer at the defeated and humiliated Sandy Jones, and, more importantly, the still-queen Elizabeth Trump. Eddie followed his wife proudly in a tight *International Male* shirt. Sandy rose graciously with a smile.

But a loud clash of thunder put a stop to things immediately. The lights flickered again, this time for a few seconds longer, and Elizabeth became disoriented. Tripping over a power cord, she fell forward with a yelp and pushed Sandy back toward the banquet table. Sandy grabbed for anything to keep herself from falling to the floor, and one of her hands inadvertently landed on Elizabeth's crotch.

When the lights came back on, there was such a look of shock from Sandy, such a look of fear from Elizabeth, that everyone there knew something horrible, fabulous, and interesting had happened.

"*You're a man!*" Sandy cried aloud.

The crowd gasped. Elizabeth stared back at Eddie. Eddie fainted. They had been discovered. This was the Gay Porn Wives Club, not the Gay Porn Transvestite Husbands Club! (That was down the street.) If Elizabeth had had an operation and become a woman, that would have been different. *But this?*

A crowd of women hovered over Eddie, who lay unconscious and spread over a table. "He needs mouth-to-mouth!" one of the women cried. A fight broke out between the club members as to who would get to resuscitate him.

Sandy pushed Elizabeth from her, the former president's face crowned in distress. Sandy held out her hand in a sign of "reconciliation." She knew now Elizabeth would have to resign.

JAMES and Rick sat in the Jeep long after everyone else had already left the game. The rain poured steady but not as heavy.

After James had finally been pulled off Seth, Rick found a blanket in the Jeep to wrap around his muddy, naked, soaked partner. Seth had been hurried away. Rick drove himself and James to a coffee shop in silence and then returned to the scene of the throwdown with their warm drinks. James drank his coffee gingerly.

"I acted like such a fool," James finally spoke above the rain. "I could have killed him."

"He told you the truth, didn't he?" Rick asked, reaching over and stroking James's matted hair.

James nodded. "You should have heard the things he was saying about you. Actually, scratch that. You shouldn't hear any of it. It was filthy and wrong and childish." James was loosening up, gripping the blanket less tightly.

"Will it make you feel better to tell me?"

"First off, he tried to act as if he was just interested in some fun." He gritted his teeth. "He asked if we could threesome, and if you could be bottom for both of us!"

"Charming."

"I tried to pass it off as a piece-of-shit joke and told him not to kid around like that about you. But then he told me you'd be better off with him. He said it all straight-faced, dead serious. He had some reasoning like you've got drama, and I don't deal well with drama, and he deals very well with drama. Some bullshit."

"Drama?" Rick tried to sound offended. "I don't have.... Yeah, I guess I do."

James looked gently on Rick. "I like your drama."

"So is that when you attacked him?"

"No. He kept looking over at you during the game, and he looked so determined to get in your pants. His dirty jokes combined with the spirit of rugby, and all the primordial, manly he-beast feel of the game...."

Rick shook his head. "Testosterone."

"What?"

"That was testosterone you could have used on me, and you wasted it out there on the field kicking Seth's ass." He leaned over, gave James's cheek a kiss, and then wiped his mouth of the mud and grime.

"I made the Sacred Band of Thebes lose their first game. So much for being undefeated."

"Well, you certainly would have won."

"Yeah. If the game hadn't been called off because of me. Like I said, I'm a fool."

"Well, then we're well-suited for each other. Remember, I thought all this time that Seth was trying to get in *your* rugby shorts."

"Blech! Not my type at all."

"I know. Mine neither."

They sat in the Jeep, watching the rain wash down the windshield, feeling that things were slowly coming back to normal.


CASSIE and Vera played a friendly game of Go Fish in the front parlor to wait out the storm. They had lit candles; Cassie still had out many of the ones she had used for her "show." The lights had flickered due to the weather as they played but never stayed out for any length of time. It was getting on in the evening, though, and neither of them particularly relished the idea of playing cards in pitch dark.

"And candles are so much more evocative than flashlights," Cassie commented.

Cassie was also worried about Jason. She had not heard from him since he left. It wasn't that she expected him to call and tell her where he was, but in a storm like this it would have been nice to know he wasn't lying in a ditch somewhere. Whatever reason he had left so early that morning for, it was important to him. Cassie was secretly hoping it was a boyfriend or a getaway with friends, something to signify that he was adapting to a new life.

Before either of them knew what was going on, as Vera proclaimed "Go fish," the large bay window of the parlor was smashed, imploding inward. Vera and Cassie jumped to their feet, thinking it was the storm intensifying, something tornadic. Then they saw a figure stumbling in through the shattered frame.

"Jefferson," Cassie gasped in recognition. He held a gun. "Vera, run!"

"Vera!" shouted Jefferson, aiming the gun before she could move.

Cards were blowing everywhere, and candles were being snuffed out by the wind and small gusts of rain. The lights flickered and dimmed fiercely.

"You broke my heart!" Jefferson cried as if he was a community theater version of James Dean or Marlon Brando come in from a storm designed by Tennessee Williams. He was drunk, and his eyes were crazed and dilated.

"Sorry, Jeff," Vera spoke cautiously. "Things had to be done."

"Yes! And things still have to be done." He waved the gun carelessly. "I'll hate to do them, but they have to be done." He stepped toward Vera. "I loved you. I was in love with you."

"Jefferson, it would have never worked out," Vera said. "There are things you might not like about me. Beautiful things you could never understand."

"You were a man. I know." He was slurring. "I was disgusted at first, but... I love you, Vera! I could have forgiven you for it."

"Forgiven me? You asshole, mother-fucking rapist...."

"Vera!" Cassie tried to keep her from angering the gun-wielding drunk.

"But instead," (he seemed not to notice Vera's insults) "you team up with this murderer... er... er." He shook the gun momentarily at Cassie before returning his attention back to Vera.

"She didn't kill Jackson," Vera stated.

"Vera!" Cassie tried to hush her again.

Again, Jefferson seemed not to hear what Vera was saying. "Because I love you," he said, "I'm going to kill you first. You won't need to suffer anymore, you heartless cunt!"

Vera looked at him with a mixture of disdain and fear. "Lucky Vera," she said dryly.

Jefferson cocked the gun. "Goodbye, lover," he said.

"No!" Cassie screamed, jumping toward him. He reeled about, pointing the gun at her, and a shot rang out. Vera screamed, thinking Cassie had been shot, and initially Cassie thought so as well. But then Jefferson dropped the gun and screamed in pain as he fell to the floor clutching his shoulder.

Cassie and Vera stared at each other, confused. Jefferson lay on the floor, weeping and wailing like a child. The ladies were frozen for a moment, trying to sort out what had happened. Vera helped Cassie to her feet. Finally, their attention focused on the shattered bay window. There, Asha Fields stood just outside of it, still holding a gun.

"FBI," she shouted above the storm. "Are you all right, ladies?"

BY THE time the police had arrived, the storm had lessened quite a bit. The flashing lights of the police cruisers made certain everyone on Jasper Lane was watching the cul-de-sac from their front windows or on the sidewalks under large umbrellas. They all witnessed Jefferson Bloom being taken by the cops into an ambulance, ranting and hollering about the murderess and the transvestite.

"I knew there was something strange about that man."

"Was he insane this whole time?"

"A crazy man, right in our very midst!"

"I'm glad we put off having children. This isn't the neighborhood for it."

Of course, no one would know for certain what had happened. At least not until the next morning when Cassie would make sure absolutely *everyone* knew the selected details of the ordeal.

"Cassie always has the best stories," Melinda would be heard to grumble. "The good stuff never happens to me."

Jasper Lane was still gawking and whispering in excitement as Jason Bloom came home. At first there was a conversation with the cops over who he was, but then Cassie saw him, and she and Vera ran to him. They embraced in the rain.

The entire street seemed to sigh a big, hugging "*Aww!*"

As convenience would have it, it was at this moment that Terrence and Chris returned home to Jasper Lane as well. Terrence, unwilling to wait until he got to his own house to find out what was going on, pulled crooked into David and Cliff's driveway. They were watching from inside Cliff's Hummer, eating trail mix and drinking beer. (It was a better view to the excitement than inside the house.) Terrence jumped from the minivan and pulled open the driver's door of the Hummer in a frenzy. Cliff stared down at him in annoyance with a mouthful of assorted treats.

"What's happened?" Terrence squealed. "What did I miss, bitches?"

David poked his head around Cliff's chest. "*So* much!"

*The next day...*

CASSIE and Vera sat beside each other at coffee the next morning. The rain clouds were gone, and the sun shone down as it should on Jasper Lane. As promised, the tradition Melinda had so counted on was picking up right back up where it had ended. Indeed, to Melinda's delight, Cassie and Vera seemed to be closer than ever. They seemed on the verge of tears more than once, and this would occur by simply looking at each other. Cassie relayed the previous night's events as only she could, with all the right gestures and perfect emphases.

"Isn't it wonderful?" Melinda asked Becky as they walked down the hill to their own homes afterward. "That crazy man brought them closer than ever. I mean, I know they had made up before that, but surely now they realize how important they are to one another."

Becky found herself wishing she could tell Melinda the truth, but she kept quiet. That was Cassie or Vera's story if they so wished to tell her. "Are we speed-walking this afternoon?" she queried instead.

"Of course!" Melinda chirped.

Once Becky and Melinda had gone, Cassie and Vera headed downhill themselves to visit one of their neighbors. They had to know just how deep in shit they were. Asha Fields had explained the night before that she was off-duty FBI but had noticed Jefferson trudging toward the cul-de-sac in the storm and became suspicious. Neither Cassie nor Vera had the mind the previous night to question her as to why she had a gun with her.

Asha answered the door in a T-shirt and sweats. "Ladies," she said with a nod. "How are you this beautiful morning?"

"Good," Cassie answered. "Thankful."

"Inquisitive," Vera added.

"Oh?" Asha said with an innocent grin.

They didn't know what to say exactly. "We're so grateful," Cassie expressed once again. "But there is something…."

"Would you like to come in? Keiko's at your friend's studio filming, but I can make some coffee that doesn't taste too bad."

"We just had some, but thank you," Vera answered. "Asha, I'll just get down to it, honey. The man across the street…."

"Jefferson Bloom." She looked at Cassie as she said his name. "Bloom's a very common name around here, isn't it?"

Cassie and Vera were startled that she knew who he was. But then, she was FBI. Who knew what she knew?

She continued. "Horrible man. I've been watching him for a while now. I think to the point that I might have drawn some suspicion to myself. Never trusted him. I did some private investigating into his past. He's done all sorts of things. Rape, attempted rape, molestation. It's about time he was locked away. He won't be getting out for a very long time."

"Attempted rape?" That had hit close to Vera's own experience with him.

"Yes. I'm surprised no one's gotten him sooner. He's not a very smart man. If he had done something like that to me, I would have found a way to get him put away. And if I knew of someone who he had done something to and they were trying to put him away, I certainly wouldn't get in their way."

"You wouldn't?" Cassie asked.

Asha winked. "No. I wouldn't. It's rare, but sometimes looking the other way is the right thing to do."

"You know what?" Vera said. "I think we could do with more coffee after all. Couldn't we, Cass?"

Cassie smiled. "We sure could!"

Asha gestured them past her. "Well, then come on in! Keiko will be so proud that I'm finally making friends."

THE Boys sat on David and Cliff's front lawn in their short shorts and sunglasses enjoying midday margaritas and the welcomed sun. The world was drying off. David, Rick, and Terrence sipped and gossiped and talked about their neighbors as they drove, jogged, or walked past. The UPS man came by, and Terrence turned red.

"I'm so glad I had my tongue ring removed," he remarked.

"So, there will be no more whoring it up?" David asked him.

"Not as long as Harry's in my life." Terrence sighed dramatically.

"What will we talk about at parties now, David?" Rick queried playfully. "Terrence's exploits were always the best tales."

"I'm a grown-up now!" Terrence proclaimed. "I have a son, remember?"

"Where is our little Christian?"

"He and Patrick Gold went somewhere. I dunno. Wherever kids go these days."

Rick took a drink. "Church."

"Where?" Terrence was horrified, but Rick and David laughed. "Rick made a funny. How charming."

"We's three married girls now," David said, settling back into his lawn chair.

"Well, I'm not popping out any babies," Terrence said. "Not with this body."

"Me neither," Rick agreed.

"Cliff neither."

The afternoon wore on pleasantly, and, bit by bit, the moist lawn was laid with other prints from other lawn chairs.

Cassie and Vera were the first asked to join the Boys as they came back from a longer-than-expected visit with Asha Fields.

"Margaritas?" David asked.

"Where are the chairs?" Cassie replied. "Have we got a tale to tell you, boys!"

Sandy strolled by with Amy in a stroller.

"Madame President," she was greeted.

"Would you happen to have a virgin daiquiri?" she asked as she joined them. Amy kept the Boys entertained on the blankets. She loved her gay uncles.

Melinda and Becky were delighted to have a break in their speed-walking to indulge as well. "We can just walk a little extra speedy to burn these drinks off," Melinda assured Becky.

And finally, the looming figure of Cliff, home from the day's shoot and still wearing his loincloth, drove up the drive. "I think I might just wear this to the Fourth party this year," he said, stepping down from the Hummer and strolling to David's side. "What do you think, Sandy?"

"Tasty," she replied.

The spontaneous lawn party went on into the evening. James arrived soon, as did Steve, giving their respective spouses a kiss. Vera yelled down the street to Asha and Keiko to come join them, and they did, though Asha was never one for parties.

"How many friends do we really need?" Asha asked as Keiko pulled her along.

Patrick and Chris came back home, Patrick always surprised to see Melinda drinking.

"I think I'm drunk," she whispered in her son's ear, somewhat concerned.

"Well, it's about time!" Terrence hollered, overhearing what she had said. Overhearing because he was listening.

Cassie even called her home for Jason. He hadn't left the house all day, and she didn't want him to miss out on the fun. She was ecstatic when he told her he would be there shortly. That he just had something to do first.

Yes, the residents of Jasper Lane were quite content on this early summer day. Their laughter filled the air, floating through backyards and across dinners. Even Jason could make out his mother's cackle coming in through his bedroom window in the cul-de-sac. He smiled, looking out at the garden, which had once harbored a buried secret. He would have fun this evening because his mind at last was going to be getting some peace very soon, and he had that to look forward to.

"I'm going to make it to that camp you wanted me to go to after all, Daddy," he said to the air. "But maybe not in the way you would have wanted. I tricked them, you see? They hired me on." He looked back to his bed. "Can you believe that? Your little gay boy is going to cause one hell of a ruckus."

He walked slowly to the bed as if conversing with it, and stopped in front of it with a superior gaze.

"You look fabulous, Daddy!" he said.

On the bed, perfectly painted and decorated with rouge and jewelry, was the skull of Jackson Bloom.

## Suburbilicious: Vignettes from Jasper Lane

*Two weeks later...*

STEVE and Sandy Jones's Fourth of July costume party was, as usual, a huge hit with the neighborhood. Music played from a set of even larger speakers than Steve had used at previous parties. He could afford bigger things now. He was the head of a company, after all, and was doing very well. Lights were strung through the air, attached to a special netting. A buffet table of scrumptiousness Sandy had personally picked out was constantly surrounded, and an open bar was stocked with the finest alcohol and tastiest liquid treats. There was plenty of help this year as well. The ladies of the GPWC were only too happy to offer any assistance they could offer after Sandy had rescued them from Elizabeth Trump's tyranny.

Sandy and Steve talked with everyone they could. Amy was asleep, being watched by the babysitter inside the house. (Luckily, she was a very good sleeper.) Sandy had come upon the patriotic idea of dressing as a revisionist Molly Pitcher, the Revolutionary War heroine. She wore a ragged dress, torn and stained with gunpowder, but one sleeve was cut so that it caused her left tit to hang out. Not wanting to be too lewd, she covered her nipple with a fringe tassel. ("Not terribly accurate," she complained to Steve.) Steve was dressed as the cannon which Molly Pitcher helped to fire. The costume didn't take much imagination to design, and Steve was happy for that. But it was shocking to the more prudish partygoers.

"Nice cannon," David said as he peered down at Steve's prosthetic crotch.

David and Cliff had, as usual, stopped by early to help the Joneses with the decorations and food. As promised, Cliff wore his costume from the film. He was Manwhore all evening, a tight little loincloth and little else. David was dressed in a kilt of sorts and sandals as Manwhore's new companion, Slutbutt. ("He's going to be in the sequel," Cliff assured him.)

"Looking to get into porn?" Steve teased David.

"I get into porn every night." David winked at Cliff and gave the big guy's fleshy ass a tight squeeze. "And by 'into' I mean—"

"We know what you mean," Sandy laughed.

The truth was, though, after the Manwhore trilogy was completed, Cliff was seriously thinking of giving up porn. Nothing would get him back into it this time. He wanted to focus on bodybuilding as a career for a while before it got too late in life. The ability to be a muscular behemoth only lasted so long. He knew David would support him in whatever path he chose. ("You mean your ass might be all mine for a while?" David said teasingly.)

Steve and Sandy had themselves just begun talking of a change in their own lives. They acknowledged things weren't the same between them since Amy, and they needed to fix that. The notion of a trip with just the three of them came to Steve. Not a short vacation, but a long trip, long enough to repair some things. They were going to start seriously looking into it after the Fourth of July party.

Across the party, the swirling laughter of the guests almost drowned out the music. Asha and Keiko arrived dressed as The Avengers. Keiko was clad as Emma Peel, and Asha made a reluctant John Steed, though she rather liked the suit.

"Getting to know people is a pain in the ass," she remarked to Keiko. Secretly, however, she liked her new neighbors. Still, her naturally suspicious personality would not let her get too close to anyone new without a struggle.

Becky Ridgeworth, dressed as a very voluptuous Mae West in a screaming-red dress and boa, greeted Asha and Keiko as they entered. She quickly got them caught up on the latest gossip. Becky had recently found herself thinking quite a bit about Jasper Lane's newest homeowners. She began to think about being with a woman, and it wasn't at all that bad a notion. ("Lord knows, I can't find a man that's worth anything around here.")

A few feet away, Terrence and his date Harry stood as matching cowboys talking to James and Rick. Harry's son and Chris were off with Patrick somewhere in the crowd. Together they were the Three Musketeers and enjoying the parts. The cowboy costume was the only look Harry was completely comfortable with. Terrence had tried to convince him to arrive together as The Ambiguously Gay Duo or some other superhero to satisfy Terrence's fetish, but Harry wouldn't agree to it. At least not now.

"Next year," Terrence said to himself.

The very next weekend Harry and Terrence were going to spend three days together at a state park. But Terrence had had enough of becoming one with nature for a while, so they would be getting a very comfortable room at the park's inn. Terrence was determined to make a go at this relationship no matter how much it frightened him.

"So you get to stay on the rugby team?" Terrence asked James as the four of them bobbed and weaved to the music.

"They can't afford to lose him," Rick answered for James. "He's the best player on the team." James's arm was wrapped around Rick. Neither Rick nor James was the costuming type, and everyone knew this, but the guys were obliged to dress up for their hosts. James simply wore his rugby outfit, his muscular legs attracting much attention. Rick came as a crazed rugby fan with a painted face and a T-shirt specially made that screamed SACRED BAND OF THEBES.

"Once Seth quit ,there was really nothing else they could do," James said. "The team couldn't afford to lose two players as rough as us."

"They're all scared of him, though, especially the straight guy, Will."

"And he's the one that has the least to worry about unless he decides he's gay and starts hitting on Rick."

In the back of James's mind, he kept the image of Coby at the front door. James never told Rick his former boyfriend had shown up that morning. But he trusted Rick, and if anything had happened between Coby and him, Rick would say so. Still, James was hoping Coby would come by uninvited again, just so he could give Rick's ex a little talking-to.

The star of any Jasper Lane party, however, was Cassie Bloom. Her original idea for a costume was that of the Marquise de Merteuil from *Les Liaisons dangereuses*, but after her recent rescue by the FBI she and Vera decided to go another route. Cassie was Angie Dickinson, Police Woman, and Vera was Foxy Brown, complete with a fabulous afro.

They were talking to Patrick, who had separated momentarily from the other two Musketeers.

"It's so good to have you back," Cassie said.

Both Vera and Patrick heard the bittersweet-ness in her voice. Jason had left a week before for a job. He wouldn't say much about it; only that it was very important, that it would give him purpose again. At the last he hugged his mother and smiled. "See you soon," he promised.

"Where's Melinda?" Vera asked. "I want to see her costume." She looked around, interested to see what Melinda would consider a costume.

"She's still getting dressed. She'll be here soon." Patrick grinned. "She's gonna blow you away. I picked her costume out myself."


MELINDA had protested. How could Patrick expect her not to? She hadn't wanted to come in costume at all to the Joneses' party. Melinda Gold didn't wear costumes. Maybe it was some of the old Melinda remaining in her still, but she just didn't see it as proper for a grown woman to be seen parading about in public dressed so extravagantly.

# Suburbilicious: Vignettes from Jasper Lane

"It doesn't have to be extravagant," Patrick urged her. "I bet you already have something we can throw together. You could be a washer woman or something."

Melinda stayed seated on the sofa, admiring him in his own costume as he headed to her bedroom to find an outfit for the evening. She hadn't dressed up last year. Why should she this year?

She took a drink from her coffee (which she realized she was consuming quite a bit of lately) and wondered what sort of ensemble her son would come up with for her. As she sat pondering this, she suddenly remembered something, and her eyes went wide.

Melinda screamed "Oh my God!" at the very same time as Patrick did upon finding the dominatrix suit at the back of her closet. She rushed to her room. "Patrick!" she screamed on the way.

"I found your costume," Patrick said. "And I don't want an argument."

So she agreed to it, but only if he promised to eat healthier. "If you wear this tonight," he said, "I won't have so much as a piece of candy for a month."

By this she understood he meant that this would take effect after the Joneses' party.

Once more she got into the dominatrix outfit, and once more admired her own form. Maybe she'd even turn a few heads at the party.

Patrick left early along with his fellow Musketeers. Melinda picked up her whip and headed to the door. Before she reached it, though, the doorbell rang.

"Did you forget your keys, Patrick?" she called as she answered it. "Bethany!" she gasped, staring into her sister's face.

Bethany looked her sister up and down, the dominatrix ensemble clearly a surprise. "We've got to talk," she said.

"Can it wait? I'm headed out."

"I've found our mother," Bethany replied.

"Nanna? Yes. The old crone's in some depressing apartment across town now. I had my reasons for kicking her out, and I don't want to hear a word about it."

"I found our real mother. We were kidnapped, Melinda."

ERIC ARVIN resides in the same sleepy Indiana river town where he grew up. After graduating from Hanover College with a Bachelors in History, he has lived, for brief periods, in Italy and Australia. He's survived brain surgery and his own loud-mouthed personal demons.

Eric loves company. Visit him at his blog

http://daventryblue.blogspot.com/.

Don't miss these other titles by Eric Arvin from Dreamspinnerpress…

www.dreamspinnerpress.com